Books by Lisa Jackson

Stand-Alones

SEE HOW SHE DIES
FINAL SCREAM
RUNNING SCARED
WHISPERS
TWICE KISSED
UNSPOKEN
DEEP FREEZE
FATAL BURN
MOST LIKELY TO DIE
SINISTER
WITHOUT MERCY
YOU DON'T WANT TO KNOW
CLOSE TO HOME
AFTER SHE'S GONE
REVENGE
YOU WILL PAY
OMINOUS
BACKLASH
RUTHLESS
ONE LAST BREATH
LIAR, LIAR
PARANOID
ENVIOUS
LAST GIRL STANDING
DISTRUST
ALL I WANT FROM SANTA

Colony Series
Written with Nancy Bush

WICKED GAME
WICKED LIES
SOMETHING WICKED
WICKED WAYS

Cahill Family Novels

IF SHE ONLY KNEW
ALMOST DEAD
YOU BETRAYED ME

Rick Bentz/Reuben Montoya Novels

HOT BLOODED
COLD BLOODED
SHIVER
ABSOLUTE FEAR
LOST SOULS
MALICE
DEVIOUS
NEVER DIE ALONE

Pierce Reed/Nikki Gillette Novels

THE NIGHT BEFORE
THE MORNING AFTER
TELL ME
THE THIRD GRAVE

Selena Alvarez/Regan Pescoli Novels

LEFT TO DIE
CHOSEN TO DIE
BORN TO DIE
AFRAID TO DIE
READY TO DIE
DESERVES TO DIE
EXPECTING TO DIE
WILLING TO DIE

Books by Alexandra Ivy

Guardians of Eternity

WHEN DARKNESS COMES
EMBRACE THE DARKNESS
DARKNESS EVERLASTING
DARKNESS REVEALED
DARKNESS UNLEASHED
BEYOND THE DARKNESS
DEVOURED BY DARKNESS
BOUND BY DARKNESS
FEAR THE DARKNESS
DARKNESS AVENGED
HUNT THE DARKNESS
WHEN DARKNESS ENDS
DARKNESS RETURNS
BEWARE THE DARKNESS
CONQUER THE DARKNESS
SHADES OF DARKNESS

The Immortal Rogues

MY LORD VAMPIRE
MY LORD ETERNITY
MY LORD IMMORTALITY

The Sentinels

BORN IN BLOOD
BLOOD ASSASSIN
BLOOD LUST

Ares Security

KILL WITHOUT MERCY
KILL WITHOUT SHAME

Romantic Suspense

PRETEND YOU'RE SAFE
WHAT ARE YOU AFRAID OF?
YOU WILL SUFFER
THE INTENDED VICTIM
DON'T LOOK
FACELESS

Historical Romance

SOME LIKE IT WICKED
SOME LIKE IT SINFUL
SOME LIKE IT BRAZEN

And don't miss these Guardians of Eternity novellas

TAKEN BY DARKNESS in YOURS FOR ETERNITY
DARKNESS ETERNAL in SUPERNATURAL
WHERE DARKNESS LIVES in THE REAL WEREWIVES OF
VAMPIRE COUNTY
LEVET (ebook only)
A VERY LEVET CHRISTMAS (ebook only)

And don't miss these Sentinel novellas

OUT OF CONTROL
ON THE HUNT

Books by Lisa Childs

THE RUNAWAY
THE HUNTED

Published by Kensington Publishing Corp.

Afraid

LISA JACKSON
ALEXANDRA IVY
LISA CHILDS

ZEBRA BOOKS
KENSINGTON PUBLISHING CORP.

www.kensingtonbooks.com

CONTENTS

RETRIBUTION

by
LISA JACKSON

Lucy froze.

Hiding in Mama's bathroom.

Holding Mama's special scissors, unable to escape.

How many times had she heard, "Don't touch Mama's things" from her mother, and now she was going to be caught.

She bit her lip. She wasn't supposed to be in Mama's suite, and she especially wasn't supposed to be stealing the scissors, but she needed them to trim her own hair, which Mama insisted couldn't be cut.

She was used to sneaking into Mama's room and going through her things, playing dress-up, pretending to be a big-time movie star like Mama, who had changed her name from Christy Smith to Tina Champagne the day she'd landed in Hollywood—or so Lucy's older sister, Marilyn, had confided. When no one was looking, Lucy had slipped into Mama's superhigh heels, donned her sparkly sunglasses, put on her lipstick, and tried on her hats. Lucy was familiar with everything in Mama's wardrobe and had lots of time alone to explore and touch, especially the items she was forbidden to, warned against. Even when Mama said, "That's expensive, don't touch Mama's Fabergé egg pendant, oh, no, no, no," or "That bracelet is diamonds, dear, a gift from your father who gave it to me so I wouldn't divorce him, well, it didn't work, now did it? But please, Lucille, leave it be," or "You know you shouldn't be going through Mama's drawers, not even this nightstand. That gun is loaded, so hands off, missy. It's very, very dangerous, but Mama needs it for protection. Dear Lord, Lucy, am I going to have to put a lock on my door?"

But she never had.

And now, if Mama were to come into her bathroom . . . Lucy would be in big, big trouble. Slowly, silently, she backed away from the door that was only open a crack and into the shower room. Heart pounding, she sent up a prayer to God that Mama would go right to sleep.

Then Lucy could sneak down the hallway to her own room.

Mama was rustling in the bedroom, the frame creaking slightly as she settled into her canopied bed with its twinkling fairy lights, the radio playing softly, a tall glass of her clear drink, Mama's "nightcap" or vodka, as Marilyn had told her. Now the glass was nearly drained, a few ice cubes melting.

Good!

If Mama would just fall asleep, then—

She heard footsteps in the hallway and silently cursed her older brother and sister. It would be just like Clark and Marilyn to come bursting into Mama's bedroom and ruin everything.

The door banged open.

"What the—?" Mama said, obviously surprised. "What're you doing here?"

"I live here," a gruff male voice said, and Lucy's heart sank. *Ray.* Mama's boyfriend, her "boy toy," as Marilyn called him.

"Not anymore." Mama's voice was firm. Harsh. Even now, it made Lucy cringe. "Get out."

He was big and muscly, his teeth a slash of white in a jaw that always looked like he needed to shave, and he didn't walk so much as swagger.

Lucy didn't like him, didn't like the way he looked at her.

"I'm not goin' anywhere," he said, slurring his words. "We need ta talk. We got problems, we both . . . we both know it."

"Our 'problems' are because you can't keep your hands off other women. Younger women. Much younger women."

"Thaaas what I wanna talk about—"

"Leave now, Ray. Or I'll call the police."

"C'mon, babe, you don't mean it."

"Try me."

Lucy's throat went dry, and though she knew it was crazy, she inched forward in the darkened bathroom to the doorway where she could peer with one eye into the bedroom, lit only by the fairy lights vining over the crossbeams of the canopy. Mama was lying in her usual spot, her silky sleep mask pushed over her forehead, her red hair poking out at all angles.

Ray stood next to the bed, that knowing smile pinned to his face, a drink in one hand.

But Mama wasn't buying it. Lucy saw the fury in her mother's face. Tina Champagne didn't like to be bothered when she'd gotten ready for bed, her face slathered in some kind of miracle antiaging cream. Mama never allowed anyone to see her less than "camera ready." Lucy knew it, and her sister and brother knew it, and stupid Ray should know it, too.

But Ray was pushy, and crude, thinking he could sweet talk or bully his way into Mama's good graces. He couldn't. Not anymore than Tina's other three husbands had been able to when Tina had decided to divorce each of them.

Ray swirled his drink, ice cubes clinking. With the other hand, he reached for Mama's head, snapped off her mask, and tangled his fingers in her thick red curls, drawing her face closer to him, to his waist, where his T-shirt pulled from the waistband of his Levi's.

"Don't," she warned.

Lucy's fingers tightened over the shears.

"Come on, baby. Relax." He started rubbing his hand over the back of Mama's neck, drawing her closer. "You know you want it—"

Mama spat through clenched teeth, "I said, 'Get out, Ray,' and I meant it." She pushed him backward. Hard. Then opened the drawer to her nightstand and riffled through it frantically.

"Wha–?" He stumbled, slipping on the thick, faux fur of the white carpet. His shoulder hit the wall with a loud crash and the house shuddered. Someone down the hallway yelled. Ray tried to stand, got tangled in the cord for the fairy lights. The room was suddenly pitch black.

"Mom?" Marilyn yelled over the sound of running feet.

"Are you okay?" Clark yelled from the corridor.

"Get the hell out! Now!" Mama said into the darkened room.

"You fucking bitch," Ray growled, and Lucy, her eyes trying to adjust to the darkness, sensed him climbing to his feet, heading toward the bed.

She opened the door and slipped through, her fingers holding the shears, point side down in a death grip.

"Stay away from me!" Mama warned. "Ray, I've got a gun and I'll use it. You know I will!"

"I thought you were going to call the police," he taunted, his voice a snarl.

Mama ordered, "Don't!"

Lucy rushed forward.

Mama screamed as the door to the bedroom flew open, allowing in a sliver of weak illumination from the night-light in the hallway.

"Oh, Jesus!" Marilyn gasped, running inside. "Stop. Oh God, stop!"

Clark was a step behind. "What the fuck?"

Lucy saw Mama pinned to the mattress in a tangle of bedclothes, Ray atop her. Mama was struggling. He had his hands on her throat. Lucy cried out and, raising the scissors high, flung herself at the bed. Airborne, she steeled herself, then, as she landed, plunged the scissors deep.

Cascade Mountains, Oregon
Now

"Let's go! Come on! Hurry, hurry, hurry!" Breathing hard, Lucy glanced over her shoulder. Her seven-year-old daughter was lagging again, caught in the wonder of the forest in the snow, oblivious to the fact that a blizzard was on its way and, worse than that, *he* was coming. "Come on, honey," she said, trying to hide the urgency in her voice as she pulled on the rope attached to the sled carrying what was left of her life. "It's not that much farther."

That was a bit of a lie. They still had half a mile or so to trudge uphill on this steep trail to the cabin, hidden deep in the woods. Even so, it wasn't far enough. No place on this earth could ever be far enough. But it would have to do. For now. Until she could figure out something else.

The cold fear that had propelled her here kept her going, forced her to keep trudging ever upward, through the thickets of pine and fir trees, their branches laden with a blanket of white, the vine maples skeletal, their leaves long gone, the vibrant colors of autumn exhausted.

Had the circumstances been different, had she and Renee come up here for a Christmas holiday, to enjoy the peace and solitude of the Cascade Mountains in winter, she would have felt differently about the quaint, isolated cabin. Lucy, like her daughter, would have stopped for a minute and taken in the breathtaking scenery, the soft touch of snowflakes on her cheeks, the icy breath of wind tugging the hair from her cap.

But she couldn't.

Not now.

Maybe not ever.

"Come on!" she urged again, more sharply, as her daughter dawdled in the snowfall. "Grace, get a move on."

Grace, springy brown curls showing around the edges of her white cap scowled. Gold eyes squinted. "That's not my name."

"For now it is . . . My new name is Elle, and you're Grace."

"You're not Elle. You're Lucy."

"Lucille—Elle is the last part of my name. And Grace is your middle name."

Her child glowered at her.

"I told you, it's a game."

"It's a dumb game. I'm Renee," she asserted, her face red with the cold.

There was no use arguing. "Just hurry up, Whatever-your-name-is."

Keep it light, she's just a child. She can't possibly understand. And it was a little over-the-top. Each of them with an alias, so if and when they came across someone, their names were not immediately recognizable. "Tell you what, when it's just the two of us, I'll be Mom or Lucy and you be Renee, but if we see anyone, you're Grace. Got it?"

"Got it." Renee wrinkled her nose but didn't argue and trudged along after the sled, keeping to the path her mother was breaking through six inches of snow. As she plowed on, Lucy eyed the sky, saw only white, the clouds indistinct through millions of tiny flakes. Bring them on.

The more they fell and covered her tracks, the more likely they could escape.

But for how long?

He will never let up, never let you go.

She couldn't let herself go there.

One day at a time.

That was her mantra.

And for now, the cabin, whatever shape it was in, would be a place to hide for a while, just to regroup. Hopefully it would be a haven.

Oh God, please.

"Come on," she said, hating the snap in her voice.

"Where's Merlin?" her daughter called, searching the veil of falling flakes for the dog.

"He'll keep up. He's part Malamute. They love the snow and the cold. Come on, now." Lucy marched forward, up the hill, dragging the sled of necessities, enough food for two weeks, clothing and sleeping bags, her cell phone and iPad, not that there was wireless at the cabin. The electronics were for an emergency if they were to work. Only then.

Who are you kidding? Your whole life is an emergency!

"Can I ride?" Renee asked, eyeing the already full sled.

If it would make the trek go faster, then fine. "Sure."

Renee hopped on, and Lucy put all her weight into dragging the sled uphill to the cabin to which she had no legal access, a place she'd only discovered by eavesdropping on a private conversation.

" . . . it's my uncle's," one of her coworkers at the junior college had confided to a friend while Lucy had been taking pages out of the printer. As the machine had hummed, spitting pages into the tray, Lucy had listened to Cindy, the blond. They knew each other a little, had worked together for a couple of years. Cindy, though married, had kept her maiden name. "It's an empowerment thing," Cindy had confided when they'd attended a conference together and had ended up roommates at the Holiday Suites in Reno. "I like the sound of it. Cynthia Jacoby. Sure beats the hell out of Cynthia White–I mean, how Disney does that sound? My husband didn't seem to mind. He's kinda new age, I guess you'd say."

"Where did you say the cabin is?"

"Up in Oregon. Near Mount Hood, but it's like, so remote you almost have to hike into it, and there's nothing up there, and I mean *nothing*. It's a decent-size and got running water, I guess, and electricity, but barely. My uncle says the power's always going out in storms. He said I could go up there any time. Even left a key up there. Get this." She'd laughed. "It's hidden, like nailed to a tree or something. A tree with a split trunk, I mean, *as if . . .*"

And then Lucy hadn't been able to hear the rest of the conversation as the two coworkers had walked away from the printer area to the cafeteria. Later, at her desk, Lucy had done more than a little research on the internet, checked county and state records, along with personnel info that she shouldn't have had access to, and zeroed in on this place, the owner being Winston Jacoby, which, now that she had dragged her daughter and dog up here, she seriously hoped was correct.

What if you're wrong?

What if the cabin isn't where you think it is?

What if it's inhabited?

What if it's falling apart?

And worse yet–

What if he *finds you?*

Steadfastly, she pushed those worrisome questions aside. She had a plan, albeit a flimsy, hastily created one, but as long as she kept to it—

"Is Daddy coming up here?"

Ian.

Oh. God.

She stumbled.

Caught herself.

Ignored the stab of pain cutting through her heart.

Kept moving. "No, honey," she said as they crested the top of a steep rise and the fir trees gave way to a clearing with a rambling, dilapidated cabin, the original structure having been added onto over the years, or so it appeared. "Not this time."

"But I was supposed to be with him at Christmas," Renee pointed out.

"I know. Change of plans."

She felt her daughter's suspicious glare cutting into her back. "That sucks."

"I know."

"What the—?" Her daughter's voice was filled with wonder as she gazed at the large cabin. Or was it dread? "We're—we're going to live here?" Renee asked incredulously, flinging herself from the heap of supplies and dashing forward.

"That's the plan."

Renee's eyes lit up. "Cool."

Lucy doubted she'd think it was so cool when she

found out there was no internet, hence no Wi-Fi for her daughter's iPad. "Yeah," she lied, hiking the rope to the sled higher on her shoulder, "very cool."

But not bucolic, nor quaint, nor the least bit cozy. The center of the cabin, which looked the oldest, the original building, Lucy guessed, rose like a behemoth, two tall stories with a narrow porch over the front door, and from the center structure sprang wings that were mismatched, as if they'd been built in different decades, judging by the windows and graying siding. No paint had ever touched the weathered exterior, but the thick covering of snow softened some of the sharp angles.

"Kinda weird," Renee observed.

Very weird. But Lucy didn't say it. Instead, she patted her daughter's head and said, "I'd call it unique."

You wanted remote, a place to hide where no one can find you, didn't you? Looks like you got it.

Now, if she could just find the key.

San Francisco, California
Now

"Lucy, damn it. Pick up!" Ian muttered tautly. He was walking down the steep streets of San Francisco, cell phone pressed to his ear, the rain pelting, the wind fierce, his rage shooting through the stratosphere. He dodged other pedestrians, their umbrellas turned to the wind, and stepped around a woman balancing a take-out cup of coffee, her phone, and a poodle on a tight leash. But the phone went to voice mail and he knew his wife wouldn't return his call. He jabbed the cell into his pocket and, thoughts churning, walked the five blocks to his office.

He waved at the receptionist, then rapped twice on his partner's door, stepped inside, and found Zhou in her zenlike office with its view of the Bay and the Golden Gate Bridge. "I'm taking some time off."

"What're you talking about?" Jun Zhou was in her midforties and as fit as she had been when she'd left the military after putting in her twenty years with army intelligence. Her black hair was pulled into a tight bun, her dark eyes assessing as she sat at a circular desk complete with three computers, several cacti in ceramic pots, and not a paper out of place. A yoga mat was rolled into one corner, and aside from calming views of the ocean, a wall contained copies of her law degree and a display of the medals she'd been awarded during her military career.

"Lucy," Ian explained, hands on the back of one of the side chairs. "She's AWOL."

Jun's eyebrows drew together. "Do I have to remind you that she's your *ex*-wife? She might need some time alone. Or at least time without you butting in? I know I hate it when one of my exes tries to interfere in my life."

"I'm not interfering. She has Renee."

"And—?"

"And I haven't heard from my daughter in three days. We usually FaceTime every night that she's not with me."

"But she's not due to stay with you for what? Another couple of days?"

"Tomorrow."

Leaning back in her chair, she looked up at him. "You don't think you're pushing the panic button?"

"No." He shook his head, ran a palm nervously around the back of his neck. "Something's wrong."

Jun nodded, unconvinced. "Even so. If she doesn't want to talk to you . . . isn't interested in your help."

"I don't care. As I said, she has Renee with her, Jun. So I'm outta here. And if you could help me track her down . . ."

"Don't know what you're talking about."

But they both did. Jun was a computer genius of the highest order and had worked as a protegee with the government when she was barely out of high school, then was recruited into army intelligence. She knew the ins and outs of the internet and security codes and back doors into systems. If anyone could find a trace of Lucy, it would be Jun. That was why they worked so well together. Neither one was afraid of bending the law to its breaking point.

"I'll send you Lucy's info," he said as he walked to the window and glanced out at the gray day beyond.

She said, "Won't be necessary."

"You already have it?"

She didn't answer, didn't need to.

"And Ray Watkins?"

"Child's play, Ian." She eyed him. Her cell phone vibrated, humming against the top of her desk. She ignored it. "What really went down the night Tina Champagne was attacked?"

They'd never discussed it, mainly because Ian didn't really know what had happened, even though he'd tried for years to piece it together.

"She attacked him. Right? That's what I read on the internet."

"I think so." But the details were sketchy. Ian had pored over court records, testimony, police reports, depositions, crime scene accounts, anything he had been able to find as, he suspected, had Zhou. Details of the attack had been murky, with Ray Watkins himself taking the stand and describing what he'd claimed to remember: He'd come to Tina Champagne's home, let himself in, found her nearly passed out drunk in her darkened bedroom, and they'd gotten into a "hell-raising" fight about his lack of attention to her. The bruising around her neck was from his attempts to revive her when he'd been attacked by all of Tina's children, one—and he didn't know which—had a pair of long, sharp scissors that he wrested away after he'd been stabbed, his face and eyesight in one eye ruined, Tina herself nearly dying from wounds to her neck and torso. A gun had gone off, Tina's pistol, and she'd ended up being the one shot, the bullet nicking her carotid artery, her recovery nearly miraculous. There were smudged prints on the gun, but the only ones that could be lifted had been Tina's own.

Had someone else fired the shot?

Tina couldn't remember, and Clark and Marilyn had both been too confused. They only knew that Ray seemed to be attacking their mother and they'd tried to physically restrain him, but the bedroom had been dark, filled with screaming and cursing and stone-cold fear.

It had been Lucy's testimony, an eight-year-old, traumatized child who could barely answer any questions when placed on the stand, who had whispered, white-faced, that Ray had tried to kill her mother.

As far as Ian knew, she'd never varied from that testimony, never filled in the blanks, never confided in anyone, her husband included.

Now, as Zhou waited for an explanation, he wished he

had one. "Lucy's always said he would come for her, and now that he's out, she could be right."

"Or she could be paranoid."

"I don't think so," he said, though he had always wondered about Lucy's stability. Outwardly strong, there were cracks in her armor. She'd been traumatized as a child by not only being involved in a horrendous, tragic, and sensationalized crime, but also by then being sent away, out of the country. "Keep me posted."

"Sure."

She shouldn't have surprised him.

But Zhou always seemed to.

Maybe he was naiver than he'd like to admit, or she was just that good. He'd bet on the latter.

"What about the Dalton case?" she asked.

"Put Martinez on it. Or whoever." And he was gone. Leaving her in her faux zen environment to deal with the headaches of their private investigation firm. If there was one thing he knew about Zhou, it was she was laser-focused and efficient. Ian was damned certain she could handle just about anything.

Including finding some trace of his recalcitrant ex-wife.

Los Angeles, CA
Then

Blood.

Everywhere.

Mama moaning as men lifted her from the bed to a stretcher.

The scissors.

Where were they?

"Honey, are you all right?" Some woman in a uniform was talking to her, but someone else was screaming too loud, so she couldn't hear. Too loud. Shrieking and . . . Her throat was raw and she realized it was her own voice that she heard. She was shaking, her hands covered in blood, splatters on her nightgown.

"Come with me. Come on, honey."

"She can't leave." A male voice. Deep. Concerned. From a tall man with dark skin and gray stubble for his hair.

"Like hell." The woman, with short brown hair and freckles, picked her up. "She's a child. I'm Detective Lorna Davis. You hear me? Lorna."

Suddenly mute, Lucy couldn't answer. Her throat was raw. Her heart pounding. Her mind swirling with horrifying images. And she was sticky with blood. His blood. Mama's blood. Maybe her own blood.

"Lucy, honey, I'm with the police. And I've got you. You're going to be okay." The woman hiked her upward on her hip, Lucy's long legs dangling beneath her nightgown.

"But—" the man said.

"A child, Tony!" the woman said, cradling Lucy as best she could. "And that's her mother."

"Noooooo!" Lucy let out a cry as she saw the men hurrying Mama away on a stretcher. Mama wasn't moving, her skin an ugly shade of gray, blood soaking through her nightgown.

"Shhh. Honey. Shhh," Lorna whispered, and Lucy was reduced to sobs and hiccups. "There ya go. It'll be okay."

"Move it," one of the men carrying the stretcher said,

and they hurried off, out of the bedroom and down the stairs. Lucy heard the heavy tread of their fast-moving footsteps.

"Where are the others?" Lorna asked, still holding Lucy. "The teenagers?"

The man answered, "The son's in the living room. Daughter's in the kitchen. We split them up to check out their stories, see if there's any discrepancies."

"And the boyfriend?"

"Not here."

"Shit! He was here. That's what the neighbor said, the one who called it in. They saw his car in the drive."

"He took off." The man was worried, deep lines creasing his cheeks and fanning from his eyes. "We'll get him."

"Probably halfway to Mexico."

"The call came in fifteen minutes ago. He couldn't have gotten far. We'll pick him up." But he didn't sound sure.

"So what the hell happened here?" Lorna asked. "What *really* went down?"

"Nothing good," he said, eyeing the blood-soaked mattress and stained bedclothes beneath the canopy of still-twinkling lights. "We'll see what the kids have to say." At the landing, the male cop touched the woman on the shoulder, stopping her. "It might all depend upon what this one has to say." He nodded toward Lucy.

"Oh, Jesus, Tony. Don't even go there." The woman's arms tightened around Lucy, and she repeated, "She's just a little kid."

Cascade Mountains, Oregon
Now

The key wasn't where she'd thought it should be. But this had to be the place. She'd looked up Jacoby on the records for the county and there weren't any others besides Winston Jacoby.

Lucy let out a disappointed huff and saw her own breath fog in the cold.

There was no tree with a split trunk and the snow was falling wildly now, wind blowing, drifts piling along the cabin's foundation. If they couldn't find shelter, they would freeze and she wasn't about to let that happen. Worse case? She would break into this godforsaken cabin through a window.

"I'm cold," Renee complained just as the dog finally came bounding through the snowdrifts, his thick, gray-and-white fur dusted with snow, his tongue lolling from one side of his mouth.

Me too. "Just a sec," Lucy said, worrying that her information had been wrong. She'd overheard the conversation and made a mistake or she was in the wrong spot and then she spied it, not a split trunk, but actually two trees growing out of an old stump. She trudged to the stump, brushing off the snow. Searching with gloved hands, she ran her fingers over the mossy surface, once, then again, and discovered a rusted key wedged deep into the rough bark.

Thank goodness for small favors.

She had to take off her gloves to force the key into its rusted lock, but once she did, the door swung open and the welcome smell of dry dust hit her nostrils. The cabin might be dirty, but at least it was dry and dusty rather than moldy and dank.

With the dog and Renee in tow, she explored the rambling building with two staircases, the main one near the front door by the great room and a narrow back set of steps off the kitchen that led upward to the second floor and downward to what seemed like a root cellar, which housed the furnace and shelving filled with mostly empty jars. As she ran her flashlight over the glassware, she didn't want to think about what the filled jars that had been abandoned here held. She spied an old wooden chute connected to an opening with a cover, a place where coal or firewood or whatever could be delivered straight into the cellar. A small stack of firewood remained, an ax buried in a stump used as a chopping block, bits of wood surrounding it.

She checked, making certain the chute door was latched, along with the two, small, grimy windows, then returned to the kitchen, which was separated from the living area by a peninsula. A butcher-block counter ran beneath a bank of cabinets that, when checked, were found to be mostly empty.

The whole cabin felt as if it had been forgotten. The dust thick, the yellowed newspaper left in a box near the stone fireplace dated eight years earlier. The beds were unmade, a single sheet draped over each one, the bedding in the closets covered in dust and grime, spiders nesting in the corners of the ceiling and God-knew-what-other-creatures inhabiting the darkened nooks and crannies.

It took over an hour to set up, but yes, thankfully, the

electricity was working. Another blessing, and water ran in the sink and fixtures in the kitchen and both bathrooms. *All the comforts of home*, she told herself, and even built a fire with dry wood stacked on a lean-to just off a small back porch. She cleaned as best she could, unloading the sled of the camping goods she'd hurriedly packed, including two slim, thermal sleeping bags, dried food, short skis, and snowshoes.

And a gun.

She'd brought a pistol, the little baby Glock she'd purchased upon returning to the States when she was just eighteen.

As night was falling, she locked the doors and barricaded them with furniture. Then she huddled with her daughter and the dog as the embers of the fire burned down to coals that cast dancing, blood-red shadows over the log walls of the main room. She'd already drawn down the shades on all the windows that had coverings, though two with broken blinds she'd had to leave exposed.

How long would she be able to hide here?

Another day?

A week?

Indefinitely, or until someone who owned the place, Jacoby, saw the change in his electric bill? Or a snowshoer hiked by and saw the lights . . .

No, no, no! Just until you figure out a plan.

And what will that be?

I don't know. But I'll think of something.

Lucy glanced down at her sleeping child and prayed she wasn't kidding herself. She had to brace herself for the inevitability that he would find her.

And when he did?

She would have to be ready.

Because there would be hell to pay.

San Francisco, California
Now

"I don't know what you want from me, Ian," Marilyn said, her mouth pulled into a tight knot of disapproval. Lucy's sister was standing in the foyer of her townhouse, a wrought-iron security door firmly between them, the wind and rain pummeling the porch where Ian stood.

"I want to know where my wife—where Lucy is."

"Even if I did know, why would I tell you? And re-member—she's not your wife anymore." The look she sent him was scathing. Tall and curvy, with her blond hair tied away from her face, her arms folded defensively under her breasts, Marilyn waited. She, unlike his wife, favored their mother, with full breasts, a nipped-in waist, Kewpie-doll lips, and wide, blue eyes. She'd been named after Marilyn Monroe. And the name fit. Usually. Not so glamorous today, though, as she stood without makeup in pajamas and a bathrobe.

"I'm worried," he said.

"Too little, too late." Her lips pursed decisively. She'd determined she was judge and jury all rolled into one.

"Does Clark know?"

Marilyn rolled her eyes and let out a dismissive breath. "Does my brother ever know anything? Come on, Ian."

"I don't think you're giving him enough credit. Wasn't he Special Ops in the army or intelligence or something?"

"Or something."

"So he knows a lot."

"Not about Lucy." She wasn't budging.

"She has Renee with her."

Marilyn's eyes slid to the side, as if she were considering.

"This isn't like her," Ian said. "We have our differences, yeah, I know, but when it comes to Renee, we're pretty much on the same page. Something's wrong."

"You don't know that."

"But you do," he charged, seeing the hesitation in her eyes.

"Look, all I know is that she's needed to get away for some time. She was having those nightmares again. She told me that much. And that she was starting to remember."

"Remember?"

"What happened the night Ray Watkins attacked Mom. But who knows? It's been a lifetime ago, she was just a kid, so is she really recalling new details? Or is it all fantasy, you know, in her mind? But that's it. She didn't tell me anything else."

Nope. She was lying. The little twitch at the corner of her lips gave her away.

"Is she safe?"

"How would l know?"

"If she's in danger—if she's risking my daughter's—"

"They're not in danger! They're safe. I—I'm sure of it," she said, though she didn't sound certain of any damned thing. Then, before he could argue, she added, "Don't put me in this position, Ian. It's not fair."

"Nothing's fair in this world."

Her eyes narrowed. "You're a fucking asshole, Ian."

She was about to close the door.

He snaked an arm through the bars of the security gate and grabbed her arm. "Wait! He's out. Ray Watkins. You know it. I know it. Hell, the whole damned world knows it. That's what this is all about! That's why she ran!"

"Ray did his time. Paid his debt to society, right? Isn't that the way it works? You're the lawyer, you should know. It's been twenty-five years. So he got out early, a few years off the original sentence for good behavior. And I hear he's turned religious. Found God and Jesus." She yanked her arm back and he let go. Glaring at him, she said, "Isn't he some kind of minister, leads a men's group at the penitentiary or something?"

"But Ray was focused on Lucy. Sent her letters for years."

Marilyn's eyes turned dark for a second, then she flipped up her hand, as if she were shooing away a bothersome insect. "Those letters stopped years ago."

"Did they? Or did she just quit talking about them?"

"You tell me. You were married to her."

He didn't respond. They both knew Lucy Champagne McKenna struggled with her past and kept her secrets.

"What about you, Marilyn? Did you get mail from him? Did your mom?"

"I wasn't the one whose testimony sent him to prison. And neither was Tina. Good Lord she was still too weak to testify at the trial."

"So you did get letters?"

"Only one. When he first got in. It just said he was innocent and that he missed me."

Ian wondered. The defiant jut of her chin said otherwise, and also warned him that the subject was closed.

He took another tack. "Look, if Lucy's running from him, I can help." He held her gaze. "You know I can."

"Oh, for the love of God, Ian." She yanked her arm back. "I told you all I know. If anyone would know where Lucy is, it's probably Mom, and good luck with that!" Casting him a final disparaging look, she slammed the door in his face.

Los Angeles, California
Then

" . . . we find the defendant guilty as charged," the heavy-set foreman of the jury said in a booming voice that anyone in the filled courtroom, including Lucy, who was huddled against Aunt Beth, could hear distinctly. Voices murmured around her, the room with its high ceilings and blond woodwork buzzed with electricity. And Ray, who had been standing behind the narrow table, nearly col-lapsed.

"I'm innocent!" he insisted, bracing himself on the table. "I didn't try to kill her!" And then he looked over his shoulder and found Lucy's eyes. She shrank back at the sight of his disfigured face, the jagged, still-red scar running from his drooping eye where the scissors had cut his flesh.

Lucy swallowed hard and managed to hold back a scream, but that scar seemed to pulse with his anger. She'd heard the cops had caught him at his apartment, his car already filled with his belongings, blood on every-thing, the night that Mama almost died.

"The kid did it!" Ray accused, nearly spitting. "That little weirdo came in with a knife or something and hacked the hell out of us. And she got the drawer open.

She knew where the gun was because she was always snooping around, going through Tina's things. I swear on my mother's grave, I didn't try to kill Tina. I love her." Beneath his navy suit jacket, his shoulders heaved and his voice broke. "I love her. I didn't do it. It was the kid." A police officer tried to shepherd him away, but he screamed, "It was the kid! I don't know why Tina wouldn't say so."

Because she couldn't. Still hospitalized, her memory muddled, her voice only a rasp, she'd withdrawn and retreated, leaving her children with strict, by-the-book, children-should-be seen-but-not-heard Aunt Beth.

People pushed and shoved behind them, but Lucy didn't pay any attention as Ray turned, his gaze searching until it landed on her again. *I'll get you for this*, his eyes seemed to say. "She did it! That little liar!" He pointed a long, accusing finger in Lucy's direction, and the scar throbbed.

"Sweet Jesus." Aunt Beth, along with some uniformed officers, bustled Lucy along with her sister and brother from the courtroom. Even so, Lucy heard the questions shouted at her:

"Is he telling the truth?" a sharp female voice.

"Did you find the gun?" another man with a nasal tone.

"Shouldn't you be charged?"

Another, this time a man with a foreign accent: "Lucille. Honey! Over here. Did you try to kill your mother?"

"Stop it! Of course she didn't," Aunt Beth, taller and willowier than Mama, shouted at them. "And she's too young to go on trial. What're you thinking?"

"But if she tried to kill Tina Champagne," the woman's voice cut in.

"She didn't!" Aunt Beth insisted as she took Lucy by the shoulders, half-pushing her down the row of seats, past the gawking onlookers. "Oh, I knew this was a mistake!"

They were shuffled outside a side door and down a long hallway to a winding staircase. "Come on, Lucy!" Aunt Beth tugged on her hand, and they walked through a doorway, outside where the sun was high and baking the concrete. Police officers escorted her quickly to a waiting car.

Aunt Beth tumbled into the front passenger seat of the Mercedes while Lucy and her siblings filled the back, and Melvin, Mama's stout business manager, took the wheel from an attendant. Before they were even strapped into their seat belts, Mel hit the gas and tore away from the curb, rounding the corner. Lucy climbed onto her knees and peered through the back windshield to spy a throng of people still gathered on the wide, front steps of the courthouse.

"Get down," Aunt Beth admonished. "Lucy, buckle up! Mel, did you even think about a booster seat?"

"Other things on my mind." Lucy, as she was pushing the seat belt buckle together, saw Mel reach across the space between the two front seats to pat Aunt Beth's hands. "It was worth it, really. You'll see. Once *Autumn Heat* premieres."

Marilyn rolled her eyes and gazed out the window while Clark glowered and stared straight ahead at the back of Aunt Beth's head.

"But to take a child into a courtroom, one who . . ." Aunt Beth was shaking her head and reaching into her purse for a bejeweled cigarette case. She withdrew one of her long slim "ciggies."

"I wish you wouldn't," Mel said as he slowed for a stoplight.

"It's been a rough day." She pressed a button to lower her window, lit up quickly, blew smoke out the window, then, after another two puffs, stubbed out her barely smoked cigarette in the ashtray and rolled the window up again.

"Better?" he asked.

"No." She, too, looked out the side window at the wide streets packed with all kinds of cars, trucks, vans, and buses. "That courtroom was no place for a child."

"Come on, honey. She'll never remember this," he said, fiddling with the radio, while Marilyn muttered, "Move over," to Lucy. "I can hardly breathe."

Lucy ignored her older sister, just like she ignored Clark, whose leg was shaking, as it always did when he was nervous.

"She takes in more than you know," Aunt Beth argued under her breath. "She's always creeping around and watching. She hears and sees everything. It's . . . it's disturbing." She gave a mock shudder. "Creepy. Ever since . . . you know. She's been . . . odd . . ." Aunt Beth lowered her voice. "She never cried. I told you that, right?"

They were talking about her. Lucy knew it. And she'd cried plenty. They just never saw it. She would never let them see it.

"It's over," Mel said with a satisfied smile growing beneath his mustache as he patted Aunt Beth on her knee, his ring—gold, with a yellow stone that cut into his fat finger—catching the sunlight streaming through the bug-spattered windshield.

"You don't know that." She shifted away.

"Sure I do," he argued but returned his hand to the steering wheel.

The summer sun beat down mercilessly, heat shimmering in weird-looking waves in the distance.

Lucy had to squint.

Aunt Beth slid a pair of her Jackie O sunglasses onto her nose.

As Mel fiddled with a knob that controlled the air-conditioning, Aunt Beth snapped on the radio and punched through the stations until she found something she liked—a song Mama had sung, about a mockingbird and a diamond ring.

It made Lucy sad.

But it seemed to cheer up Aunt Beth. Calmer, she said to Mel, "All I can say is that the movie better do well."

"A sexy thriller starring Tina Champagne, released after the scandalous tragedy that cut short her career and nearly took her life? It would only be better if we could get her to come out for it, you know, wave to her fans. Give them something to juice them up."

"Ugh. She'll never. Not unless you can find a miracle worker of a plastic surgeon and couple it with a Nobel Prize-winning psychiatrist."

Mel smiled wide beneath his brush of a mustache. Lucy caught his image in the rearview mirror. "It doesn't really matter. We just got ourselves a ton of publicity, the kind you can't buy." He winked at Lucy in the mirror, as if the two of them were in on some private joke, and she just stared at him, not sure why, but knowing that she hated him.

She hated him a lot.

Cascade Mountains, Oregon
Now

"I want to talk to Daddy," Renee asserted after a long night in the cold, drafty cabin. The adventure, if that's what you would call it, had worn off, dying like the embers of the fire in the predawn hours. Lucy was second-guessing herself as she cuddled close to Renee, who had crawled out of her child-sized sleeping bag sometime after midnight to slip into Lucy's, snuggling close. Lucy kissed the top of her daughter's head. It had been reckless to drive up here, almost crazy. If she wanted to hide, she could have done it in any city away from San Francisco, right? And maybe she should have driven south, to a warmer climate.

Like LA? her mind nagged.

No. She'd avoided that city and the surrounding area like the plague, never wanting to go back to the place where she'd been taken away from her mother.

"Mommy, I said, I—"

"'—you want to talk to your father.' I know." Lucy glanced out the window, where the shade was broken, and she could look outside to the still-dark morning. She then checked her watch. Five thirty-seven. "It's too early. He's sleeping."

"How do you know?"

"Well, I guess I don't, but I think so." She remembered waking up early to the sound of Ian's soft snoring, his arm flung carelessly around her, his dark hair tousled. With Renee—no, Grace—asleep in the next room. Life had seemed simple then. Warm. Safe. And now . . . She climbed out of the shared bag, shivered, and rubbed her hands down her arms. "It's really early. You stay here with Merlin and I'll get the fire going again."

She threw on her jacket and her boots and, following her flashlight's beam, walked onto the back porch. The storm had stopped somewhere in the night, the snow piled high, a slice of moon offering a bit of silver light that glinted on the freshly fallen flakes. Trees, their branches laden, were flocked with the snow, and icicles glinted in the cold light, shimmering from the eaves.

A winter wonderland, she thought, if not for the ever-present feel of danger whispering through the fir trees and bringing goose bumps to the backs of her arms.

She searched the horizon, looking for half-buried foot-prints in the snow, or a glint of glass or metal, any hint that someone other than her or her daughter were nearby, but the slope of the mountain was calm, the nearest cabin a quarter of a mile downhill, according to the map she'd perused before driving here. She carried in two armloads of wood and was able to start the fire using the still-warm coals from the night before.

Renee had fallen into slumber again, and after Merlin had walked outside to scope the perimeter, do his business, and lap water from a dish Lucy had placed near the side door, he joined Renee, curling into a tight ball atop her sleeping bag.

Lucy went to work, scrubbing and cleaning. She'd found the valves on the pipes, then run water through them, cleaning out any debris that may have collected, and scrubbing the sinks until the water ran clear. The electricity might be working, but the lights had flickered twice, threatening to go out. She'd turned on the water heater, then drained the pipes again to get rid of the rust and dirt and bugs or whatever might have clogged them. The house, with its old, lumpy couch, small, round table, and café chairs would have to do. She only planned to be here a week, maybe less. Just long enough to get her thoughts together and plan her escape.

You can't run forever.

"I won't," she said aloud, and Merlin lifted his head to look at her. "Just talking to myself," she said, and the dog settled down again.

And where will you go, then? You can't take Renee away from her father, no matter what name you give her.

"I'll figure something out," she whispered to herself. Maybe she would return to Europe. Not Austria—he might look there—but Paris, possibly, or Madrid, or Florence, cities large enough to get lost in, places where no one knew her identity. The opposite of this lonely isolation. As she tended the fire, brushing ash back into the firebox, the flames began to crackle and burn bright. Lucy glanced to the sleeping bag where her daughter's hair, a tangle of brown curls, was visible against the stark white of her pillow. Ian wouldn't allow her to take Renee out of the country.

Never.

She could plead and beg and threaten and cry, but he wouldn't budge.

Nope. Europe was out. Mexico was out. Canada was

out. Probably most spots in the United States were out. New Zealand? Japan? Egypt? Was there nowhere safe?

No.

The truth was, she would have to confront the past.

No matter how painful it was.

A Transatlantic Flight
Then

"Someone will meet us at the airport in Salzburg," Aunt Beth said nervously again as she half-crouched near Lucy's seat on the airplane, an aisle seat, four rows back from first class, where she and Mel were ticketed.

"I don't want to go to Australia," Lucy complained, not for the first time on the long trip.

"It's Austria, dweeb. Not Australia." Marilyn was seated next to her and flipping through the pages of *People* magazine, the one with Madonna and some guy she was marrying on the cover. It was old, and Marilyn wasn't really reading it, just using it to cover up the fact that she had a newer copy of a magazine she called *Cosmo* tucked into the old, beat-up cover. *Cosmo* was a magazine that Aunt Beth would definitely disapprove of. "Big difference. Like it's in Europe. You know. A country. Not a continent." She pulled her Sony Discman out of her carry-on bag that had been tucked below the seat in front of her.

"Like you know everything!" Lucy said.

"I do. At least more than you. Like we're going to boarding school in Salzburg, Austria, which is like the end of the world."

"You're just mad cuz you'll have to be away from Nathan!" Lucy shot out and saw her sister wince, then blink, fighting a sudden rush of tears at the mention of the boyfriend with whom she'd been forced to break up.

Marilyn muttered, "Stop it!"

"Why didn't Mama come?" Lucy demanded.

"Oh, honey, you know why," Aunt Beth said with that there-there tone that Lucy hated, the one Marilyn said was "patronizing."

"Mom's sick."

"But she's getting better," Lucy said, repeating what they'd told her, and then she saw it, that knowing look that passed between her older sister and her aunt. "Isn't she? That's what you said."

"These things take time," Aunt Beth said, and offered one of her sad, almost smiles as she scooted closer to allow a stewardess to pass by.

"How long?"

Marilyn let out a huff. "God, Lucy, don't be a baby, okay? You're eight years old, for God's sake, almost nine. No one knows."

"It's been a long time!" Once again, Lucy had the feeling that she was being left out of an important conversation, if not lied to. "Really long. And why is she sending us to Australia?"

"Austria!" Marilyn said loudly. "Salzburg's in Austria! *That's* where we're going!"

A woman a row up in a red hat turned to stare at Lucy in a way that said she was accusing her of being a brat. So what?

"I just want to know why Mama doesn't want us!"

"Oh, get a life! It's not that she doesn't—"

"Girls! Hush. Enough!" Aunt Beth glanced around to the passengers nearby, the closest ones a bald man and a pudgy woman, each with a thick English accent that Lucy had overheard as they'd ordered their meals.

Slipping a new disc into her player, Marilyn sent her sister an oh-grow-up look, then adjusted her earphones to sink into the teen angst of Nirvana. "It's her fault," she said. "She's weird."

"Marilyn!" Aunt Beth shot her oldest niece a sharp look.

Lucy's sister lifted a shoulder. "It's true."

"Don't be silly." Aunt Beth gave Lucy a pat on the shoulder and whispered, "Not much longer and we'll be in Salzburg."

Who cares? Lucy thought. She was tired and grumpy, sick of Barbie dolls that she hated anyway. She swung her legs and hit the seat in front of her, and a man in a hat turned and glared at her.

"Stop it," Marilyn warned, pinching her arm.

"Ow!" Lucy shrank away from her sister and actually held back from sticking out her tongue because Marilyn was sure to call her a baby again and Lucy hated that. She sat glumly for the rest of the flight, tapping the toe of her shoe on the seat in front of her just to bug her sister and watch the old guy in the hat turn his head more than once to stare at her as the jet's engines droned in the background.

She turned back to her Barbies and made a face. Just last week, upon learning about this trip, Lucy had found her blond Sun Jewel Ken doll and his date, long-maned Glitter Hair Barbie, dressed them up in a tux and long gown, and pretended that they were walking the red carpet, as if they were at the premiere of one of Mama's

old movies and Lucy's favorite, Tina Champagne in *Love
Goes Rogue.*

Going to that movie was the last thing that particular
Barbie and Ken had ever done as a couple.

Later that night, Lucy had decapitated them both.

Cascade Mountains, Oregon
Now

"Lucy? Looooocy? I know where you are," the shapeless,
dark figure whispered, stretching out her name and darting through the shadows. "You can't hide from me.
Loooooocy."

"No!" she tried to cry, but the word wouldn't come,
was stuck in her throat.

Run!

But her legs wouldn't move. It was as if they were
mired in quicksand, and when she raised her hands she
saw that they were covered in blood. Thick, warm, sticky
blood.

"Loooooocy," the figure hissed, and she tried to scream.

Lucy's eyes flew open, and for a second she didn't realize where she was. She blinked and focused on the dark,
unfamiliar room.

Renee! Where was—? Oh God.

Reality came crashing back and she knew she'd been
dreaming, that her nightmares had returned. Her daughter
and the dog were beside her on the floor, sleeping, not so
much as stirring.

But Lucy's heart was pounding, her nerves jangling
from the too-real images. Her watch told her it was barely
three in the morning, that there were hours until daylight.
Around her the old house moaned and settled in the wind.

She put another chunk onto the fire. Flames crackled and popped.

Shivering, she looked through the window.

The nightmare left her uneasy and brought her thoughts to the night it had all started, when Ray had attacked Mama. That was the way it was, right? Ray had come into the bedroom and started the fight. Mama had been in the bed, drinking and . . . She tried to remember, caught flashes of that horrid night:

Hiding in the bathroom.

Hearing the fight.

The fairy lights showing the anger on Mama's face, and Ray looming over the bed before they dimmed.

Even now, so many years later, Lucy felt her heart pounding.

She remembered running from her hiding spot in the bathroom, leaping toward the bed, the narrow scissors raised.

Just then, the hallway door opened.

"Oh, Jesus!" Marilyn rushed in. "Stop. Oh God, stop!"

"What the fuck?" Clark yelled.

Lucy plunged the scissors deep.

Ray yowled in pain, but he still had Mama pinned down. "You little bitch."

Someone was trying to pull Lucy off, and she heard the distinctive sucking sound of the scissors being yanked from flesh. Someone's hand grabbed the scissors, pulling them from her grasp.

Mama . . . Mama was still writhing beneath a cursing Ray.

Something shifted.

Lucy thought she saw an arm raise, the scissors winking in the barest of light from the doorway before being thrust downward.

Mama screamed again. Gurgling. Coughing. Frantic. Fighting for her life. And . . . and . . .

"And what?" Lucy said aloud in the cabin as the dark memory surged and receded, teasing her as it always did. "What?"

Blam! In her mind's eye, she saw the flash of the gun as it was fired. Point-blank into the tangle of bodies on the bed.

"Oh God," Lucy whispered now, dropping her head into her hands, her fingers digging into her scalp. This was where the memory always stopped. She never could remember any further. Squeezing her eyes, she tried to force the rest of the night back to the forefront of her mind, but she couldn't. There was just dead space. The next thing she recalled was the female officer, Lorna Davis, cradling her and carrying her down the stairs after Mama was hauled off on the stretcher.

"Damn it." She pounded the floor in frustration, and Merlin raised his head.

Stop, Lucy. Don't wake Renee. Get a grip.

But that was the problem. Her grip was slipping, her memories still buried. No amount of psychoanalysis had brought them forward. Not Sister Rosa at the school in Salzburg. Not a counselor when she'd returned to the States, not even the hypnotherapist she'd sought out in desperation when she'd felt her marriage was falling apart and blamed the trauma she'd suffered as a child. All dead ends.

She'd testified to what she remembered.

Because of it, Ray Watkins had spent a quarter of a century behind bars.

Don't dwell on it. Make a plan. For God's sake, do something. Hiding here is not the answer.

She made instant coffee and told herself not to let it get to her, but she knew Ray Watkins hadn't forgotten her. He'd somehow managed to find her address and sent her letters from prison, all written on white-lined paper and in pencil. Some had been poems, some had been drawings, and all of them had been friendly, at least on the surface, but Lucy had thought there were hidden messages on those carefully crafted pages. Were there eyes in the weeping willow tree that climbed up the side of one page, ghoulish orbs with severed flesh in the swirling trunk? And the vines that decorated another missive—were they twined branches circling the poem, or were they arms and hands interlocked and struggling?

Was she making more of it than was there?

No, she told herself, because somehow, someway, Ray had kept up with her, sending her a congratulatory letter after her marriage to Ian and then again, a month after she'd delivered Renee Grace into the world. Since that day, he'd always sent a letter that arrived the week of Renee's birthday, making note of the milestone of each passing year. Consequently, Lucy had both looked forward to the celebration of her daughter's birth and dreaded the arrival of the heart-stopping note.

He'd never written anything directly threatening. No. But it had been there. Lucy had read between the lines, felt the unspoken menace of his words, she thought, sipping from her mug.

Each day since driving up here, she'd walked down the hillside, over a mile to the spot where she'd parked her car, and there, she'd start her Toyota RAV4, ensuring that the battery wouldn't die. She was also able to recharge her phone while searching the internet for any sign of Ray Watkins. She always brought her daughter with her, much to Renee's delight, as she, too, could connect to the web, though, of course, she wasn't allowed to text or call anyone.

That would have to change.

Maybe later today.

Renee had to be allowed to contact her dad or Ian would go out of his mind. For that she should be thankful, she supposed, as her own father had been such a disinterested ass.

Since his release, Watkins hadn't tried to reach her.

She'd checked her email, but nothing.

She'd also flipped through news information, but his leaving the prison had gotten little notice. In a quarter of a century riddled with outrageous scandals shown daily on television or the internet and social platforms, what had happened between Ray Watkins, a small-time thug, and a B-movie actress whose star had faded decades earlier, was of little interest to a new generation.

But the calm was chilling, the radio silence deafening.

She might have thought it was over but for that last, final letter she'd received, just a week earlier. Another missive on white-lined paper with his address, including cellblock and the warning "Inmate Mail" on the plain envelope. Again, penciled vines encircled the page, slate-gray leaves and twined branches, some looking so much like ropes, the leaves joining like a noose surrounding a simple message:

I've missed you.

And, of course, a reference to a Bible verse had been attached.

Her stomach had dropped when she'd received the letter.

And that's when she'd run.

Which was her go-to in any stressful situation.

She'd left Ian twice in the eight years they'd been married, each time after a huge fight that she'd started. Both times she'd returned for home the next day and sworn she would never take flight again. Both times she'd lied.

Had she been foolish?

Had she been overly reactive?

Probably. But she couldn't be too careful. She slid a glance at her daughter. So precious. So beautiful. And so damned vulnerable.

Lucy's throat grew tight as she watched Renee sleep.

A few more days. She stared out the window, heard the wind howl and rattle the thin glass panes. They had enough supplies to last a couple more days and then she'd decide.

But she couldn't stay here forever.

The old, patchwork house shuddered, overhead beams creaking.

She glanced from the fire to the window and her heart stopped.

Through the frosted pane, she saw his face.

Etched against the icy glass was the watery visage of an indistinct figure.

She started.

A man.

Outside.

Oh Jesus.

She scrambled to her feet and snagged the rifle from the mantel, felt in the pocket of her vest for the shells. The image faded as the fire shifted, the shadows no longer shaped into the image of a face at the window, and she realized no one had been standing outside peering in. All she'd seen was the twisted bole of a fir tree and her own face reflected in the pane, her own wild imagination creating the image of the monster she hadn't seen in a quarter of a century.

Ray Watkins wasn't up here on the frigid slopes near Mount Hood.

The danger that existed was her own loose grasp of reality.

For God's sake, Lucy! Pull yourself together.

Los Angeles, California
Now

The last person Ian expected to see at Tina Champagne's hundred-year-old North Hollywood home was Clark Rivera, Lucy's half brother, but here he was, standing in the arched doorway and towering over Ian by a good two inches. Like his father, Clark was swarthy-skinned with black hair cut in a short military cut. His eyes were light brown, his nose hawkish, his attitude suspicious. "Well, whaddaya know," he said in the supercilious tone Ian had always found irritating. "My ex-brother-in-law. In the damned flesh." Clark seemed as surprised and disappointed as Ian was.

"Hey, Clark."

"You here to see Mom?"

"Yeah."

"Does she know it?"

"I called. Left a message with her assistant."

"Oh. Angie, right?" Clark was nodding, agreeing with himself. "Okay, then. She's out back, near the pool," and before Ian could comment, held up both hands, palms out. "Don't even ask, okay? It's her thing, part of her daily ritual, rain or shine, summer or winter. I learned a long time ago to just run with it."

"Fair enough. I'm here looking for Lucy," Ian explained.

"She's not here." Clark shook his head. "Barking up the wrong tree, Ian."

"I was hoping your mother could tell me where she is. Or maybe you."

"Oh, whoa." He held up a hand, palm out. "Leave me out of it."

"She's missing."

"And it's not the first time my kid sister went MIA. I thought you two were divorced."

Ian's jaw tightened.

"I'll take that as a 'yes,'" Clark said with a knowing look.

"Do you know where she is?"

"I haven't talked to Lucy since . . . well, since you two were married." His eyes narrowed. "Why the fuck do you care where she is?"

"She's my—she was my—wife. And Renee's mother."

"So file a Missing Persons report. You were a cop once if I remember correctly. And then an Assistant DA, right? So you know how the drill goes. Look, I've gotta run. I'm picking up some script for Mom at her agent's and, again, don't ask me why it's not being emailed, for the love of God, but . . ." He pulled a pair of Ray-Bans from his pocket and slid them over the bridge of his nose. "I'm just the errand boy today."

"You work for Tina?"

"Just a part-time gig until I get a job. Got an interview with a high-tech security firm tomorrow, as a matter of fact. Flying up to San Jose tonight. Interview in the morning, but for now, for at least one more day, I'm Tina Champagne's fuckin' errand boy. Story of my life."

And he was off, half-jogging to the Jeep Wrangler parked in the circular drive, its soft top off, its roll bar exposed. Clark climbed in, started the engine, and, with a chirp of tires, roared through the open gates.

The door to the house was still standing open, so Ian knocked on the dark panels and stepped into the cool interior with its white plaster walls, dark overhead beams, and a series of arches leading from one room to the other.

Sharp footsteps echoed on the dark tile floor, and a petite woman wearing a gray tunic and open-toed boots, her hair pulled back in a tight bun hurried into the foyer. "How did you—oh, you're the ex-son-in-law," she guessed. "I've seen pictures. We talked on the phone earlier." She extended her hand. "I assume Clark let you in. Angie Morales, Ms. Champagne's assistant. She's expecting you. She's out back." She led the way through a living room with a tiled fireplace and a baby grand piano and through French doors to the pool area.

Tina Champagne was waiting.

Lounging by her pool, wrapped in blankets, sunglasses covering part of her face, a big, floppy hat shading her forehead against Southern California's weak winter sun, she lifted a hand in greeting. She was still beautiful, he thought, though much of her retained youth was due to the skill of some of the best plastic surgeons the Golden State had to offer.

Sandal-clad feet stretched in front of her, a cup of coffee sat next to an ignored paperback on a small table.

"Ian," she greeted, her voice raspy, forever altered by the attack. She tossed off the blankets to stand and give him a hug complete with air-kisses. She was wearing a frothy sundress and shivered, rubbing her suddenly bare arms. "Sit, sit." She motioned to the matching chaise on the other side of the table. "Angie can get you coffee or something stronger."

"I'm fine." He sat on the end of the lounge as she settled back into her blankets, then stared across the water to the pool house, a casita replicating the main house, including its arched porch and tile roof. A groundskeeper was sweeping dried leaves off the decking surrounding a raised hot tub and a waterfall.

"I expect you're here about Lucy," Tina said.

"You know she's missing."

"I know she said she needed some time away. Didn't she say the same to you?"

"Quick text. No answer when I called."

"She left me a message, too."

"But didn't say where she was going?"

"No. Our relationship wasn't exactly close."

Not exactly a news flash. Now his flight to LA seemed

like a frivolous wild-goose chase. He'd been grasping at straws, but he was running out of options.

Tina said, "The truth is, I haven't seen her for months. I've barely met my only granddaughter. I think, though she's never admitted it, that Lucy never forgave me for sending her to Austria, though, why in God's name I can't imagine. As if I could have taken care of her in my state." She pursed her lips, still full and glossy, any fine lines carefully Botoxed away. "Her father and I agreed that boarding school would be best."

Her father. The long-absent Hamilton McKenna. He'd never been a part of Lucy's life, not as far as Ian knew. And was now dead. Heart attack after overdoing it in the gym.

"And you're not afraid of Ray Watkins?" he asked.

"God, no." She lifted her shades to stare directly at him with eyes as aqua as the water in her pool. "That's over. Ancient history. I haven't heard from him in twenty-five years and I don't see that it's going to change."

"He attacked you."

Shrugging, she settled the glasses back on the bridge of her nose. "So I'm told. I mean, yes, of course, but Ray insisted it was Lucy, though that seems unlikely. She did have the scissors, but the gun—?" Absently, she touched her neck where the tiniest of scars was still visible. "She knew where it was, of course, all the kids did, and Ray, too. Unfortunately, I don't remember. The whole night is a blur. A horrible, ghastly blur." The same words she'd told the police when she'd woken up in the hospital room. Maybe she'd been nearly passed out drunk, or perhaps the trauma of it all had placed a mental block on those memories, but Tina Champagne had always insisted that she didn't remember anything of that night. It had been

Lucy's testimony that had sent Ray Watkins to prison for half of his life, Lucy whom he blamed.

"You were fighting that night. You and Ray."

She let out a little laugh. "We always fought." With a smile, she added, "I fought with all of my husbands."

"Ray wasn't your husband."

"No, after Hamilton, I learned my lesson. Husbands are fine for the most part, they can be fun and attentive and . . . well, you know . . . the in-the-bed part, but exhusbands, which they invariably become? They're angry and petulant, and expensive." She sighed. "Such greed." She smiled again. "But still good in bed. In fact, if anything, a divorce tends to make them a little more thrilling. Edgy, you know?"

He did. Hadn't his own ex-wife become even more attractive now that she was no longer married to him? He'd never thought he'd taken Lucy for granted, but now he wondered about that as he stared at this woman he hardly knew. His ex-mother-in-law, who had lit out from Missouri at the age of eighteen to find fame and fortune in Hollywood. And she had. Working her way up from waitress to acting as a real-life Disney film character at Disneyland to eventually a TV ad, then a soap opera part, and finally a big, breakout movie. Along the way she'd picked up husbands and had children she named after the Hollywood legends she adored as a child: Clark Gable, Marilyn Monroe, and, finally, her third after Lucille Ball.

Lucy had hated that bit of information when the press got wind of it.

"What was the fight with Ray about?" he asked.

"I wanted him to leave," Tina said. "And he didn't want

to go. I remember that much. Ray wasn't very good at taking 'no' for an answer. Couldn't believe it was over."

"But it was."

"As far as I was concerned, yes." Tina's chin inched upward and she adjusted her sunglasses, her hand trembling a bit. "He . . . he and I saw our 'relationship,' if that's what you could call it, differently."

"How so?" he asked.

"He didn't think it was exclusive."

"And you did?"

A tic developed near her temple. "Yes . . . and I didn't like the way he . . ." She cleared her throat. "I suspected he was . . . involved, that's the delicate way of saying it. I thought he might be involved with my daughter."

"Your daughter?" Ian repeated.

"Not Lucille, of course, she was . . . a child. But he couldn't keep his eyes or his hands off Marilyn." She said it bitterly, as if the betrayal still stung, as if Ray's interest in her teenaged daughter was less about Marilyn's innocence, youth, and vulnerability than about her own damaged pride. "That was . . . over the line. My daughter?" Her lips flattened. "Off-limits. If Marilyn's father had ever found out, he would have killed Ray."

Marilyn Armstrong's father, Sean, had once been a stuntman with a penchant for Jack Daniel's whose trigger-sharp temper had gotten him thrown off more than one movie set.

"But he didn't?"

"Not that I know of. Unless Marilyn told him, which, I suppose she could have. Sean and I never talk. Never. Only through lawyers. Like I said, 'greed.' Sean, he was expensive. Good-looking. Oooh. So handsome, but he knew it. Aspired to be a leading man, but it never happened. He was jealous of my success. Anyway, the upshot is that we don't speak, so the subject of Marilyn's dalliance with Ray never came up."

"Dalliance?" Ian repeated.

"She flirted with him, outrageously. It was embarrassing. Worse, of course, is that Ray was attracted to any pretty young thing. Including my daughter."

"They had an affair?"

"Close enough. I don't know the details. Don't want to know."

But Ian suspected she did. He said, "Lucy is scared of Ray."

"I know, and I understand, but it's been years," Tina said, shoving her sunglasses upward to nest in her red hair. "Years."

"Still. She's had nightmares for as long as I've known her. About that night."

"I know, I know. She's been to psychologists and counselors, psychiatrists, you name it." Tina looked off into the middle distance, to a place only she could see, and for a second a flicker of sadness appeared in her eyes, but it quickly vanished as Tina's chin inched upward, almost defiantly. "I've done what I can for her, but the only one who can fix Lucy is Lucy. She's irrational. I mean, I understand that she was traumatized. Good Lord, we all were, and she was so young, but we're not the people we were then. None of us." Tina frowned, her eyebrows knitting, and he spied a few unwanted wrinkles appear on her near-flawless skin. "Why would Ray come after her now?"

"Because he's finally out and he promised he would."

"She's the only one who claims that. Something about her reading his lips in the courtroom. As if a child her age could do that, especially that one with her overactive imagination!" After dropping her sunglasses back down again, she reached for her coffee cup, took a sip, and scowled. "Cold." Then she sighed. "Anyway, Ray's been behind bars forever. I would think he would want to experience freedom and let the past go. Start over. Find a new life."

"Sometimes people feed on their need for revenge."

Sculpted eyebrows rose behind the rims of her dark glasses. "I hear he's found God. Why on earth would a person who is at peace and supposedly at one with his maker go out of his way looking for revenge?"

"Maybe he's an eye-for-an-eye kind of guy."

"And maybe, just maybe, Lucy has blown this all out of proportion. It wouldn't be the first time, now, would it?"

Salzburg, Austria
Then

"Hurry along, Lucille," Sister Anna encouraged, the skirt of her habit rustling, her rosary dangling from the rope at her waist, her shoes clicking as they reached the staircase that wound upward, stained-glass windows allowing in filtered light that cast colorful shadows on the stone steps. "It's not a good idea to keep Sister Maria waiting."

Lucy had trouble keeping up. She wasn't supposed to run, but Sister Anna's strides were long and she mounted the stairs quickly, holding up her skirts, making short work of the two flights to the headmistress's quarters.

She'd been pulled off the playground, where she and the other girls had been playing tag, chasing each other on the manicured lawns that surrounded the castlelike structure that was St. Cecilia's School for Girls.

The ceilings on the third floor were vaulted and dark, and Sister Maria's office was on the end of a long corridor.

She sat at her massive desk, an ample woman in her late fifties, her white coif framing a face with apple cheeks and a prominent chin. Spectacles sat on a small nose and the eyes behind the wire-rimmed lenses were dark and bright and intuitive. The crucifix hanging from her neck was large and seemed to wink in the lamplight. A fireplace burned softly in one corner.

"Sit, Lucille," she ordered in English, her German accent making the words sound stern to Lucy's ears. She then nodded to Sister Anna, who swept out of the room and closed the door with a soft click.

Lucy took a seat on one of the tall, high-backed chairs facing the desk and wondered what her unknown sin was. She'd never been called to the headmistress's office before and was certain she was in deep trouble. Maybe she'd been caught cheating on her math exam, or there was a chance someone had ratted her out for throwing out "good food" into the garbage, or had Beatrix Chevalier complained because Lucy had made faces at her during choir?

The woman behind the desk sighed and looked at her kindlier than Lucy had expected. She'd heard Sister Maria was a stern taskmaster, was inflexible, that her word was law, and anyone who disobeyed her or broke the rules was in for unspeakable punishment and trouble.

"How are you doing?" she finally asked and seemed curious.

"Fine."

"You fit in here with the other girls."

Was that a question? A *trick* question? Lucy had only been here six months, didn't really know what to expect. "Sure," she said, and realized she was swinging her feet, so she stopped and sat erect, hoping her uniform wasn't stained from the gravy she'd splattered at lunch.

"Any problems?"

"Nah . . . I mean, no, Sister." Lucy glanced away, to the window where, through the paned glass, she caught a view of the Alps, snow-covered peaks slicing up to the blue sky. She swallowed hard and met Sister Maria's gaze again.

The headmistress was nodding, as if having a private conversation with herself. She stood and walked over to the massive bookcase that loomed behind her. Every shelf was stuffed with hardbound tomes, and she seemed to study each, but Lucy thought she wasn't seeing the binding, but was turning something over in her mind.

I'm in for it now, Lucy thought, remembering that Mama had once said that the quiet snakes, those that didn't rattle or hiss, were most likely to strike, the deadliest. Her throat grew tight and she was sweating, her fingers gripping the arms of her chair so tightly her knuckles bulged and showed white, and damn—er, darn it, her legs were swinging wildly again. Once more she forced them to be immobile.

The headmistress returned to her chair, opened the desk drawer, and, as if she were throwing dice at a gaming table, flipped two wobbling, colorful objects across the desk.

Lucy's heart froze.

She stared at the rolling heads of her Barbie and Ken

dolls as they stopped before her, Barbie's hair a wild mess, Ken staring straight up.

Lucy thought she might be sick.

"These are yours."

Not a question.

Not a trick question.

A statement.

"Found in your pillow."

Could she lie and get away with it? Insist the disfigured doll parts didn't belong to her? Denial formed on her lips, but when she looked up and met the nun's cool, unyielding stare, she held her tongue and swung her leg.

"This is disturbing, Lucille," Sister Maria said in a soft voice. "But . . . you've been through a lot and . . . I've prayed on this, and I've spoken with your sister—"

Lucy's head snapped up and she felt tears spring to her eyes. Marilyn would tease her mercilessly for the rest of her life if she knew . . . but it seemed like it had already happened.

"I want you to talk to Sister Rosa," she said. "She's a doctor, you know."

A doctor? But she wasn't sick.

"A . . . counselor. Someone you can open up to." Sister Maria offered a small smile. "I think it would be good for you to spend some time with her."

Lucy stared at the doll heads, but didn't dare pick them up. She understood intuitively that would be a mistake, so she sat on her hands because she wanted to touch them, to rub them. She knew it was weird to keep them, but they reminded her of why she hated living so far away from her home in California.

At the thought of the stucco house surrounded by

palm trees, she felt an all-too-familiar pang and tried to ignore it.

And wished like crazy that she could leave with the heads, but she glanced up at Sister Maria and knew that doing so would be a vast, irreversible mistake, so she contented herself with staring at them and tried not to think what would happen once she met with Sister Rosa.

Cascade Mountains, Oregon
Now

"I'm freezing," Renee complained as night settled over the old house.

She was sitting cross-legged on the blankets in front of the fire, its golden shadows shifting across her face.

Lucy, who had been heating soup on one of the two burners of the kitchen stove that worked, nodded. "I know. Me too."

Five days on the mountain, sometimes with near whiteout conditions and the firewood almost gone. The old furnace was rumbling, and though it had started out smelling as if something dry was burning, it was now somewhat working, though never raising the temperature of the rooms above the midsixties. Not that it mattered. She and Renee camped out in the main room of the house, the doors to the wings shut tight and locked because she didn't like the idea of anyone slipping in through a window or creeping along a back hallway unnoticed.

She'd made this central area their fortress, barricading themselves inside.

Do you know how paranoid that sounds?

"I'm bored," Renee announced as Lucy returned to the

living room and placed one of the mugs she was carrying on the scarred coffee table they used as their dining area, game table, and footstool. "Here ya go." She sat on the floor and braced her back against the sagging couch. "You're just mad because you lost at Battleship." She'd brought several pocket-size games along with a deck of cards, but they'd played them all over and over again.

"I hate that game." Renee turned her head and leveled a steady gaze at her mother. They'd played cards, made snow angels, and dug a snow fort outside, where Renee had insisted they leave a flashlight to shine onto the icy ceiling and walls, which now, with the continued blizzard, had become a cave, buried in the powder. They had also counted the icicles hanging from the eaves and explored the extra bedrooms of one wing of the house, with its connecting closets. The second wing was little more than a storage area, a rabbit warren complete with skis and snowboards and hiking and hunting gear. In one of the cupboards she'd discovered the hunting rifle with a scope, a bayonet, and ammunition, all of which Lucy had confiscated and kept with her at all times. The rifle was now, unloaded, on the mantel.

Ready.

Just in case she needed it.

Please, God, that she didn't.

"When are we leaving?" Renee asked as she stirred her soup, the spoon clinking against the sides of the cup.

"Soon."

"You said that yesterday."

"Yeah, I know. But I mean it."

San Francisco, California
Now

Ian tossed his jacket over the back of the desk chair in his bedroom and stretched. He didn't know what he'd expected when he'd visited Tina Champagne, but something more than what he'd gotten. He sensed that all of Lucy's family—Tina, Marilyn, and Clark—knew more about his ex-wife's whereabouts than they were admitting. But that was par for the course. They'd never liked him. And Tina, bless her twisted heart, had cautioned him about her daughter.

"She's not your normal girl, Ian," she'd said, warning him off by phone after he and Lucy had eloped. Of course it had been too late, and with Renee on the way, the point was moot. "She's been through a lot. Trauma."

"We'll be okay," he'd assured his new mother-in-law.

Tina's response to their quickie marriage had been echoed by her older children. Skepticism? Yes. Resentment? Maybe. Suspicion? For certain.

They'd met Marilyn for lunch in Newport Beach, at a café with outdoor tables scattered beneath wide umbrellas. Marilyn, already seated and sipping a mimosa, the stemmed glass glistening in the sunlight, had surveyed Ian from behind oversize sunglasses. "So we're family now, I guess." She'd shaken her head. "You met at a seminar?"

"He spoke at my college. Criminal law," said Lucy.

"Huh. Criminal law. And you're going to be a teacher?"

"An interest of mine. You know that."

"Yeah, you like criminal anything. It's weird, Lucy," Marilyn had muttered, then, when Lucy didn't rise to the bait, asked, "And so what happened with you two?" She waved her glass back and forth to indicate both of them. "Love at first sight and bing, bang, boom, you get pregnant and married? I hope you know what you're doing." She'd said it to Lucy, but somehow he'd felt the words had been meant for him.

Clark had been stationed overseas at the time and they hadn't met until the next year, after Renee was born, but the attitude was the same. Befuddled at the marriage, not all that interested in the baby.

Yeah, theirs had been a strange marriage, but he had trouble believing it was over. And now . . .

Now his phone jangled on the bedside table.

A number he didn't recognize.

But he answered. "Hello?"

"Hi, Daddy!"

Renee! His knees buckled at the sound of his daughter's voice.

He dropped onto the corner of the bed, relief flooding through him. "Hey, baby. How are you? Where are you?"

"In the mountains!"

"What mountains?"

"I don't know, but we drove a long time. It was sooo boring."

"Oh, sweetie, I've missed you."

"Me too, Daddy! We made snow angels and a snow fort, even with a light, and Merlin got lost," she said all in a tumble, eager to share with him, then added, "But this place is gross!"

"Gross? How?"

"Yeah, like weird and creepy. Like a . . . like a haunted house."

"That doesn't sound good." Where the devil were they?

"I know. Mommy's got all the doors locked. Like she's scared."

Jesus.

"Daddy, I want to come home."

He felt his heart crack. "And I want you to come home. When are you coming back?"

"I don't know . . . Mommy?" He heard muffled conversation, as if Renee had turned her head away from the phone, her voice saying, "Daddy wants to know when we're going home."

A beat. Silence. Then, "I'm not sure." Lucy's voice, too, was muffled from afar, and a deep emotion stirred in him. Anger, yes, but longing as well. God, he'd loved her. Once upon a time. That the feelings still lingered pissed him off.

Voice still indistinct, Lucy said, "We'll go home soon."

A lie, he thought. She had no plans. He knew that.

"Honey," he said into the phone, trying to get his daughter's attention. "Renee?"

"Yeah?" his daughter was back.

"Can you put Mommy on the phone for just a sec?"

"Okay." Again her voice became indistinct, but he heard, "Daddy wants to talk to you."

Boy, did he, and he wanted to yell and rant, but he told himself that would be unproductive, that he needed information, not her immediate response of ending the call, so he fought the fear that was beginning to crawl through him.

"Hey," his ex-wife said, and the soft sound of her voice caused a physical reaction, an eroding of his resolve.

"Where are you?"

A pause that stretched too long.

"Lucy?" he prompted. When she didn't immediately respond, he pushed, "I need to know. As Renee's father." He didn't say the rest, but the unspoken threat of his parental right, possibly to the point of getting the police involved, was out there.

"In Oregon, okay?" she finally admitted. "In the mountains."

"Where in the mountains?" Oregon had tons of mountain ranges all throughout the state.

"At . . . at a friend's cabin."

"What friend?"

"You don't know her. Someone I work with."

His jaw tightened and his free hand clutched the bedspread, wrinkling the quilting. "Lucy," he said as calmly as possible, "where are you?"

Another few seconds of silence passed as she hesitated, and Ian thought he might go mad. Finally, she said in a rush, "I—I can't say, Ian. You—you know why."

"Because of Ray Watkins."

"Yeah."

"And you think I would tell him, or that he would be listening in . . . Lucy, listen, you can't run and hide from him, even if he is a threat—"

"He is!"

"Don't you think you'd be safer with me? Here?"

She didn't answer.

"With people around?"

He heard a sigh. Felt her indecision.

"I don't know."

"Does anyone know where you are?"

She hesitated a second too long. "No. Not really."

"You told someone."

"I had to. In case something happened."

"Who?" he demanded.

"My aunt."

"Beth," he said, thinking of Beth Smith, who had not, unlike her sister, changed her name to Champagne.

"I have Renee with me. Someone had to know."

"Didn't you think I was the logical person?"

"Of course."

"But—?" he prodded, anger coursing through his blood.

"But you would have come up here."

"Damn straight."

"And Ray would have followed you."

"You don't know that." Ian released the bedspread and tried to remain calm, to sound steady. "Being holed up in the mountains alone—what were you thinking?"

Lucy let out a long breath. "I guess maybe I panicked."

"Way more than panicked," he said, and tried to keep his voice even, his worry disguised. "I'll come for you."

"No!"

"Lucy—"

"No, Ian. Just for once listen! We'll come back in a few days. I promise. We will. Once I know what I'm going to do. How I'm going to handle this. But I needed space, you know. Distance. To figure it out. I know. I know I've had years to think about it, but it was always in the future, not real, and then . . . and then it happened. He was released. Early! As I said, I freaked out, and so we're up here now, but I thought, I mean, I just wanted Renee to talk to you so that she could connect and you would know she's okay. And there was bound to be a lot of press around with Watkins being released, everything dredged up again. . . . I didn't want her to go through that. She's too young."

"But—"

"Has he contacted you?" she asked suddenly.

"No. Why would he?"

"I don't know. That's just it. I don't know what he'll do."

"Lucy, this has got to stop."

But she kept asking. "What about Mom or anyone else? Marilyn? Clark? Aunt Beth?"

"Not that I know."

"But you're monitoring him." It wasn't a question. When he didn't immediately respond, she said, "Jun, the woman you work with, Jun Zhou, she's like an intelligence whiz, right? That's what you told me. That she can hack into any computer system, that nothing was sacred or off-limits, right? Does she know where he is?"

"Okay, you're right. We've checked. As far as I know, Ray Watkins is at his sister's house in Fresno, starting up some religious group meetings for ex-cons."

"You believe that?"

Did he? Ian walked to the window to stare through the rain-spattered glass to the lamppost illuminating the street three stories below. A woman was huddled against the rain, walking a small dog, passing through the pool of light. "From all accounts, it's what's happening."

"Don't be fooled, Ian. Whatever Ray's up to is a scam."

"And you know this how?"

"Because it's Ray Watkins, and running a con is all he knows. I—I really have to go. I've only got so much power." Then her voice was indistinct again, "Hey, Renee, say 'goodbye' to Daddy."

A moment later, Renee's small voice came over the wireless connection. "Mommy wants me to say goodbye. And now I 'member. I saw Mountain Hoodie, isn't that right, Mommy? When we were driving here?"

"Just tell Daddy goodbye." Lucy's voice was strained.

"Mommy says I have to go."

"I heard that," Ian said.

"I don't want to."

Ian's throat tightened. "I know."

"Daddy, can you please come get me?"

He felt as if he'd been hit in the gut. "Sure, honey. I just need to know where you are."

"Let me have the phone," Lucy said, then more loudly, as if she'd wrestled the cell away from their child, "Goodbye, Ian."

She clicked off.

He immediately called her back.

She didn't answer.

He tried again.

This time he was certain the call didn't go through. Lucy had turned off her damned phone.

Cascade Mountains, Oregon
Now

"I hate you!"

Renee's harsh words echoed through the old cabin and

cut deep into Lucy's soul. They were uttered in anger and frustration, she knew, but they hurt nonetheless.

"You're just mad."

"No. I *really* hate you." And to prove her point, Renee upended the little table, scattering the Uno cards from their last game and sending Lucy's half-drunk cup of coffee sailing across the room, to shatter against the floor.

"Stop it. Ren—Grace, don't!"

"It's stupid that we're up here! I want to be with Daddy."

I do, too. That thought surprised Lucy. Gave her pause. She did miss Ian. And not just because of Ray Watkins; no, that just put an edge on the need, to the thought that she'd been rash when she'd divorced him. But this was not the time to second-guess herself.

Once they were through this current nightmare . . .

But will you ever be?

Yes, yes, of course. She would make certain. "Come on, help me clean this up," she said, and Renee, still petulant and sending her dirty looks, picked up the cards while Lucy righted the table, gathered the big pieces of the destroyed cup, and wiped up the coffee that probably would stain the area rug. So she could add property damage to trespassing, breaking and entering, and whatever other crimes she'd committed.

Get it together!

She held on to the rapidly disintegrating rags of her patience. "Look, I know you miss Daddy, and I promise, we'll go home soon."

Renee still gave her the cold shoulder and cuddled with Merlin instead.

San Francisco, California
Now

Zhou was wearing yoga pants, her hair pulled back in a tight ponytail when Ian met her at the office. "This better be important," she said. She settled into her desk chair and started switching on computer screens. "I was on my way to a very important spin class."

"I need to find my wi . . . Lucy."

"You have any clues, or is this a needle-in-a-haystack kind of deal?" she asked, fingers already flying over the keyboard.

He handed her his phone. "This is the number of the phone that called me. Probably a burner."

"Got it." She entered the number in her computer. "Any clue to where she is?"

"Just that she's in the 'mountains' of Oregon."

"That narrows it down," Zhou said sarcastically.

"She's in a cabin."

"Please." She rolled her eyes. "How does that help me?"

"Possibly near Mount Hood. Renee said Mountain Hoodie, but I think—"

"Yeah, yeah. Got it." Zhou's fingers worked fast, clicking the keys.

"It's owned by an uncle of one of her coworkers at the junior college."

"Got a name?"

"No."

Her gaze moved from the first screen to his face. "For the love of God, Thompson, I'm a hacker not a miracle worker."

"That's all I've got. I'm heading up there."

"Where?"

"To the place you find," he said. "Call me with directions."

"If I find a place."

"You will," Ian said and took off, taking the stairs to the first floor of the building and the parking garage. Minutes later he was wending his way through traffic and crawling across the Bay Bridge, red brake lights a steady stream ahead of him, blocking his path, causing the seconds of his life to tick by.

Ever since speaking with Lucy and Renee, he'd felt an ever-rising sense of panic, an urgency to get to them, as if his ex-wife's paranoia were infectious and could be transmitted over a wireless cell phone connection.

Stay calm. Everything's fine. You talked to them less than an hour ago.

But the pressure on his chest was intense and he found himself weaving in and out of the lanes, his fingers drumming on the steering wheel, the need to get to his family overwhelming.

You don't even know where they are.

Not true. Oregon was a vast state, yes, but he knew he had to get north and fast, at least cross the damned state line. "Come on, come on," he heard himself saying out loud, willing the traffic to lessen, but the clog didn't disperse, and only after a soul-gouging hour was he able to punch the accelerator of his Tahoe and put the Bay area in his rearview.

Less than two hours later, Zhou called him.

"You've found her," he said.

"Maybe. We'll see. But I did find a connection." She told him that she'd located the cell tower from which

Lucy's call had pinged. She'd also broken into the personnel records of the school where Lucy worked and found a name that she cross-referenced against names of property owners who owned parcels of land close to said cell tower. "I'll text you a map of the area and the cabin owned by Winston Jacoby, who just happens to be the uncle of Cynthia Jane Jacoby, who works in the same department as Lucy at the community college. And that's all I've got. If I turn up anything else, I'll call."

"Thanks, Jun. I owe you."

"I'll add it to your ever-growing tab."

"Do that, and while you're at it, keep an eye on Ray Watkins," he said and she gave a snort.

"Already done."

Salzburg, Austria
Then

"We have a bit of a situation," Sister Maria admitted and returned to the desk. She sat down, opened a drawer, and retrieved a fat manila envelope, which she placed on her desk.

How many times had Lucy sat in this very chair, often being reprimanded, sometimes being guided, always told to find her spirituality by the headmistress. She wasn't sure of the exact number, but at least twice a year, she figured, and now, at eighteen, she'd been at the school about a decade, so somewhere around twenty. She wondered vaguely if it was some kind of record.

This, the centuries'-old grounds with its school, chapel, and cathedral had been her home, her sanctuary while Tina Champagne's house in California was a place for vacations and time between semesters. And now she was leaving. As much as she'd hated being sent here as a child, she was now feeling some reluctance at returning to the States.

"Since you've graduated, and are of age, Sister Rosa and I think it's time."

"Time for what?" Lucy asked. She'd come a long way from the timid, scared eight-year-old who had first sat at the headmistress's massive desk. Or the girl who had petulantly attended Sister Rosa's counseling sessions, pretending disinterest, though all the while curious about what the psychologist who had become a nun thought about her. Sister Rosa had been in her twenties when they'd started with Lucy's sessions, a woman not much older than Clark had been, and over the years Lucy had learned to trust Sister Rosa with her kind, dark eyes and quick, easy smile, a flash of white against coppery skin.

Now, as Lucy reached for the envelope, the nun placed her hand over the far edge, pinning it against the polished surface of the desk, not yet releasing it. "I want you to know that I've prayed a lot, Lucille. For you. When your family asked that you be boarded here, I understood your mother's plight and the . . . situation that sent you and your sister here. It was agreed that you would be here not only for your education, but your protection as well."

Where was this going? Lucy eyed the envelope.

"We, here at St. Cecilia's, have kept our part of the bargain."

"And?"

"And in so doing, we've kept something from you."

"What?" Lucy asked, a needle of dread pricking deep into her heart.

"These. Sister Rosa and I have discussed this and, again, prayed on it, and because these are legally your property, we are giving them to you." Her eyes behind the wire-rimmed glasses held hers as she released the packet. "I'm a believer in the theory that 'forewarned is fore-armed.'"

Lucy picked up the envelope, her skin crawling as she lifted the flap and saw the Barbie and Ken heads atop a bound bundle of white envelopes. She slid the envelopes out.

"Letters?" she whispered, not understanding. She'd been getting mail here every week. "You stole my let-ters?"

"Kept them," she said gently. "We were always going to give them to you. It was just a matter of finding the right time." Her voice was grave. "That was the problem, Lucille. There never was a right time. Nor is there yet, I fear."

The top letter was legible, her name in block letters written in pencil above the address of the school, a stamped warning—Inmate Mail—catching her eye.

"What are these?" she whispered, her hands trembling. There had to be fifty envelopes, maybe more. All the exact same size.

"Correspondence we thought it best, for your protec-tion, not to show you."

The return address included numbers and a cellblock, along with Raymond Watkins's name.

Lucy's heart turned to ice.

"We can burn them if you like," Sister Maria said, motioning to the fireplace in the corner.

"No." Lucy shook her head and stood. She was going to read every word the monster had written. At least once. "As you said, Sister, 'Forewarned is forearmed.'"

Cascade Mountains, Oregon
Now

Night was again cloaking the mountains.

After their fight, Renee had fallen asleep in her sleeping bag on the floor near the dying fire, and Merlin was curled up next to her. Lucy sat, propped against the couch, staring at the embers, her arms surrounding her jean-clad knees.

It had been hours since she had spoken to Ian on the phone. Since that conversation, she'd turned off the damned burner phone, just so he couldn't call her again and she wasn't tempted to answer. The sound of his voice had taken her back to another time and place, to the years of carefree abandon, college in Colorado, her first job teaching in a private school in San Francisco, and meeting Ian at a fundraiser, benefit dinner that she'd been forced to attend. Ian Thompson had been one of the speakers and appeared as uncomfortable as she. They'd talked briefly that night, he'd shown up at her school the next day, and . . . well, the rest was history, whirlwind romance, unplanned pregnancy, eloping to Las Vegas for a quick wedding. Not exactly a fairy tale, but her story. And though she was now divorced, she had a wonderful, if stubborn daughter, whom she loved with all her heart.

Yet here she was, trespassing and hiding out in a stranger's cabin, wondering if she, as so many people near her thought, was irrational and fearful to the point of paranoia.

Crazy or sane, you need to stay safe, to keep Renee safe. If you look like a mental case to the outside world, what do you care?

The shadows of midnight were creeping in.

Again.

The wind was picking up, howling through the trees.

Again.

Lucy doubted she could sleep.

Again.

The old timbers creaked, and for a second she thought she heard footsteps over the storm. But that was nuts, right? Just her imagination. Still, she had to be certain. "Come on," she said gently, touching the Malamute on the back of his head. "Let's go outside. Check things out. Come."

Taking the rifle with her, she pointed the bayonet in front of her as she let the dog out and, from the porch, watched as he sniffed around the edges of the house and the path leading to the snow cave. While Merlin searched for squirrels or rabbits or whatever, she eyed the area around the cabin, where their footprints were covered in the icy powder of the ever-falling snow and the drifts were piling high against the rough walls of the house.

She spied paw prints from the dog and a trail of other small, deep impressions, probably from a deer.

No human footprints.

And yet she didn't feel that she was alone. The back of her neck tingled, suggesting that someone or something was watching her. But she saw no eyes staring at her through the swirling snow, no dark figure lurking at the tree line.

Overactive imagination. You're here alone with your child and dog. That's it.

She was about to go inside, but took one last look around, turning slowly to survey the white landscape, her cheeks pummeled with sharp crystals.

The wind was brutal, coming in icy blasts that rattled the windows and screamed around the corners of the house.

In seconds, despite her down jacket, boots, and wool cap, she was cold to the bone. Shivering.

"Come," she said to the dog, and followed him into the house, where the fire was dying, the edges of the room muted and shadowed. How long could she stay here? Sooner or later she'd be found. Someone was bound to see the lights or smell or see the smoke curling up from the chimney, or the heat exhaust from the furnace. Or someone might come across her car, and then there would be that pesky but incriminating electricity bill.

Also, her food was running low.

And she'd promised Renee they would return soon.

If Ray Watkins was really intent on chasing her down, wouldn't he have already shown?

Hiding wasn't solving any of her problems, just prolonging them. And what would happen if she got caught here by the owners? She stared through the window to the dark night. Soon, within the week, she'd leave.

And go where?

Ray could be waiting for you.

Biding his time until you return.

With Renee.

Her throat went dry and she tamped down the panic that kept rising in her. Maybe returning to California had been a big mistake. She thought of the years of torment he'd inflicted, the weekly letters, always without rancor, sometimes poetic, oftentimes apparently thoughtful, and often with a Bible verse attached, but they'd always given her chills and she'd seen through the normal words to the deeper, more-sinister subtext.

And that last letter:

I've missed you.

But there was more. The accompanying Bible verse that had been included in his letter and was unfamiliar to her. Did it, like so many of the others, she suspected hold a secret message for her? She couldn't look it up on the internet, not now, but she'd seen a Bible in the bookcase in an upper bedroom. As Renee slept, she climbed the main staircase, the steps creaking under her weight. The upper hallway was dark and colder. She didn't want to risk flipping on a light because it might be visible, a beacon in the night.

Using a flashlight, she located the bookcase, stuffed with dusty tomes in what was the largest bedroom. A faded rug covered the planks of the floor; the bed, draped in a floral sheet, positioned against the far wall. She let the beam shine over the faded books, and there on a lowest shelf, she found what she was searching for: a Bible. It was old and worn, its spine broken, several of the thin pages falling free. King James version.

She flipped through the pages quickly, finding Romans and turning to the passage:

For he is the minister of God to thee for good.

*But if thou do that which is evil, be afraid; for he
beareth not the sword in vain: for he is the
minister of God, a revenger to execute wrath upon
him that doeth evil*. Romans 13:4

Fear as cold and bleak as the night swept through her.

The message was clear. Ray Watkins considered himself the minister of God, the revenger and executioner.

From habit, she sketched the sign of the cross over her chest, then hurried quickly to the lower level. Had she made the right choice coming here? Was it safe? Should she take Renee and the dog and leave, hide out in a city filled with people rather than this isolated cabin?

She checked on Renee, then double-checked all the doors and windows before settling in front of the fire again. She, Renee, and the dog were barricaded. Safe. She just needed to get through one more night; then she would call Ian in the morning. Meet him somewhere. Find a new hiding spot.

Maybe you don't need one. Maybe Ray Watkins sent that last letter and is moving on with his life.

She didn't believe that for a second.

Then call Ian back. Call him now.

She picked up the burner phone, thought it over, and slipped it back into her pocket.

She'd been half-crazed when she'd left him and filed for divorce, certain that he'd been cheating on her. Now, though, she wasn't so sure. Or perhaps, because she was facing a life-and-death situation, whether he'd had an affair or not wasn't so big a deal.

Who're you kidding? If the guy can't be faithful, he's not worth your time. . . .

She settled in next to Renee, listening to the fire hiss and pop and knowing sleep, tonight, would be elusive.

As it had been ever since Ray Watkins had been released from prison.

She thought of him as a young man. His swagger, his bravado. How he'd loved being the eye candy escorting Tina Champagne to openings of her latest movie, or at restaurants, or hosting parties at her home. But there had always been a rough side to him, and a glint in his eye that had bothered her, even as a girl. Something about the way he treated Mama, the way she let him treat her.

Much later, Lucy had learned from Marilyn that he'd had a wandering eye, that he'd cheated on Mama, and that was the reason Tina Champagne had sent her daughters abroad. Marilyn had explained it all before she'd left the boarding school for college in France.

"It's probably my fault," Marilyn had explained while packing her bags in the small dorm room she'd occupied for the past two years. Wearing a yellow dress Aunt Beth had sent, one Marilyn had declared, "gross, but at least not a uniform," she was searching through the piles of clothes still on her stripped bed.

"Your fault?" Lucy sat on a stool near the arched window over the desk, while all of Marilyn's things—her clothes and jewelry, a diary, and her makeup kit—were being shuffled haphazardly into two suitcases.

"Yeah. My fault." Marilyn flipped her hair over her shoulder. "Where the fu–where's my brush? Damn it, it was right here." She began rummaging through the small piles.

"What do you mean?"

"Oh, it was because Ray was into me, y'know."

"Into you?" Lucy repeated.

"You saw it," she declared. She turned her head to stare at Lucy and arch her eyebrows. "I mean, like *into* me. As in physically."

"What?"

"That's what pissed Mom off. Y'know, cuz I was only like seventeen."

When Lucy just stared at her, Marilyn added, "You're *such* a child."

"Almost nine."

"Going on three. Where's my brush?" She began throwing in the neatly folded blouses and sweaters and a pair of jeans, all she had with her other than the navy blue uniform of the school. "Did you take it?"

"No."

"You're sure? Cuz I know you're a little klepto. First my ring. My ruby ring." Her eyes narrowed on her. "Did you take it?"

"Your brush?"

"My *ring*. I haven't seen it for like three days!"

Lucy asked, "You liked him?"

"What—who? Oh, Ray?" She shook her head as she pulled the thin mattress from her bed. "Not really. I just did it to piss Mom off, and it worked. But he was only a few years older than me, y'know. Oh—there it is!" She scooped up the brush. "How'd it get . . . ?" Again she looked over her shoulder to meet Lucy's gaze. "You hid this here, didn't you? You're such a little head case. I know what you used to do to your dolls. To mine! I found them, you know, the naked bodies. Of those Barbie and Ken dolls."

Lucy didn't respond.

"You hid them in *my* underwear drawer. Who does that kind of thing? What kind of freakoid are you?"

Lucy asked, "You did it with him?"

"Did it? Oh, like had sex?"

"Yes. With him."

She hesitated, then shook her head again, but Lucy suspected she was lying. Marilyn always lied. In the two years they'd been at St. Cecilia's, the nuns hadn't been able to change her older sister or make Marilyn more holy, or whatever it was they were supposed to do.

Lucy charged, "You like getting into trouble."

Marilyn rolled her eyes. "Maybe. I guess I'm just a 'rebel' or a 'naughty girl.'" Her eyes danced as she'd made the air quotes. And then she threw her brush into her bag. "Just keep your hands off my stuff, okay? If you get out of this prison and we see each other again, like in another lifetime? Remember: hands off!" With that she stuffed all her clothes into her suitcase just as Aunt Beth appeared, the scents of perfume and cigarettes accompanying her.

"Ready?" she asked Marilyn.

"Oh yeah." Marilyn zipped the last bag closed, then cast Lucy a too-bad-for-you look and stepped into the hallway, her footsteps quick and retreating on the wood floors, the smaller bag rolling loudly behind her.

"I have to go now, honey," Aunt Beth said, taking the time to give Lucy a hug. "It's been so good to see you." Aunt Beth had been in Salzburg for the three days during

Marilyn's graduation ceremonies. "I'm settling Marilyn into an apartment in Paris. Can you imagine? What eighteen-year-old girl doesn't dream of that?"

Lucy had answered, "I want to go home."

"I know."

"I want to see Mama."

"And she wants to see you, too. But she's still not well, Lucy, and it just wouldn't be a good idea, you know? She's trying to get her career going again, too, and . . ." She didn't finish because they both knew it was all a lie. Mama wrote letters. Mama called on the phone. Lucy went home for vacations. But for some reason Mama didn't want her living with her. Aunt Beth probably knew why, but she just wouldn't say. Marilyn had told her it wasn't just because of Mama's life-threatening injuries.

"Nah," she'd explained when Lucy had brought it up after vespers. She'd caught Marilyn heading back to her dorm and asked about it. "Mama was hurt, yeah, but she got better. We'll both see her soon. She didn't just send us clear over here for our protection, you know. That wasn't it."

"Then what was it?" Lucy had asked as Marilyn headed for the wide staircase.

"She was jealous, silly! Why do you think?"

And then she'd dashed up the stairs, ignoring the sisters' dark looks and shushing noises. That was the trouble with Marilyn. She always broke the rules.

"It's okay," Lucy lied to Aunt Beth, and though she felt tears sting the backs of her eyes, she wouldn't let them fall.

"Oh, baby." Aunt Beth hugged her tight. "I love you."

And then, dabbing at her eyes, she'd left, dragging the larger roller suitcase, her footsteps echoing hollowly from the corridor until there was nothing but the sound of the church bells tolling loudly, as if counting off the hours of Lucy's life.

She turned to stare out the window, to the grounds and the long drive that encircled a fountain at the front entrance of the school. She waited until the bells stopped ringing and she'd spied Aunt Beth hustling Marilyn in her yellow dress off into a waiting car. Marilyn didn't even look up.

As the car drove away, past the fountain and down the lane to the main gate, Lucy removed the treasure from her pocket, eyed the blood-red stone, and slipped the ring easily onto her finger.

Central Oregon
Now

Ian pushed the speed limit.

Despite the snow flurries and icy patches on the road.

He'd driven steadily north along I-5 until his GPS directed him inland through mountainous Central Oregon, where snow was falling steadily, still hours from the Mount Hood forest and his destination. He only hoped Lucy and Renee were there.

You should get the police involved.

And tell them what? That my ex-wife, who has a history of paranoia, is missing, even though she called me and told me she was fine, even though I spoke to my daughter just last night, even though, by all accounts, Ray Watkins, the ex-con whom she feared, is tucked inside his sister's home in Fresno, probably leading a prayer meeting or something. Even though this isn't the first time my wife has gone missing and each time returned unscathed. She's my ex. Remember? That's what she wanted. Because she thought I was having a damned affair. That was my fault, too, idiot. So I didn't end up sleeping with Jenna, I was tempted, wasn't I? A friend of a friend who showed interest in me when my wife was distracted. What's that called? Emotional infidelity.

He put the brakes on that line of thinking. It would get him nowhere.

On the outskirts of Bend, still two hours from the Jacoby property, he found a twenty-four-hour gas station/minimart. The refuel light was already glowing on the dash, so he pulled off to fill his tank, grab a prewrapped deli sandwich, and a cup of coffee and stretched his legs in the snow-covered parking lot before climbing behind the wheel again.

The coffee was bitter but hot, the ham-and-cheese sandwich flavorless, but he kept driving, his fingers tight on the wheel, his thoughts on his wife. He'd known she was damaged when he'd married her, had read about her, but had fallen in love with her quick smile, sharp wit, and deep, if slightly dark sense of humor. There had been quirks, of course, little jagged edges, an overly curious interest in all murder mysteries, no matter how grisly. Ian had been a cop. An assistant DA. He, too, was intrigued by the inner workings of the criminal mind, of the puzzling out of bizarre mysteries, but with Lucy it had been deeper, almost as if she thought she could understand what made the deviant mind tick.

Ian drove into the mountains. The road narrowed.

Snow piled high on the sides of the road that had once been plowed but now was covered in white again. The beams of his headlights reflected off patches of ice, his wipers struggled to keep up with the blizzardlike conditions.

Headlights bore down upon him, nearly blinding him in the rearview. A pickup roared past, spraying up road sludge, his wipers struggling with the dirt, ice, and grit.

His phone rang, the screen lighting up the interior of his SUV.

Zhou's name and picture flashed on the screen. Why would she be calling at 4:17 in the morning?

It had to be bad news.

He answered, his dread mounting. "What's up?"

"Just want you to know," Zhou said, her voice stern. "The cell phone that Ray Watkins purchased when he got out hasn't moved. It's still at his sister's house."

"That's good, right?" he said slowly.

"Not sure. The men's group session he was leading last night was canceled; I double-checked. Basically because Watkins was a no-show."

Ian's dread spiked. "Have you talked with his sister?"

"No," Jun admitted. "She's not answering. I had Gonzales drive over there and look around. He couldn't see in the upper-story windows, but no one answered the door. He saw a cat inside, wandering, but that's it."

Ian's guts tightened. "Keep looking."

"Will do. I've got a call in to his parole officer. Waiting to hear back."

Ian's fingers tightened over the wheel. He thought of Lucy. Of Renee.

"When's the last time anyone saw him?"

"Don't know. Maybe two days ago. Like I said, I'm waiting to talk to his PO."

"Hell."

"I have the license plate and make of the car. But the police won't be interested, because there's no hint of foul play. Just so you know, though, be on the lookout for a five-year-old Ford Explorer. White. California plates," and she rattled off the series of letters and numbers for the vehicle. Then she said, "It could be nothing. Brother and sister out for a drive."

"Or?" he said, the acid in his stomach crawling up his throat.

"Or," she admitted. "It could be trouble. Big trouble."

Cascade Mountains, Oregon
Now

What was it about that night?

Lucy closed her eyes in the darkness, trying to force the memory of the attack to the surface. As always, it only teased her with dark, disjointed, and blurry memories. She'd sliced Ray's cheek; she knew that because he'd been strangling her mother . . . right? And Marilyn and Clark had rushed in, trying to separate Ray from Tina. Someone—Mama?—had reached into the open drawer of the night table and pulled out the gun.

As it had fired, Lucy had caught a glimpse of the scissors being plunged into Mama's neck. Fingers clenched around the handle, a ring with a dark, red stone encircling one finger.

Marilyn.

Marilyn? She couldn't believe it. Marilyn had plunged

the blades into Mama's neck? But that couldn't be . . .
Ray had been choking their mother. Had Marilyn meant
to stab him and in the dark been confused and—

Craaack!

The sound was sharp.

Like glass splintering.

The images of the night of the attack faded.

Merlin shot to his feet, ears pointed forward, his gaze
fixed on the window with the broken shade. The hairs on
the back of his neck stood on end, his tail stiff. A low
growl rumbled deep in his throat.

Heart clutching, Lucy searched the darkness.

"What's wrong?" Renee asked, her eyes blinking open
to stare at her mother, worry in her eyes.

Oh God, she hated what this was doing to her daughter.
The toll Lucy's paranoia was causing Renee. "Probably
nothing," Lucy said, not believing it for a second.

"Then why do you have that gun?"

She was freaking her kid out.

"Shhh." She was on her feet, her eyes fixed on the
window where the gathering darkness was a cloak and the
glass panes reflected the interior with its soft golden light.

But who, if anyone, was outside?

No one.

But the dog was still on guard, every muscle tense, his
eyes laser focused on the window.

Silently, Lucy slipped a shell into the rifle's chamber.

The wipers were barely keeping up with the snowfall
as Ian angled off the main road leading over Mount Hood,

to what was little more than a lane that cut through the woods. Tire tracks had flattened the fresh snow, and every so often he caught a glimpse of a cabin through the stands of fir trees, but the predawn hours were quiet and still, the forest seemingly unoccupied. He drove across a single-lane bridge that spanned a creek that was nearly iced over, only a trickle of water visible.

Could Lucy have picked a more isolated spot?

Squinting, he scanned the darkness and nearly missed the opening in the trees, where a spur of this desolate lane angled upward. Twin ruts, covered with ice and snow, looked as if they'd been made by a single vehicle.

But not long ago.

His cell phone rang, again lighting up the interior.

Zhou.

His stomach dropped.

"Yeah?" he said, answering as he kept his eyes on the road.

Zhou's voice came through the speakers. "Just giving you a head's-up. I called Watkins's parole officer and he checked on the sister's house. No one was there."

"No one."

"Not his sister, not Watkins. But they did find blood."

"Blood?"

"Yeah, enough that they don't think it was a paper cut. Serious blood in an upper hallway. Enough that there were footprints in it, and the cat's paw prints as well."

"Watkins's sister?"

"Don't know. That's what the cops are assuming."

"Shit."

"Be careful," she said. "I already told the detectives you're at the Jacoby cabin, that you're searching for your ex-wife and that in my opinion, somehow Watkins figured out where Lucy is."

"Christ."

All of his worst fears crawled through his guts.

"And I told them Lucy had Renee with her."

His jaw clamped down hard.

"They want you to back off. They've got a possible homicide, and they want to handle it. Police matter. You got that."

"Message received."

"Good. Be safe."

He clicked off. No way was he standing down.

He punched the accelerator, fear streaming through his veins. What if Watkins reached them first? What if even now his ex-wife and daughter were being hunted down by the ex-con? What if it was already too late?

"Jesus, no," he whispered as the snow deepened and his tires slid a little. He eased off the gas and the wheels responded again as images of Watkins teasing and brutalizing and then killing his wife and daughter tore through his mind.

No.

Rounding a sharp turn, he spied a vehicle parked outside a large cabin, an inch of snow already covering it.

Lucy's Rav?

No . . . his heart dropped when he saw that the SUV was a white Ford Explorer with California license plates. Even in the dark, he could make out the series of numbers and letters, and the sick feeling in his gut only got worse.

Ray Watkins was already here.

* * *

"You're scaring me." Renee climbed to her feet and started for the window.

"Get behind the counter!" Lucy ordered. "Go into the kitchen. Like we practiced."

"Why?"

"Just do it."

"Oh God. This is *so* lame!" But Renee did as she was told, walking into the kitchen area and hiding behind the bank of cabinets. "Mom?"

"Sssh! Stay there! Don't move!"

"Mom—"

"I'm serious, Renee. Don't argue!"

She'd already hidden her Glock in the pocket of her jacket. Now, Lucy removed the bayonet from the rifle and placed the knife underneath her jacket, only her sweatshirt separating her skin from the cold, deadly blade. She hiked the rifle onto her shoulder and killed all the lights, then slid her feet into boots near the back door. She waited, her eyes adjusting to the dark. Everything was still, the dog beside her, nose to the door, ready to bound outside.

Her mouth was dry as sand as she saw how stiff and attentive Merlin was.

It's probably just a deer.

Or . . . even an elk.

You've seen tracks.

It could even be a rabbit.

Or it could be a person, a monster who wrote letters from prison all dressed up in vines and Bible verses.

And what about Marilyn? Now that she'd remembered her sister's part in the bloody confusion, she couldn't stop thinking about it. Did Marilyn not remember? Why hadn't she said a word?

Stop it. Concentrate. Someone could be out there.

Her pulse was pounding in her ears as she cracked the door. Merlin bolted through, then Lucy slipped into the darkness herself, hiding behind the ever-dwindling pile of firewood. The snowy landscape showed no signs of an intruder, but the rush of the wind was loud, the snow swirling and dancing from the dark sky.

You're safe.

Renee is safe.

Calm down.

But her heart was thudding, every nerve strung tight.

Slowly, she moved around the perimeter of the cabin searching the darkness, squinting against the icy pellets of snow, the dog at her side, the wind blustering and blowing, howling through the trees. Merlin wandered out to the edge of the forest along a path they'd broken earlier, past the snow fort that was now nearly buried in a thick, white blanket, just another hillock near the ice and snow-encrusted evergreens rimming the clearing. She saw a broken tree branch, splintered from its trunk but still hanging, probably what accounted for the noise that had frightened her.

Again, her lurid imagination was overriding her sanity.

Cold to the bone, she walked backward, up the steps of the rear porch, her eyes on the forest, never daring to look away as she slipped back inside.

"Renee?" she said. "Sweetie? I'm back."

But something felt off in the cabin.

It was too still.

Was her daughter hiding? Frozen in fright? Had Lucy

freaked out her daughter to the point she couldn't speak? "Honey," she said, her hand going to the wall switch to turn on the light. "It's okay."

"Is it?" a deep male voice said, and as she spun, a gloved hand clamped hard over her mouth while, with his other hand, he stripped her of the rifle and reached into her pocket, withdrawing her baby Glock. "I don't think so."

Crouching so that no one could see him in a mirror, Ian approached the vehicle cautiously. It seemed abandoned, the snow piling ever higher on the roof, trunk, and hood. How long had Watkins been here? Ears straining, heart thudding, eyes scanning the snow-covered landscape, Ian half-expected someone to jump out at him. He saw the footprints, fresh from the looks of them, heading up the mountain, but he paused at the white Ford and peered through the frosty glass of the windows. It was dark in the interior, but there was no movement.

Using the flashlight on his phone, he shone the bright beam through the icy glass to the empty driver's seat and the passenger seat.

Then he brushed snow from the rear window, illuminating the back seat.

The beam landed on a person. Instinctively, Ian raised his gun, only to realize that the man lying face up on the back seat was dead, his wrists and ankles bound with zip ties. His face ashen, his tongue lolling from his throat, his eyes fixed, and the ugly, jagged scar that ran from his drooping eye down his cheek where Lucy had tried to kill him, was all too visible.

Ray Watkins.

In the rotting flesh.

"Jesus," Ian whispered, backing up and nearly tripping.

What about Lucy?

Renee?

He didn't bother checking for a pulse.

Ray Watkins had been dead for hours.

And whoever had killed him was now stalking Lucy and Renee.

Ian punched in Zhou's number as he began running up the path to the Jacoby cabin. At the sight of another vehicle, he clicked off.

Heart clambering, he recognized his ex-wife's RAV4 and paused to look inside, to brush off the ice and snow and shine his light through the windows, all the while bracing himself, telling himself that he might find Lucy or Renee, trussed and killed as Watkins had been.

Please God, no.

But the interior was empty and he prayed the truck, too, had no body stuffed in it as he raced up the hillside, his heart thundering, the icy pellets of snow raining down.

Clark?

Clark was attacking her?

Why?

And where—oh God, where the hell was Renee?

Lucy struggled, but her half brother held her fast, one arm pinning both of hers, pressing her spine to his torso, his other hand forcing the back of her skull against his chest, his hand firmly over her mouth.

"Surprised?" Clark whispered into her ear, causing her skin to crawl. "Or have you remembered? Mom and

Marilyn both said you were recalling what happened that night." He let out a huff of disgust. "That's too fucking bad. Y'know? I thought we'd gotten past that, but between you and Ray Watkins, I couldn't take a chance."

What was he talking about?

"I know Mom thinks Ray pulled the trigger and that you stabbed her—by mistake, of course—so I'm safe with her and Marilyn, who'll never talk because she stabbed Mom that night and let you take the blame. You knew that, right? Marilyn was mad at Mom for stopping her from seeing Ray. I think Marilyn did it on purpose. But you . . . I couldn't be sure."

Clark shot their mother?

"I was really trying to shoot Ray because I hated that prick, and I never thought I'd have the chance to put him out of the picture permanently. That was my chance, y'know. But in the dark, in all the craziness, the gun went off and . . . well, you know the rest."

Lucy's mind whirled. She did know. She did.

Mama had nearly died, but survived her injuries. Ray was disfigured, but went to prison. And Marilyn and Lucy were shipped off to boarding school, Marilyn knowing she'd stabbed her mother, Lucy thinking she was the guilty party. There had been no clear prints on any of the weapons, except for her mother's on the gun. No real evidence. The only credible witnesses were Tina Champagne and her children, who had all agreed that Ray Watkins had initiated the attack and tried to strangle his lover.

And now?

Holy crap!

Where the hell was Renee?

As if reading her thoughts, Clark asked, "Where'd you stash the kid?"

He didn't know? Instinctively, she glanced to the peninsula of cabinets that were her daughter's protection.

Clark picked up on it. "In there?" He nodded toward the kitchen, and Lucy's heart sank. She shook her head, her hair scraping against the zipper on his jacket, but he wasn't buying it. "Let's take a look-see, shall we?" He walked her toward the cabinets, his hand hard over her mouth and nose. Her heart was jackhammering with dread, pumping adrenaline wildly into her bloodstream. He couldn't, wouldn't, harm his own niece, would he? But the deadly calm of his intent, the slow, determined dragging of her over to the kitchen convinced her otherwise.

As they turned the corner, Lucy braced herself.

"Oh, Renee," he said in a singsong tone. "Come on out. Uncle Clark is here."

They rounded the corner and Lucy expected to find her daughter cowering where the cabinets met the stove, but the area was empty, the only sign that anyone had been there the door to the basement still slightly ajar.

"Son of a bitch," Clark said and reached for the door.

In that instant, when her arm was free, Lucy bit down hard on his gloved hand and heard her brother suck in his breath in shock. In the same instant, she reached under her jacket for the bayonet. She grabbed it, felt the skin on her stomach slice open, almost painless. She whirled, stabbed blindly, jabbing, swinging crazily, cutting through

the down of his jacket, causing Clark to jump backward
and blood to bloom over the white stuffing.

"You *bitch*!"

He fumbled for the gun—*her gun!*—and she dived for
the kitchen door to the basement, half-tumbling down the
stairs. If her daughter were here . . . but no . . . the
coal/wood chute door was unlatched! The only light came
through the small window, the glare of snow, but as her
eyes adjusted to the darkness, she stumbled over boxes
and chunks of wood. She heard him on the stairs, saw the
beam of a flashlight.

"I know you're down here, Lucy. Come on out."

Shit!

The wind was whistling and she heard it in the chute.
Renee had gotten out! That was what mattered.

But how long would her daughter survive in a blizzard?

And if Clark survived, wouldn't he track her down, hunt
her, and then . . . Lucy almost cried out at the thought. She
couldn't let that happen. Wouldn't. The phrase *over my
dead body* ran through her mind and she decided, *if that's
what it took, so be it*.

"God, it's cold down here." He sounded out of breath.
Maybe she'd wounded him more than she knew.

She backed up, her calves hitting the edge of the chopping block.

With the ax.

Clark was slowly arcing the beam of his flashlight over
the interior.

Give me strength.

"You cut me, bitch." He sounded almost amused.

Quietly, she bent down, picked up the bits of wood

around the chopping block, and flung the biggest piece toward the chute. *Clack!*

It hit.

Now would he buy it?

"What the fuck?"

He swung the light toward the chute.

"Gotcha," he said under his breath.

Her nerves so taut she could barely move, she grabbed hold of the ax handle and tested it, pulling it from the stump. As he limped over to the end of the chute, she raised it over her head. He bent down, pointing his gun and flashlight into the opening, ready to kill her or her daughter.

Lucy didn't think twice.

She swung down.

Threw all of her weight behind the blow.

With a sickening thud, the blade buried deep into Clark's back.

"Oooogh!" He crumpled, his head still in the chute, his body unmoving.

Shaking, she stepped backward, nearly falling over a chunk of split wood. His body slowly slithered backward to the floor.

"Oh God. Oh God . . ." She blinked, staring at the unmoving body. His flashlight had rolled on the ground and ended up shining a light on his surprised face. Her stomach roiled and convulsed and she wretched.

Renee! You have to find Renee!

She started for the stairs just as she heard the sound of frantic footsteps overhead.

"Lucy!" Ian's worried voice reverberated through the cabin.

"Ian!" She nearly collapsed with relief. He was already halfway down the stairs. "We have to find Renee."

"Got her." Ian appeared at the top of the stairs and met her halfway.

"Don't look," she said.

"Who?"

"Clark. Not Ray Watkins. I don't even know how he knew where to find me."

"I think Watkins knew and Clark got it out of him. Watkins's dead. In his sister's car."

"Oh God. Where's Renee?"

"Outside, with Merlin. I found her in some kind of hole."

"The snow fort." Lucy nearly collapsed with relief. "She must've gotten out through the firewood chute and hid there with the dog."

"Let's go get them, before the police arrive. They're on their way."

They stepped outside into the frigid night, where the blizzard still raged. Upon spying her mother, Renee dashed from beneath the cover of the surrounding forest, kicking up snow as she flung herself into Lucy's arms.

"Ooh." Lucy sucked in her breath. Pain burned through her abdomen where the bayonet had sliced her skin, but she didn't let go of her daughter. There were hurdles to overcome. She would have a mountain of charges against her, everything from trespassing to murder, she supposed, but it would all sort out. Somehow. She'd make sure it did.

She heard the sound of sirens before she saw the strobe of red and blue lights barely visible through the snowfall.

Ian placed an arm around her shoulders, and for once she didn't shrug it off. Maybe it was time to take another look at him. For tonight, at least, she'd cast off her doubts. Tonight, the nightmare was over.

San Francisco, California
Now

As rain drizzled down the windowpanes and holiday music played softly from the radio, Lucy eyed the Christmas tree, its warm lights glowing in the townhouse in San Francisco, the only home her daughter had ever known.

Renee was carefully rearranging the ornaments, adding older, forgotten angels and reindeer and whatever else she could find from an old box she'd found in the attic. Lucy had let her do the decorating as she was still recovering. The slice in her abdomen from the bayonet had required thirty-three stitches. The wound wasn't deep, but it was long, and it still hurt like hell. It was a miracle they were even celebrating the holiday this year, Lucy thought, as the past week had been a flurry of police interviews, doctor visits, depositions, and explanations. The police were still looking into Ray Watkins's sister's brutal death. Her body was found in her home, but it was still undetermined whether Ray had killed her or Clark had. The prevailing theory was that Clark was behind it all, and though Ray Watkins had intended to track down Lucy, Clark had used him, taking him hostage to find his little sister. No one knew what Clark really intended, what his ultimate goal had been, or how he'd planned to get away with it, but it was over. Thank God.

As for Lucy, it seemed as if she still had her job; the Jacoby family wasn't pressing charges and had agreed to take a few thousand dollars for repair and cleanup of their cabin. Aunt Beth, tired of "all the drama," was keeping her distance, but Lucy believed that relationship could be mended. The press was at least under control, though that was temporary, and Lucy was estranged from both Marilyn and her mother. They both blamed her for Clark and Ray Watkins's deaths.

So, what else was new?

"Wonderful," she muttered under her breath.

"What's wonderful?" Renee moved a tiny angel to a higher branch. How fitting. Closer to heaven.

"The season. Haven't you heard those song lyrics about it being the most wonderful time of the year?"

"That's not what you were talking about."

True.

Renee said, "I thought you were going to make us cocoa."

"Coming right up." She pushed herself out of the chair and walked carefully into the kitchen, Merlin at her heels.

"Make enough for Daddy," Renee reminded her. "He texted. He's on his way over."

"Okay."

Ian. What are you going to do about Ian? Now that he's proved himself, been by your side throughout this ongoing ordeal, and now that you no longer believe he cheated on you, are you going to give him another chance?

The jury was still out on that one, but she thought she might give it a go. What did she have to lose? The odds were better than fifty/fifty that she'd let him into her heart again. The truth was, she wanted to.

"Oh, there, listen." The strains of *It's the Most Wonder-*

ful Time of the Year began to play as she found the tin of instant cocoa and began heating water in the microwave. "Told you."

"Hey, Mom?"

"Mmm?"

"Ick! Gross!"

"What?" She looked across the living area to the tree and her daughter, who was opening the lid of a box that Lucy had nearly forgotten existed.

"What're these?" Renee's face twisted into an expression of disgust as she pulled two heads from the ornament box. Glitter Hair Barbie and Sun Jewel Ken. And on Renee's finger, a ring with a ruby stone that was slightly too big. "Should I hang them on the tree?" She looked skeptical.

"Better not. Might freak out your dad," Lucy said. She thought about reprimanding her daughter and saying something like, "You know better than to touch Mommy's things."

But she didn't.

And she wouldn't.

Not ever.

GHOSTS

by
ALEXANDRA IVY

CHAPTER ONE

Chicago, Illinois
Now

The mansion on Lake Shore Drive in Chicago wasn't the biggest or the fanciest home in the elegant neighborhood, but it was one of the most admired. Over a hundred years old, it was built out of iconic red bricks, with a large turret and stunning views of Lake Michigan from the wide balconies on each of the three stories.

Shelton Taylor purchased the house in the early eighties, more as an investment than as a place to raise a family. The savvy businessman never made a decision that wasn't calculated to improve his portfolio. Still, he'd allowed his ex-wife and daughter to live there even after he'd left Chicago to expand his business in Singapore.

Parking her van next to the curb, Rayne Taylor climbed out and studied the impressive structure. This had been her childhood home, but she always felt like a stranger when she came here. Maybe because her parents divorced when she was eight. Or because her mother had remarried a man who had no interest in children, and she'd been packed off to St. Cecilia's School for Girls in Salzburg, Austria, by the time she was ten. Or because when she'd graduated from St. Cecilia's she'd returned to the States to go to art school in New York City, and from there had spent the past ten years traveling around the country, painting the landscapes that captured her attention.

Her van was more a home to her than this sturdy structure.

With a shrug, Rayne climbed the steps to ring the bell. Several minutes passed and Rayne briefly wondered if her mother was still in bed. It was just past eight a.m. and the older woman never liked mornings. At last, there was the impatient click of stiletto heels on a marble floor and the door was yanked open to reveal a tall, painfully slender woman with bleached-blond hair pulled into a smooth knot at the base of her neck and an oval face that was carefully coated with layers of cosmetics.

Tami Taylor Jefferson might be fifty-five years old, but she was rabidly determined to appear thirty, no matter how much stretching, filling, and numbing she had to do to keep her skin smooth.

"Rayne." The older woman's green gaze narrowed as it roamed over Rayne's black curls that tumbled carelessly down her back and the pale face with big, misty gray eyes that had never been touched with makeup.

"Hello, Mother," Rayne murmured.

"I . . ." Tami cleared her throat. "I wasn't expecting you."

Rayne held up the box that was wrapped in bright red foil. "I was passing through Chicago and I thought I would deliver my Christmas present." She shrugged. "A couple of weeks late, but better than never."

"Oh. Thank you." The older woman stepped back, waving her hand toward the narrow foyer. "Come in."

Rayne stepped over the threshold and paused to set the present on a side table before removing her heavy parka and tossing it on a chair. Her mother wouldn't bother to open the gift. And even if she did, the delicate crystal ornament that Rayne had found in a charming art shop in Mexico would be shoved into a closet. The two women couldn't be more different.

As if to emphasize the point, Rayne glanced down at her soft, handknit sweater and faded jeans. They were a direct contrast to Tami's designer pantsuit and silk top. A wry smile touched her lips.

"Are you hungry?" her mother asked as a middle-aged woman in a gray dress and white apron appeared from the back of the foyer.

"No."

Rayne emphatically shook her head. She never ate in front of her mother. Rayne considered herself a normal size, but Tami was obsessed with weight and over the years she'd hounded her daughter for being too "solid" or too "stout." Thankfully, Rayne had never paid much attention to her mother's chiding. She'd accepted she was a disappointment to Tami by the time she'd entered preschool to see other daughters with their mothers. They were never going to have a normal relationship.

"Tea or coffee?" Her mother continued her role as hostess.

"Not for me," Rayne insisted. She didn't intend to stay longer than necessary.

"That will be all for now," Tami said to the housekeeper.

"Yes, ma'am." The woman turned to disappear toward the back of the house.

"We'll go into the sitting room."

Tami didn't wait for Rayne to agree as she headed through an arched opening into the long room that was dominated by the wall of windows that offered a view of the lake. Rayne arched her brows as she glanced around, her gaze skimming over the low, white sofas and matching chairs that were arranged on a white carpet with walls painted white. Even the brick fireplace had been white-washed. It was as if someone had come through and sucked away all the color.

"You've redecorated," she muttered.

"Yes." Tami paced toward a glass coffee table to grab her pack of cigarettes. "I used LeChez. They're supposed to be the best in the city."

Rayne silently translated the best to the most expensive.

"It's very . . . bright."

A brittle smile touched Tami's lips. "Mark says it's a perfect backdrop for me."

Mark Jefferson was Tami's husband. The washed-up actor had a few minor roles in the late eighties, but his true talent was conning women into giving him money, gifts, and a bed to sleep in. He'd hit the jackpot with Tami. She'd not only been willing to share her bed, but she'd agreed to marry him so he could get his hands on the generous dividends she received from her shares in her ex-husband's corporation.

"How is he?"

"Fine." Tami lit her cigarette, her motions jerky, as if

she was hiding some inner emotion. "He's flying home from Los Angeles today."

"Was he working?"

"Soaking up the sun. He claims that Chicago is colder than the arctic during the winter."

Rayne grimaced. She'd forgotten how bitterly cold the city could be in January. "He's not wrong."

Tami took a deep drag, blowing the smoke out of the corner of her mouth. There was a tension around the older woman that made Rayne wonder if all was well between her mother and her younger, overly handsome husband.

"So why are you here?" Tami abruptly demanded.

Or maybe the tension was because her daughter had landed on her doorstep, she wryly acknowledged.

"I have a show next month. I brought my paintings so the gallery can frame and mount them."

"Ah, yes." A genuine smile touched Tami's lips. She might not have motherly feelings for Rayne, but she was willing to take pride in the fact her daughter had become a world-famous artist. "I read the article about your exhibition in the *Tribune*. Do you want me to hold a reception here?"

Rayne shrugged. The reception was always the worst part of an exhibition. If it was up to her, she'd give it a miss. Unfortunately, the gallery owner insisted that she spend at least a few hours mingling with the guests.

"I think the gallery has already arranged something."

"Of course." The smile faded. "How long are you staying in town? I can have a room prepared."

"Thanks, but I already have a reservation booked at the Drake. I'll only be in the city for a night or two before moving on."

"I see."

An awkward silence settled between the two women. Rayne squashed a sigh. It was painfully familiar.

"If you don't mind, I have something in the attic I'd like to get."

Tami blinked. "The attic?"

"Yes."

"No one's been up there in years. I'll send Mary to clean—"

"There's no need," Rayne interrupted. "I don't mind a little dust."

Tami wrinkled her slender nose, but she managed to avoid glancing down at Rayne's jeans, which were clean but speckled with flecks of paint.

"What do you want up there?"

Rayne hesitated. She didn't really want to answer. The past was something she firmly believed should be left where it belonged. Locked in a dusty attic. But over the past couple of weeks, she'd been plagued with a need she couldn't shake. At last, she'd crawled into her van and driven from Nevada to Chicago, determined to clear her mind. She had to come to the city anyway. Two birds, one stone.

"Did you see the news about Tina Champagne?" she grudgingly asked.

"I know her daughter was involved in some scandal." Tami clicked her tongue. "I never did approve of your connection to that family."

Rayne didn't point out that her only connection with the actress was attending St. Cecilia's School for Girls along with Tina's daughter, Lucy. Or that she hadn't disapproved until Mark Jefferson had mentioned that he'd met Tina Champagne when he first arrived in LA.

He'd all but implied they'd been lovers, but Rayne had serious doubts the beautiful Tina had any interest in yet another pretty boy hoping to make it big in Hollywood.

"Seeing the story reminded me that I never unpacked my belongings after I returned from Austria. There are a couple of things I'd like to dig out."

She didn't mention that the item she wanted was a gift Lucy had sent to her for graduation. After the terrifying events of that day, she'd completely forgotten about it. Now she was curious to see what her friend had gotten for her.

Tami shrugged. "If you don't mind grubbing through the cobwebs, be my guest."

Rayne headed back across the white carpet, pausing at the door to glance over her shoulder. "I'll say goodbye before I leave."

"Don't bother. I have a pedicure appointment." Tami lifted a slender arm to glance at the Rolex strapped around her wrist. "I'll see you next month."

Salzburg, Austria
Then

Rayne hauled the last of her suitcases into the cramped dorm room. It was a sparse space, with two single beds and two matching desks. There were no posters on the barren gray walls, and no television or stereo system. The only beauty to be seen was out the window, where the snow-capped Alps towered over the landscape.

"Hello, mouse."

Rayne jumped at the sound of a voice coming from the open doorway. She whirled to study the tall, blond-haired, blue-eyed girl who managed to make the school uniform look as if it should be on a runway.

Natalie Scantlin. Like Rayne, she was fourteen years old, but that was where the similarities ended. Natalie was the most popular girl in school. And not just because she was pretty, or smart, or because her parents were rich. It was her vivacious personality that made her the constant center of attention.

Rayne, on the other hand, preferred to fade into the background. From the moment she'd arrived in Austria she'd tried her best to avoid attracting attention. It was a habit she'd learned after her mother had started dating Mark Jefferson. It had been painfully obvious the man didn't want Rayne underfoot, and she'd made a conscious effort to disappear.

It hadn't worked, of course. Two days after the wedding, Rayne had been packed up and sent off to St. Cecilia's.

Surprisingly, Rayne was happy at the school. Although she didn't mix easily with the other students, she loved her classes and even the nuns. Especially Sister Gemma, who'd recognized Rayne's talent in art and encouraged her to spend her free hours painting. It wasn't until the school counselor, Sister Rosa, had pulled her aside two days ago that she realized that the teachers were worried about the amount of time she spent alone. They insisted that she swap rooms and move in with Natalie, in the hopes the gregarious girl could pull her out of her shell.

Now she scowled at the girl who strolled into the room with a confidence that Rayne would never possess.

"Don't call me that," she snapped. "I'm not a mouse."

"A mouse with teeth." Natalie abruptly laughed, her

blue eyes twinkling with a humor that took the sting out of her words. "Good. Let's go."

Rayne frowned. "Natalie—"

"Nat," the girl interrupted. "Only my parents call me Natalie. And the nuns." She lifted her hand to motion toward Rayne. "Come on."

"Where are you going?"

"To the stables. Lucy said there's a new colt." She touched the camera hung around her neck. It was heavy and black and looked as if it belonged to a professional. "I want to get some pictures."

Lucy was Lucy McKenna. She was a year older than Rayne and the daughter of an actress, but she'd always been kind. In fact, she'd been one of the few girls to go out of her way to spend time with Rayne after she'd seen the way Mark Jefferson had treated her when her mother had come for a visit. She'd understood the trauma unwelcome men forced into a young girl's life.

"I have to unpack," she informed her new roommate.

"You can do that later. The light is starting to fade." Marching across the wood-planked floor, Nat threaded her arm through Rayne's and steered her out of the room. "Come on."

They headed through the narrow hallway and down the stairs to leave the castlelike structure through a side entrance.

"Maybe I don't like horses," Rayne protested, even as she was urged across the manicured lawn.

Nat angled past the looming cathedral, heading for the L-shaped stables and paddocks at the edge of the property.

"What are you talking about? Everyone loves horses."

Rayne snorted. "Are you always this bossy?"

"Yes. You'll get used to it."

"Doubtful," Rayne groused, although she wasn't as annoyed as she was trying to pretend. There was something irresistible about Natalie Scantlin. A charm that not even Rayne could ignore.

Without warning, Nat came to a halt, pulling Rayne to face her. "You're an artist, right?"

Rayne blushed. The only thing that mattered to her was her painting. Just talking about her tentative efforts made her feel oddly vulnerable.

"I hope so." Her blush deepened. "One day."

"Me too. Only I use my camera, not a paintbrush, to create my masterpieces."

Rayne arched her brow. Masterpieces? Nat obviously had no trouble believing in her own talents. "If you say so."

"My point is that my pictures would be tragically boring if I stayed in my room all day just taking pictures of the same stupid stuff over and over."

"Painting isn't the same as taking pictures."

"The medium may be different, but art is always the same." Nat spread her arms in a dramatic gesture. "Passion. Agony. The soaring highs and brutal valleys of love."

Rayne rolled her eyes. "And you're going to find all that in the stables?"

"What could be more exciting than new life?"

Rayne stubbornly refused to be convinced. She didn't want to accept that Nat's words resonated deep inside her. Or to consider the fact that she might be using her art as a means to retreat from the world, not to explore it.

"I don't paint animals."

"I've seen what you paint." Nat glanced toward the nearby Alps. "Mountains."

Rayne flinched, hurt by the girl's dismissive tone. "There's nothing wrong with mountains."

"No. They're very fine mountains." Nat grabbed her hands, giving them a squeeze. "But they only reveal your talent. If you want to be a great artist, you have to share your soul."

CHAPTER TWO

Chicago, Illinois
Now

Rayne knelt in front of the suitcases that still had the tags from their trip overseas almost fourteen years ago. After . . .

She grimaced, her mind balking at the memory of her last few hours at St. Cecilia's School for Girls and the sight of Natalie Scantlin lying on her bed, covered in blood. Once she'd flown back to the States, she'd headed straight to college, locking away the horrifying images, just as her belongings from that time had been locked in this attic.

But the moment she'd seen Tina Champagne's picture and the lurid headline splattered across the front page of a scandal rag, she'd been sharply reminded of the gift Lucy had sent to her for her graduation. It'd been packed up with all her other belongings and shipped to Chicago. She had a sudden urge to discover exactly what it was so she could send a message to Lucy and thank her.

Better late than never, she wryly conceded, opening

the largest of the suitcases. She wrinkled her nose as dust swirled through the shadows of the cramped space. Nothing but old school uniforms, her underthings, and a shower bag. She turned her attention to the second suitcase. Inside, she could see her old painting supplies, as well as the package that was wrapped in thin foil with a small bow. This was what she'd come to find.

Sitting back on her heels, she tugged at the bow and pulled away the foil. There was a jewelry box inside and she opened it to discover a small silver charm in the shape of a paintbrush. It had obviously been handcrafted, and Rayne felt a sentimental rush of gratitude as she tucked it into the pocket of her jeans. Her childhood would have been a misery without the friends who'd surrounded her at school.

Reaching out to shut the suitcase, she was distracted by the stack of paperbacks. Those didn't belong to her, did they? No. She leaned forward to study the pile, belatedly recognizing the forbidden books that Nat had gotten from a friend. She'd hidden them under her mattress, to keep them away from the prying eyes of the nuns. Rayne's hand was shaking as she pushed the paperbacks aside to discover the large wooden box that had also been hidden along with the books.

Obviously in the confusion of the crime scene, some of Nat's belongings had been mixed up with hers. Grabbing the box, Rayne placed it on the floor. For long moments she simply stared at it with her heart lodged in her throat. A part of her urged her to return the thing to her suitcase. Nat had stored her most private belongings in the box. It was no one's business what was inside. Or maybe she should wrap it up and send it to her parents.

They would no doubt be eager to have anything that belonged to their dead daughter.

Instead, she found herself slowly reaching out to open the lid.

Her breath caught at the sight of the pile of mementos. Valentine cards from her friends. A silver charm bracelet. Small tokens from a local fair. The Saint Christopher medallion one of the nuns had given her. A ribbon that was tied around a lock of hair.

Each keepsake held a memory, and Rayne was nearly overwhelmed by the flickering images of uniformed girls running through the playground. The shadowed pews in the cathedral. The picnics in the nearby woods. And the whispered giggles as she snuggled with Nat beneath the blankets on the frigid winter nights.

Fragments of her childhood that were best left in the past.

About to close the lid, Rayne noticed the photos at the very bottom. Shoving aside the jumble of stuff that Nat had collected, Rayne pulled them out. Nat had taken hundreds of pictures, but these obviously had special meaning to her.

The top photo was a black-and-white picture of the tiny colt curled in the hay with sunlight slanting through a window. The second photo was of Nat, who was standing between two teenagers, a boy and a girl who looked enough alike to suggest they were brother and sister. Trent and Brooke Orwell. They were all wearing fancy clothes that revealed that they'd been on their way to a party. And the third was of the marble fountain that was located near the gardens behind the cathedral.

Caught between the pleasure of remembering the girl

who'd become closer to her than any sister and the pain that was still raw as the day that Nat had died, Rayne didn't notice the scrap of paper that fell from between the pictures. Not until it landed on her lap.

With a frown, she picked it up to smooth out the wrinkled paper and read the words that were scrawled in red ink.

Give me what I want or die . . .

Chicago, Illinois
Now

Mark Jefferson strolled into the elegant house on Lake Shore Drive with a sense of smug satisfaction. It didn't matter that it belonged to his wife. Or that it had been purchased by Tami's former husband. In his mind, this place was the validation of what he'd known since he was a young boy living on a farm in the middle of Nowhere, Iowa. He was destined for a life of sophisticated ease.

Who cared if he'd never become a famous actor? Or that he was stuck in frigid Chicago? He had a closet full of designer clothes, he went to the best parties, and when the cloying attentions of his wife became overwhelming, he took off to LA for some fun in the sun. Not bad for a man who'd never worked a day in his life.

Leaving his bags in the foyer, Mark frowned as he reached for the small gift that had been left on a side table. What was that doing there? He strolled into the sitting room, finding his wife standing next to the fireplace with a cigarette in one hand and a glass of whiskey in the other. He arched his brows. It wasn't even three o'clock. A little early even for Tami to start drinking.

At the sound of his footsteps, she whirled to face him.

"Mark." She tossed the cigarette into the crackling flames. She knew that he hated her smoking. "I didn't hear the taxi."

Crossing the white carpet, he placed a light kiss on her cheek. "Did you miss me?"

"Of course."

A brittle smile curved her lips, but she couldn't disguise the way her gaze hungrily drank in the sight of him. He knew exactly what she was seeing. Despite the fact that he was nearing fifty, his copper curls didn't have a hint of gray and his hazel eyes still shimmered with golden flecks. His waist might have grown a couple of inches, but his morning trips to the gym made sure there was no flab, and his deep dimples maintained his boyish charm.

Halting in front of Tami, he held up his hand. The large diamonds that studded his wedding band flashed in the firelight. "If that's true, why am I finding gifts for you from some secret admirer?"

Her smile tightened. "Would it bother you if I had a secret admirer?"

He shrugged. He was an expert at this game. "If you want someone else, all you have to do is say the word and I'll be out of here."

The predictable fear darkened Tami's eyes. She was terrified of losing him. She always had been.

"It was Rayne," she said in sharp tones.

"Rayne?"

"She came by this morning and brought me a Christmas gift."

Caught off guard by the unexpected name, Mark scowled. From the moment he'd chosen Tami Taylor to be his permanent sugar mama, the one negative had been her daughter, Rayne. He didn't want to be a dad. Or have a kid underfoot. And he most certainly didn't want to share Tami's generous income with the brat.

It had been a simple matter to convince Tami to send Rayne to Austria once they were married, and thankfully, Rayne had chosen to stay away from the house after she'd returned to the States. But he always worried she might decide to repair her strained relationship with her mother. He intended to nip that nonsense in the bud. He needed Tami completely dependent on him.

"Why was she in Chicago?" he demanded.

"She had to bring some pictures for her upcoming exhibition."

"Is she going to be staying?"

Tami smoothed her slender hands down the tailored jacket of her pantsuit. She didn't seem nervous, not exactly. But there was a tension humming around her that Mark didn't like.

"I offered her a room."

Mark stiffened. "Why would you do that?"

Tami clicked her tongue. "Obviously because this is her home."

Her answer did nothing to ease Mark's annoyance. "Not really. She's been a vagabond for years. And I just got back in town," he reminded his wife in peevish tones. "It's uncomfortable having a guest underfoot."

"You don't have to worry, she's not staying." Tami glanced away, as if unwilling to meet his gaze. "She wanted to search through the attic, and then I think she said that she was going to stay at a hotel. Or maybe she was going to sleep in her van. I wasn't really listening."

Mark lost any interest in why Tami was so on edge. Instead, he clenched his hands into tight fists.

"What would she want from the attic?"

"I don't know. She said it had something to do with seeing Tina Champagne in the headlines." She restlessly shrugged. "I assume whatever she wanted was in her old school things."

"What was it?"

"I don't know. I had to leave for an appointment before she came back down." She narrowed her eyes, as if becoming suspicious of his interest. "Does it matter?"

"Of course not." He flashed his perfect smile, stepping forward to wrap his arms around his wife's tightly clenched body. He'd worry about Rayne later. For now, he had to remind his wife why she couldn't live without him. He brushed a kiss over her cold cheek. "Have I told you how beautiful you look?" His mouth skimmed toward her parted lips. "Or how much I missed you?"

CHAPTER THREE

Salzburg, Austria
Then

After two years of being Nat's roommate, Rayne had discovered that the one constant was to expect the unexpected. So, when Nat burst into the art room where Rayne was washing out her paintbrushes, she wasn't surprised. Saturday mornings were supposed to be her private time to concentrate on her paintings, but Nat was too spontaneous to accept Rayne's pleas for peace and quiet.

Shoving open the door, she waved an impatient hand. "Come on."

Rayne shook her head, pulling off the smock that had only partially protected her jeans and sweatshirt from the splatters of oil paint.

"I'm busy."

Nat impatiently marched across the room to grab Rayne's hand. "I have someone I want you to meet."

"Who?"

Nat tugged her out of the art studio at the back of the building and toward a side door. "Just come on."

They crossed the grounds that surrounded the school, seemingly headed toward the white canopy that had been erected along with a dozen tables and chairs near the garden that was just beginning to come into bloom.

Confused, Rayne at last caught sight of an older couple who were directing the numerous uniformed waiters who were moving from the nearby vans to the canopy.

"Wait. Isn't that your parents?" she demanded.

"Yep. They flew in last night for my birthday."

Ah. That explained the flurry of activity. Every year Nat's parents descended on St. Cecilia's School for Girls on the first day of May to celebrate their daughter's birthday in grand style. Rayne's lips twisted in a smile that held a hint of bitterness. Her own birthday had been two weeks before. Her mother hadn't even remembered to send a card.

"I've already met them," she reminded her friend.

"I want to introduce you to Niko."

On cue, a tall boy with broad shoulders and a slender waist stepped into view. He had the same golden blond hair as Nat, and the same perfect features. Only Niko's were sharper, as if they'd been chiseled by the hand of an artist. And even at a distance she could see the dazzling blue of his eyes.

Was that the reason her heart stopped? And why her knees suddenly felt weak? Whatever the cause, Rayne stumbled to a halt, her tummy churning with a sensation she didn't entirely understand.

"That's your brother?"

"I know." Nat heaved a sigh. "Every girl who sees him is thunderstruck. He's disgustingly gorgeous."

With an effort, Rayne forced her gaze back to her friend. "He's your twin, isn't he?"

Nat giggled. "Exactly. I'm disgustingly gorgeous, too."

It was true. There were times when Nat didn't seem quite real. She was too beautiful, too vivacious, too . . . everything.

"I'm still not sure why you dragged me out here," Rayne said.

"I think you and Niko should meet."

"Why? Is he an artist?"

"No. He's the heir apparent to the family business." Nat wrinkled her nose. "Poor guy."

"Why do you say that?"

"He's being groomed to take over the reins whether he wants to or not," Nat explained. "Someone has to keep the rest of us rolling in cash."

Rayne wasn't entirely sure what Nat's family did for their wealth. She knew they were based in Kansas City, Missouri, and it had something to do with rental cars.

"So why do you think we should meet?"

"He saw your series of paintings of the Salzach River that the nuns have hanging in the library," Nat explained. "He thought they were brilliant."

Rayne flushed. The pictures that captured the river during the four different seasons was some of her best work so far. She'd taken Nat's advice, and while she still preferred to be in the background, she'd started using the emotions she kept tightly leashed to add depth and meaning to her landscapes. It had made all the difference.

"Brilliant," she repeated the word, letting it nestle into the center of her soul.

"His exact word," Nat assured her.

Rayne turned her head, discovering Niko's piercing gaze studying her with a strange intensity. The world seemed to shift beneath her feet.

"Oh."

"He's even cuter now, isn't he?" Nat teased.

"Maybe."

"Come on." Hooking their arms together, Nat pulled her toward the boy who made her heart race.

Kansas City, Missouri
Now

Niko Scantlin was pacing from one end of his Kansas City office to the other. It had been decorated by his father to resemble an English country manor house. Lots of dark wood, sturdy furnishings, and handwoven rugs. When Ingram Scantlin had started his fleet of rental cars, he'd wanted to give the impression his company had been around for a century, not a few months. The businesses who hired his services wanted solid dependability at a reasonable price. And that was what Scantlin Fleets offered. And even when Niko had taken over and expanded into real estate, he'd left the office as his father wanted it. It didn't really matter to him. As long as he had a clear view of the downtown plaza with the large fountains and iconic Spanish-style architecture, he was happy.

After what felt like an eternity he could hear the soft sound of his secretary's voice in the reception area before the door was pushed open and Rayne Taylor appeared.

His mouth went ridiculously dry as she stepped into the office and closed the door behind her. He'd seen pictures of her over the years. Her reputation as one of America's up-and-coming artists meant she was in the news on a regular basis. But he felt as if the air was being squeezed from his lungs as she set an object on a low coffee table and stripped off her heavy parka. She was wearing a soft sweater and a pair of jeans that clung to her curves. Her long, glossy hair was tangled from the wind and tumbled down her back with glorious abandon, and her cheeks were rosy from the chilled air. It was her eyes, however, that had always captured his attention. From the very first time he'd caught sight of them.

The misty gray held a depth of emotion that she kept fiercely hidden away. The urge to tap into those passions had haunted him since he was sixteen.

Unfortunately, Nat's death had destroyed any hope for a future between them.

A hesitant smile touched her lips, as if unsure of her welcome. "Hello, Niko. It's been a long time."

"Rayne." He moved forward, grabbing her hands to give them a gentle squeeze. The sight of her stirred a nostalgic warmth. A memory of visiting St. Cecilia's School for Girls and watching Nat and Rayne together. His sister as bright and vivid as the sun, and at her side Rayne, as calm and mysterious as the moon. "How was the flight?"

"Quick," she assured him. "When I called you I didn't expect you to send a helicopter."

He shrugged. When he'd picked up his phone to hear Rayne's voice, he'd been stunned. He'd never expected to hear from her after he'd cornered her and demanded to know who wanted his sister dead. The poor girl had been in shock after finding Natalie's body and his angry attack hadn't helped.

In his defense, he'd been dealing with his own shock. And a brutal sense of loss that had never fully healed.

"It's a short trip," he said, referring to the private chopper he'd sent to pick up Rayne from Chicago. "And you sounded upset when you reached out to me."

She cleared her throat, as if embarrassed by her frantic call. "I'm not usually so emotional."

"You said you found something belonging to Nat?" he reminded her.

"Yes." She gave a jerky nod. "I was going through my old school stuff. I hadn't touched it since I came back to the States, I had no idea they'd packed a few of Nat's things in my suitcase."

"Is that what bothered you?"

"No. Well . . ." She grimaced, turning to pick up the object she'd been carrying when she entered the office. "Not entirely."

Sensing she was still upset, Niko gestured toward the hidden door across the room. "Let's discuss this somewhere more private."

He waited for her nod of agreement before he moved to touch the wooden panel that slid silently open. Together they stepped into the long, open space that had once been the boardroom. Niko had stripped away the heavy wood furniture and dark carpeting, instead filling it with a sleek couch that pulled out to a king-size bed and several matching chairs that all faced the long line of windows. There was a small kitchenette in one corner, and an attached bathroom with a shower.

Rayne smiled as she glanced around. "Nice."

"I work late too often not to have someplace to crash."

"Nat said you were being groomed to take over the family business."

It was true. As the oldest son, he'd been expected to

step into his father's shoes. When he was young he'd occasionally resented that he didn't have any choice in his future. But after Nat's death he'd been eager to shoulder the responsibility. He'd failed his sister; he wasn't going to fail the rest of his family.

"For better or worse," he murmured.

"I'd say better." Her roaming gaze at last reached the two framed paintings on the far wall. They both depicted Death Valley, but one was smeared with soft pinks and violets of dawn and the other had the harsh yellows and oranges of midday. "Oh. You have some of my work."

He stepped beside her, breathing in the sweet scent of her shampoo. "I have two more at my condo."

She appeared oddly flustered. "I had no idea."

He smiled down at her, watching the blush stain her cheeks. "I've admired your art since we were sixteen years old."

Their gazes locked, and Niko wondered if she was recalling the moment they'd met. Niko had felt an instant explosion of excitement that had never happened again. Her blush deepened before she was giving a sharp shake of her head and shoving the object she was carrying into his hands.

"This belonged to Nat."

Niko forced himself to glance down at the wooden box. A sharp pain sliced through him. "I remember. I gave it to her when she went to St. Cecilia's." He ran his fingers over the polished top. "Thank you for bringing it to me."

"It has some of her prized possessions inside," she told him. "As well as a few pictures."

"Of course." Nat had been five when their dad had

bought her a camera for her birthday. From that moment on, she'd never gone anywhere without one in her hands.

Rayne reached into the front pocket of her jeans, her face paling as she pulled out a small, crumpled piece of paper.

"It also had this."

"What is it?" Setting the box on a low coffee table, Niko reached for the paper, smoothing it between his fingers. Then, more curious than alarmed, he read the brief note. His breath abruptly hissed through his clenched teeth. "Shit."

"It was hidden between the photos," Rayne told him.

"I knew it." He jerked his head up to meet Rayne's wary gaze, a combustible combination of emotions detonating through him. "I knew Nat would never have killed herself."

Salzburg, Austria
Then

The day of her graduation had started off as one of those rare, perfect mornings. The sky was a brilliant blue and the air was perfumed with wildflowers. Rayne had gone into Salzburg with her mother to shop for a new dress, and they'd managed to spend their time together without the usual strain of pretending they weren't virtual strangers. Probably because Mark had chosen to remain at the hotel. They'd even stopped to share a cup of hot chocolate before heading back to St. Cecilia's.

Rayne had been bubbling with a sense of anticipation at the knowledge she would soon be graduating and on her way to art school as she'd walked along the familiar path that led to the dormitory.

It was then that everything had gone wrong.

"Wait." Her mother had reached out to grab Rayne's arm, the familiar tension tightening her features. "You go on. I'll see you later."

Rayne frowned in confusion. "I thought you were coming to the Senior Tea with me?"

Tami's gaze was locked on a spot at the back of the cathedral. "Mark and I are having dinner in Salzburg. I really should go back to the hotel and get ready."

Rayne turned her head, her heart sinking at the sight of the slender man leaning against the stone wall that surrounded the gardens, his gaze following the girls strolling past. Mark Jefferson.

Without waiting for Rayne to respond, Tami was scurrying across the recently mowed grounds. Like a missile zooming toward its target.

Or a woman dangerously obsessed with a man.

Shaking her head in disgust, she stomped into the dorms and headed up the narrow flight of stairs. She'd stepped into the lobby where a few of the students were already starting to gather in preparation for the events planned for the day. Rayne frowned when she failed to see her roommate.

"Hey, Erin." She motioned toward the red-haired girl with light blue eyes and freckles. Erin MacDonald had been one of her friends since she arrived at the school, both of them sharing a love for old movies. "Have you seen Nat?"

"I saw her shortly after her morning run. She said she was headed down to the stables." Erin shrugged. "But I haven't seen her since then."

"Thanks." Heading back down the hall, Rayne pushed

open the door to her room. Once inside, she paused to dump the bags of clothing her mother had insisted on buying next to her packed bags. Then, turning back, she clicked her tongue at the sight of her friend lying on her bed with her back turned toward Rayne. "Seriously?" Walking across the floor, she reached out to grab Nat's shoulders. She was going to miss all the festivities if she didn't get up soon. "You can take a nap later."

A scream ripped from Rayne's throat as Nat flopped onto her back, her sightless eyes staring at the ceiling and her white dress stained with blood.

So much blood . . .

CHAPTER FOUR

Kansas City, Missouri
Now

Rayne swallowed the lump in her throat, forcing back the memory that had haunted her for years. Instead, she concentrated on Niko, who was staring at the note as if he'd just seen a ghost.

"Did she show this to you?" he demanded.

"No. I had no idea she was being threatened."

He lifted his head to reveal his grim expression. "This changes everything."

Rayne swallowed a sigh. After finding Nat's body in their room, the next hours had become a blur. She knew that she'd been taken to Sister Rosa's office. And that the nuns had tried to question her about Nat only to be halted by her mother, who had swept in to demand that Rayne come back to the hotel with her until they could get a flight out of Austria.

She'd been waiting alone in the hallway for her mother to grab her purse and an overnight bag from her room when Niko had tracked her down. He'd obviously been crying, but there was a fierce determination in his expression as he'd adamantly refused to believe that Nat had killed herself. Rayne had been too traumatized to offer him comfort. She'd turned and fled out of the building.

Now she belatedly wished she'd considered the pain she was going to cause Niko before she'd called him.

"Not necessarily," she tried to temper his automatic assumption that this proved Nat's death was anything but a tragic suicide. "The note could have been a joke. Or just one of the girls venting."

He scowled, reading the words out loud. "'Give me what I want or die?' That's a joke?"

She hunched her shoulders, trying to ignore the chill that inched down her spine. Unlike Niko, she wasn't going to leap to conclusions. "Young boys use their fists to intimidate and bully one another. Young girls use their words, but they're equally brutal."

He was shaking his head before she finished speaking. "If you thought this was a bad joke, you wouldn't have called me in a panic."

"I was upset and I overreacted."

"You?" He arched his brows. "Overreact?"

"It happens."

"No." He stepped toward her, studying her with a brooding gaze. "I don't believe you. You've never accepted that Nat killed herself."

"None of us could accept it. Not when it meant we'd been so blind," she insisted. "Or so selfish not to realize she was in pain."

"Nat was a fighter." His tone was harsh. "I would more easily believe that she killed someone in a fury than that she'd taken her own life."

Her lips parted to inform him that there was no debating how Nat had died. The sight of her sliced wrists were forever burned into her mind. But she couldn't deny that he had a point. When Nat was hurt she didn't sulk. She struck out with a vengeance. Once, an older student had broken a window in the conservatory playing field hockey and blamed it on Rayne, who was punished by being left cleaning up the damage when the rest of her class went into the Alps to enjoy a day of skiing. Rayne was willing to forget the incident, but not her fiery roommate. In retaliation for the lie, Nat had taken pictures of the girl's private diary and posted them throughout the school.

Rayne frowned. Was Niko right? Was the reason she'd been incapable of processing her friend's death not only been the horror of finding her body, but some inner suspicion that there was something wrong? No. She shook away the strange sense of foreboding that threatened to settle in the pit in her stomach.

"I know what I saw," she stubbornly insisted. "Her wrists were slit and there was no sign of a struggle in the room. She wouldn't have just lay there and let someone do that."

Niko clenched his teeth, glancing away, as if struggling to control a powerful emotion. "When my parents flew Nat's body back to the States, I insisted on an autopsy. I was certain there had to be some other answer for her death."

"And?"

He glanced back, his eyes shadowed. "They found opioids in her system."

"Opioids," Rayne breathed in shock. "Why didn't your parents say anything?"

"They were afraid she'd become addicted to drugs and that's why she decided to kill herself."

"Never." The word burst from Rayne's lips before she could halt it.

"I agree. I think it's more likely someone slipped her enough opioids to knock her out and then sliced her wrists."

Rayne released a shaky breath. The information that drugs had been found in Nat's body changed everything. It wasn't that illegal substances were never smuggled into the school. They were teenagers who had the typical desire to flaunt authority, along with enough money to buy whatever they wanted. But never Nat. She was a health fanatic who was vegan long before it was fashionable, and up at dawn every morning to run five miles. She considered her body a temple. She would never, ever, pollute it with drugs.

Grudgingly, she allowed herself to consider the idea that Niko had been right. What if Nat hadn't killed herself? That would mean . . .

"Who?" she at last muttered. "Who would do such an awful thing?"

"That's the question." He held her horrified gaze. "Can you remember anyone who was mad at Nat? Did she say anything about being in an argument?"

Rayne shook her head. "Everyone loved Nat."

He waved the note. "Not everyone."

"There were certainly girls who were jealous of her," Rayne conceded. "But I can't imagine that would drive them to murder."

Niko paused, as if lost in his thoughts. Then, with an obvious effort, he squared his shoulders.

"You said there were mementos from school in the box?"

"Yes. Along with a few cards. Oh and some photos."

"Photos of what?"

"See for yourself."

Rayne moved to where he'd set down the box and flipped open the lid. Reaching inside, she pulled out the pictures and placed them in his outstretched hand.

He glanced down, his brow furrowing as he studied the top photo. "A horse?"

A reminiscent smile curved her lips as Rayne turned so she was standing side by side with Niko.

"She took the picture the day I moved into her dorm room."

"I suppose that could have special meaning," he said, pointing his finger toward the shadowed form at the back of the stable. "Who's that?"

Rayne leaned forward, trying to recall who had been in the stall with them. He was familiar, with his tangle of brown hair and tall, slender body wearing what looked like a uniform, but she hadn't spent much time at the stables. All she remembered was some of the girls giggling about the cute boy who tried to kiss them when he helped them saddle a horse.

At last she managed to dredge up a name.

"Henri," she said. "I don't remember his last name. He worked in the stables."

With a vague nod, Niko shuffled to the next picture of Nat standing between her friends.

"That's Trent Orwell, isn't it?" Niko asked.

"Yes, and his sister, Brooke. She was probably closer to Nat than anyone else at school."

He sent her a startled glance. "Closer than you?"

Rayne smiled wryly. There was no doubt that she'd been a little jealous of Nat's friendship with Brooke. The two were inseparable the last couple of years of school. But looking back, she accepted that it hadn't been because Nat liked Brooke more. It was just that they had more interests in common.

"We loved each other like sisters, but we were very different people," she told Niko. "She could never understand how I could spend endless hours in front of my easel, or simply stare at the mountains for an entire afternoon. She was always moving. Like a bee buzzing from flower to flower."

They shared a pained smile before Niko turned his attention to the last photo. "A fountain?" He looked puzzled. "Was this a special place?"

Rayne was equally confused. She couldn't remember Nat ever mentioning the fountain, or spending time in that particular location. And it certainly wasn't one of her best photos. It was slightly out of focus, and there was someone in the background spoiling the view of the nearby gardens.

"Not that she ever mentioned."

Niko wrinkled his brow. "Why would Nat keep these pictures in her special box? She had endless crates of photos. Most of them a lot better than these."

Rayne heaved a sigh. "I have no idea."

"Then maybe Brooke will know."

Rayne blinked at his abrupt words. "What makes you think that?"

"You said she was Nat's best friend," he reminded her. "And there might be a reason for her picture to be in the box."

He was grasping at straws. And it was her fault, she silently acknowledged. If she'd taken time to think before she'd grabbed her phone and frantically searched for Niko's number, she would never have dredged up his painful memories.

And he certainly wouldn't be considering reaching out to Nat's old acquaintances to get answers for her death.

Then again, she couldn't deny her own desire to discover exactly what had happened on that fateful day. Was it a straightforward suicide? Or something more nefarious? She wasn't nearly as confident as she had once been.

"I suppose it's worth a try."

Satisfaction rippled over his sculpted features. "Did you keep in touch with her?"

Rayne pulled out her phone, pulling up a search engine to type in a name. "Not after I left school. But her parents owned a horse farm not far from Chicago."

"Yes, I remember. Orwell Horse Farm and Stud." He smiled wryly as she sent him a startled glance at his ready memory of the place. "Nat went to stay there a few times. My dad did a full background check on the family before he allowed her to go."

Rayne returned her attention to her phone, pressing the link to the Orwells' official website.

"It's been in the family for generations. I'm sure someone there will be able to tell us where she is."

She pressed the number, putting the phone on Speaker as a female voice answered the call. "Orwell Horse Farm and Stud."

"Hello, can I speak with Brooke Orwell?" Rayne asked. She had no idea if Brooke had married or not, or if she used her husband's last name.

Thankfully, the person on the other end of the line knew exactly who Rayne was referring to. "I'm sorry. She's in the stables. Can I take a message?"

"Yes, this is Rayne Taylor, an old friend of hers from school. I'm going to be in the area . . ." She hesitated, glancing toward Niko.

Tomorrow morning, he mouthed the words.

"Tomorrow." Rayne spoke into the phone. "Could you tell her I'll stop by around ten?"

"Of course."

"Thank you." Rayne disconnected and tucked away the phone.

"We'll take the helicopter to Chicago in the morning and rent a car at the airport," Niko said in decisive tones, as if he was accustomed to giving orders and having them obeyed.

Rayne nodded. It was the quickest solution. "I have a van we can use once we get to Chicago."

"Okay."

For the first time since she'd arrived in Kansas City, Rayne felt awkward as she lifted her hand to glance at her watch.

"I need to check into a hotel."

"There's no need for a hotel," he instantly insisted. "You can stay at my condo."

She was shaking her head before he finished speaking. "I don't want—"

"Or you can stay here," he cut into her protest. "I use

this place for out-of-town business acquaintances to stay if they spend the night. The sofa opens into a bed." He nodded toward the opening to the bathroom. "You'll find everything you need if you want to shower, and I can easily have dinner sent up."

She hesitated. It was a sensible plan. She hadn't brought an overnight bag, and it would be nice to have a fully stocked bathroom, not to mention the privacy of the secluded suite. But she wasn't used to accepting help.

She didn't want to be obligated. To anyone.

"Okay," she finally forced herself to say. In part because she was just too tired to deal with locating a hotel and checking in.

Niko stepped forward, his eyes darkening with an emotion she couldn't decipher as he brushed a finger down her cheek.

"It's good to see you, Rayne. I've missed you."

The next day they were back in Chicago before the morning rush hour. They drove to the hotel where Rayne had already booked a room for her brief stay in Chicago. She quickly changed into a pair of jeans and a soft lemon sweater before they were back on the road, headed south.

They remained silent until they'd left behind the suburbs and were traveling down a County road that was lined by a patchwork of frozen fields. Rayne slowed, her gaze searching for the upcoming turn that would take them to the Orwell farm. The GPS on her phone wasn't entirely dependable in such a remote location.

"So, this is the infamous van," Niko finally broke the silence.

Rayne kept her gaze locked on the road. She was acutely aware of the large, male body settled in the seat next to her. The small span between them seemed to sizzle and snap with an unfamiliar heat. She told herself that it was because she wasn't used to having anyone in her vehicle, but she knew that wasn't true.

Only Niko possessed the ability to make her heart race and her stomach feel as if she'd just stepped off the edge of a cliff, freefalling to some unknown destination.

She cleared the strange lump from her throat. "Infamous?"

"I read an article in an art magazine that you travel around the country in a van until inspiration strikes," he told her. "It sounded very mystical."

Rayne snorted. She remembered the article. She'd been portrayed as some weird hermit who appeared from the mist with a van filled with masterpieces. If it hadn't been for the need to earn a living, she wouldn't bother to promote her art. She painted because she couldn't *not* paint, not to be famous.

That was an unfortunate side effect.

"There's nothing mystical about it," she dryly assured him. "I drive, and occasionally I see something that captures my attention. When that happens I stop and make a quick sketch." She shrugged. "That's when I decide if I want to stay long enough to complete a painting."

"Whatever your method, it produces magic," he murmured. Heat touched her cheeks and her hands tightened on the steering wheel. She hated compliments. They made her feel like a fraud. No doubt a reaction to her mother's constant criticism. Easily sensing her discomfort, Niko smoothly changed the subject. "Did you know Brooke Orwell before you went to Austria?"

Rayne forced her muscles to relax. "My father was friends with Brooke's parents." She grimaced. "My real father, not Mark," she clarified. "He brought me out to the farm a few times when I was young. I think they were the ones to suggest I go to St. Cecilia's School for Girls after my mother remarried. Brooke was already there."

"Did it bother you to be sent so far from home?"

"Not really. My parents never knew what to do with a child." The words were an understatement. Her father's only interest was in acquiring as much money as possible, and her mother was too self-absorbed to care for a baby. "And once Mother married Mark I was an unwelcome intruder in the house. St. Cecilia's was more of a home than anywhere else."

"And now you live in a van."

"Something like that."

There was a pause, as if he was considering her vagabond lifestyle. "Do you ever intend to settle down in one place?"

A small shiver raced through her. "Doubtful."

"What about a family?"

"I prefer my freedom."

"Don't you ever get lonely?" he pressed, his voice hard.

Was he bothered by her preference for the road? Probably. He'd been raised in a tight-knit family who would be deeply hurt if one of them chose to maintain a constant distance. He would never understand parents who rarely recalled they had a child.

Or the ghosts that refused to give her peace.

"I don't get lonely as long as I keep moving." She took her foot off the gas as she caught sight of the massive wooden sign that was carved with the words "Orwell Horse Farm and Stud," along with an image of a horse. "This is the turn."

Niko was thankfully distracted as they veered onto a graveled road that wound between endless white fences. Eventually they could see the stables and paddocks that were spread over several acres, along with a barn the size of a football field. Across the road there was a white, Palladian-style home with long wings on each side and a detached garage.

Niko released a low whistle. "Quite a spread."

She pulled through the open gates and up the circular drive. She parked in front of the sweeping veranda, complete with fluted columns. She didn't know if there was a separate office, but this was as good as anywhere to start the search for Brooke.

"I remember thinking we were in the middle of nowhere when I was little. I was so used to being in the city, I couldn't believe how far I could see." She glanced toward the rolling fields that seemed to go on forever. "Now I've actually been in the middle of nowhere."

"And I have the paintings to prove it," he teased, referring to her series from Death Valley.

They shared a quick smile before she switched off the engine and slid out of the van. Niko joined her as she reached the steps leading to the veranda, and together they moved to stand in front of the double doors. It was Niko who reached out to press the bell, which they could hear echo through the vast house. A few minutes later one of the doors was pulled open to reveal a tall, slender woman.

Brooke hadn't changed much since they were together in Austria. Her hair was a dark red and pulled into a smooth braid. Her skin was flawless despite the hours she must spend in the sun, and her eyes were a light brown.

She was currently wearing a pair of khaki slacks and a tailored shirt, without any jewelry or makeup. The stark style suited her natural beauty.

"Hello, Brooke."

"Rayne." Brooke's gaze traveled to the tall man standing at Rayne's side, a hint of curiosity in her eyes. "And Niko. I had no idea you were coming. Are you two together?"

"For now," Niko murmured.

Brooke stepped back, motioning for them to enter. Once they were standing in the foyer, with its heavy chandelier and the sweeping staircase that spilled onto the upper floor, she closed the door. Then she headed toward the nearest opening.

"We'll go into the study," she told them, leading them into a square room that had two walls lined with floor-to-ceiling bookcases. On the far side of the space was a heavy desk cluttered with piles of papers where a man was seated. At their entrance, he rose to his feet. "You remember my brother, Trent?" Brooke asked.

"Of course," Rayne said. Trent had transformed from a boy into a man over the past years. His once-skinny body had filled out with a broad chest beneath his cable-knit sweater, and he'd cut his red hair until it lay smooth against his head. There were even a few lines fanning out from the brown eyes that looked closer to black in the muted light.

His charming smile, however, was the same as he rounded the desk to shake their hands. "Rayne. Niko."

Rayne felt a small flare of relief. It would be much easier to question Brooke and Trent together.

"Coffee? Tea?" Brooke asked.

"Nothing for me," Rayne said as Niko shook his head.

Brooke moved to stand next to her brother, eyeing Rayne with open curiosity. "I assumed you contacted me because you wanted to use the farm in one of your paintings."

Ah. That was why she'd appeared so eager when she'd opened the door. Rayne hadn't been close friends with her and it had seemed odd that she would be excited by her visit. Obviously she'd been hoping for some free publicity for the horse farm in the form of an art show.

"We're here to ask you about Nat," Niko clarified.

"Nat?" Brooke slowly stiffened, her eyes narrowed. "I don't understand."

"A couple of days ago I found some of Nat's belongings in my old school stuff," Rayne said, taking charge of the encounter.

Niko was no doubt far more skilled in negotiations, and his people skills were a thousand times better than her own. *Everyone's* people skills were better. But his emotions were too raw to be objective. He was convinced that Nat hadn't committed suicide. And now he was searching for proof to back up his theory.

Rayne pulled out a picture from the pocket of her heavy parka and handed it to Brooke. It was the one of Nat standing between the Orwell siblings.

Brooke studied the image, her features softening, as if recalling a happy memory.

"I remember this." She glanced toward her brother. "You came with Mom and Dad for Parents Weekend."

He nodded, moving closer to Brooke as he gazed down at the photo. "There was a formal dance. I was Nat's date and she insisted I wear a tux for the event."

"Who took the picture?" Rayne asked.

Brooke furrowed her brow, as if struggling to recall the precise details of the night. "I think Nat gave her camera to my mom. It took her forever to figure out which button to push."

Rayne swallowed a sigh. There was nothing in the picture to indicate why Nat would have saved it in her private box. She was hoping it was either the occasion or maybe the person who'd taken the photo that had been special.

"I still don't understand why you drove out here," Brooke said, handing back the photo.

Rayne tucked it back in her pocket and pulled out the wrinkled note. "This was with the picture."

Brooke took the paper and scanned the stark threat. Her eyes widened, and she shot a startled glance toward her brother. Trent's own expression was carefully devoid of emotion. As if he didn't want Rayne or Niko to witness his reaction to the note.

Finally, Brooke cleared her throat and returned her attention to Rayne. "What is this?"

"Obviously a threat," Rayne said.

"From whom?"

Rayne reached out to take back the note, folding it before she slid it into her pocket. "We're hoping you could tell us."

"Why me?"

Rayne blinked at the sudden aggression in Brooke's tone. She wasn't sure what she'd expected. Shock. Or disbelief. Maybe even indifference. But her defensiveness was like waving a red flag in front of them.

Suddenly she suspected that Brooke had something to hide.

"You were her best friend," Rayne pointed out, careful not to sound accusing.

"Exactly. It . . ." Brooke's words trailed off, as if they'd dried on her parted lips. She blinked, battling back tears. "It broke my heart when she killed herself. Why would I ever threaten her?"

Rayne ignored the woman's distress. This was painful for all of them. "Do you know anyone who would have?"

"No," Brooke snapped. "Everyone loved Nat."

"Nat was my sister, but I wasn't blind to her faults," Niko intruded into the conversation. "She was stubborn, selfish, and opinionated as hell."

Brooke clenched her teeth, clearly annoyed by Niko's description of his sister. "Yes. Just like every other teenage girl at St. Cecilia's."

Trent wrapped a protective arm around his sister. "Why are you interested in an old note?"

"I'm not convinced that Nat killed herself. I never was," Niko bluntly admitted. "I want to know if my sister was being threatened before she died."

Brooke released a hissing breath, half-collapsing against her brother. If Trent hadn't been holding her in a tight grip, she would have fallen to the floor.

"What the hell, Niko?" Trent rasped, sending Niko a

fierce glare. "We all grieved for Nat. Brooke most of all. You have no right to come here opening old wounds."

Rayne didn't doubt the truth of his words. The loss of Nat was still clearly a source of pain for Brooke.

Or was it guilt? The treacherous thought niggled in the back of Rayne's mind. They'd all been devastated by Nat's death, but Brooke's grief still appeared to be as raw and deep as the day they found Nat dead.

So was it just an act? Teenage girls could be victims of their raging hormones. Even Rayne had felt out of control during those traumatic years. And friendships could transform into worst enemies in the blink of an eye. Had Nat done something that had sent Brooke over the edge?

She was pondering the horrifying possibility when Niko spoke directly to Trent.

"What about you?"

Trent flinched, as if blindsided by the abrupt question. "Me?"

"You were dating Nat."

"Hardly dating," Trent protested, an unexpected flush staining his lean face. "We lived thousands of miles apart."

Niko folded his arms over his chest, his expression hard. "She came here to spend the summer with you before her senior year."

"And?"

"Did she ever call you? Maybe mention she was having trouble with someone at the school?" Rayne hastily stepped in. There was a tension vibrating around the Orwell siblings that warned they were increasingly irritated by the questions. Even if they did know something, they were getting to the point they were going to refuse to answer. "Or even a boy from the nearby town?"

"Yes, she occasionally called or texted me," Trent ground out, glaring at Niko. "But no. She never mentioned any trouble. She was excited about graduation and looking forward to her career as a photographer. She even asked me to write a letter of recommendation for her application to the School of Visual Arts in New York."

Rayne grimaced. His words only confirmed that Nat wasn't contemplating suicide. She glanced toward the silent woman at Trent's side.

"Brooke?"

"She never said anything." Brooke wrapped her arms around her waist, as if she was suddenly cold. "And if she really believed she was being threatened, she would have told me."

Once again Rayne was struck by the edge of aggression in the woman's voice. "And you don't think she would have told you that she was thinking about killing herself?"

"That's enough," Trent growled, urging Brooke across the room. "I'm sorry, but we have a meeting in the stables with a buyer. You can show yourself out."

Startled by the abrupt end to the meeting, Rayne turned to watch the two head toward the door. She still had more questions, but the Orwells had made it clear that they were done with the conversation. Then her gaze caught sight of a large, framed picture on the wall above a glass trophy case.

"Wait," she muttered.

"Let Nat rest in peace, for God's sake," Brooke snapped.

Rayne ignored the chastisement, hurrying to inspect

the photo of Brooke and Trent standing next to a beautiful chestnut stallion. There was a large trophy on the ground in front of them, and off to one side was a man dressed in coveralls. Rayne would never have recognized him if it hadn't been the newspaper article that was framed next to the picture with a large headline:

Easy Breeze, owned by Orwell Horse Farm and trained by Henri Wagner, takes All-Around Award for best in Quarter Horses.

"Henri Wagner." She blinked in shock. "Isn't that Henri from St. Cecilia's School?"

CHAPTER FIVE

Niko turned his head toward the Orwells, watching their reaction to Rayne's accusation.

Brooke's eyes widened, something that might have been fear rippling over her face, while Trent's jaw tightened with an unmistakable anger. It was obvious Henri Wagner had left behind intense feelings. But after a quick glance, they hurriedly attempted to disguise their response.

"Who?" Brooke asked, blinking as if unable to recall the name.

"The stable boy from St. Cecilia's." Rayne reached into her pocket and pulled out a picture as she crossed to stand directly in front of Brooke. Niko hurried to join her. There was something about the Orwells that were setting off his inner alarms. He wanted to be close to Rayne in case things went sideways. Rayne held out the picture. "This is Henri," she said. "That's the same man who was your trainer, isn't it?"

There was a pause. Was Brooke deciding whether or not she would continue to pretend she didn't know the identity of her own employee? Then, she flicked a glance toward the picture in Rayne's hand and released a brittle laugh.

"Oh, yes. Henri. I'd almost forgotten about him."

"How did he get from Austria to here?" Rayne demanded.

"He knew we owned a horse farm, and when my parents came to my graduation he asked if my father would hire him," Brooke smoothly responded.

"And your father did?" Rayne arched her brow. "Just like that?"

"Henri was well-trained and eager to immigrate to the States. My father decided to give him a chance."

Niko watched as Trent's hands curled into tight fists. The man looked as if he was wishing he could punch something. Henri Wagner? Or Rayne, for asking uncomfortable questions?

"Is he still here?" Niko abruptly demanded.

It was Brooke who answered. "No."

"Why not?" Rayne asked.

Brooke shrugged. "We caught him stealing from petty cash."

Niko narrowed his eyes. He wasn't friends with the Orwell family. Nat had been their only connection. But he did know rich families and their reactions to having a servant stealing from them. They would consider it more than a mere theft. It would be the breaking of a trust. They wouldn't be satisfied without punishing them.

"You didn't have him arrested?"

Brooke shook her head. "We didn't want to make a

fuss. We kicked him off the farm without a reference. That seemed fair."

Niko snorted. They'd brought him all the way from Austria and then just asked him to leave? No way. There was something more to this story.

"Where is he now?" Niko asked.

Brooke licked her lips. She didn't want to answer. "I heard he went to jail. For all I know he's still there," she eventually muttered. "Or maybe he went back to Austria. He didn't seem particularly happy in America."

"We're done here," Trent announced in hard tones, tugging his sister through the doorway. "If you have any more questions, contact our lawyers."

The two disappeared from view, and with a rueful glance toward Rayne, Niko led the way out of the house. There was no point in hanging around. Trent Orwell had made it clear the meeting was over.

Neither spoke until they were in the van and Rayne was pulling through the gate onto the graveled road.

"They're hiding something," Niko said between clenched teeth.

Rayne nodded. "I agree. But what?"

"Maybe we should ask Henri," Niko murmured, his gaze locked on the nearby barns, which were bigger than most people's homes. "It's too much of a coincidence that he worked at St. Cecilia's School and then for the Orwells."

"If we can find him."

Niko pulled out his phone, searching for the name on the internet. "Here," he said, glancing through the top hits.

"Wagner Stables, horse training and riding lessons for all ages. Proprietor Henri Wagner. That has to be him."

"Where is it?"

Niko pulled up his map app and plugged in the address. Then he released a low whistle. "Twelve miles north of here." He pointed toward the upcoming intersection. "Make a left at the next road. It will take us directly to the place."

Rayne slowed to take the turn, her brow furrowed. "Hard to believe that neither Brooke nor Trent knew Henri had stables practically in their backyard."

"No crap. I have a friend who owns a racehorse. The boarding and training of Thoroughbreds is a specialized business where everyone knows everyone else."

"Which means they didn't want us talking to him."

Niko watched the flat pastures slide past as Rayne picked up speed. He considered the meeting with the Orwells. It'd felt like an awkward dance, with the brother and sister attempting to avoid the simplest questions as they'd hurried to find a way to end the conversation. The unease had been more than just a lingering grief at Nat's death. It'd been . . . fear. And it'd gone from bad to worse when Rayne had recognized the picture of Henri Wagner.

"The question is whether Henri knows something about Brooke and Trent they don't want exposed," he said. "Or if he knows something about my sister's death."

Rayne nodded. "There has to be a reason Nat had a picture of him hidden in her special box."

Niko made a sound of frustration. Natalie had always been bubbly and outgoing, but there was a part of her that she hadn't been willing to share with others. Not even with him. But he couldn't believe that she wouldn't have reached out if she was being threatened. She had to know that he would do everything in his power to protect her. Didn't she?

The thought that she'd hidden the note instead of calling him was gnawing at him like a cancer. If she'd only told him what was happening, he would have . . .

"I think that's the stables." Rayne thankfully interrupted his dark thoughts.

With a small shake of his head, Niko forced himself to concentrate on the cluster of buildings that were crouched together, as if trying to take as little space as possible. Or maybe they were leaning against one another in an effort to stay upright, he wryly acknowledged, taking in the sagging roofs of the outbuildings and the peeling white paint. There was an air of neglect that extended to the fence that framed the small paddock and the weathered sign that swung from a pole next to the open gate.

"Nothing compared to the Orwell farm," Niko said as Rayne pulled to a halt in front of the small house that was long and narrow, with a tin roof and a porch that had lost most of its railing.

Rayne sent him a humorless smile. "Not many places are."

"True." Niko pushed open his door, grimacing as he caught sight of the rusty nails and old beer cans scattered across the front yard. "Have you had a tetanus shot?"

"Not recently."

"Then be careful."

Together, they left the van and picked their way across the frozen ground, exchanging a glance as they climbed onto the wooden porch that groaned, as if it was considering collapsing beneath their weight. Whatever Henri's grand plan when he emigrated to America, he'd ended up in a place that wasn't much more than a crumbling shack.

Niko nodded toward Rayne, who knocked on the screen door while he leaned toward the side, trying to peer through the filthy window. He wasn't expecting trouble, but it was always possible one of the Orwells had called the man to warn him that Rayne was stirring up the past.

There was a long pause before the heavy inner door was yanked open to reveal a slender man dressed in a brown shirt and filthy khakis. He had dark, shaggy hair threaded with gray that brushed his shoulders and a three-day growth of whiskers on his narrow face. His eyes were dark and currently bloodshot, as if they'd wakened him despite the fact that it was close to noon.

"Yeah?" the man demanded, staring at them with a bleary confusion.

"Henri Wagner?" Rayne asked, studying the man. Was she trying to determine whether or not he was the same Henri she'd known in Austria?

"Yes." The man confirmed his identity, along with a hint of a German accent. "If you want a lesson, they're by appointment only. Call the number on the sign."

Niko shuddered. He couldn't imagine the condition of the poor horses in the stables. Henri didn't look as if he could take care of himself, let alone high-maintenance animals.

"We're not here for lessons," he assured the man.

"Are you lost?"

Niko shook his head. "We need to ask you a few questions."

Henri scowled. "If you're from Animal Welfare—"

"We're not," Niko interrupted, silently promising himself he was going to make a hotline report as soon as they were back in Chicago.

It was possible the horses were in fine shape. The man had worked in stables for a number of years and he might very well put the well-being of his animals over himself. But Niko wanted someone in legal authority to check out the place.

"Then what do you want?" Henri snapped.

"I'm Rayne Taylor," Rayne told him.

Henri blinked. Either he simply didn't remember Rayne, or his mind was fogged from a night of heavy drinking. By the stale stench of beer that wafted from inside the house, Niko was betting his brain was toasted.

"So?" the man muttered.

"I went to school at St. Cecilia's School for Girls," Rayne clarified.

Henri made a sound of shock. He hadn't been expecting that. Then, narrowing his eyes, he studied Rayne through the screen door. The seconds ticked past before Henri abruptly stiffened, as if he'd belatedly recognized Rayne. At the same time, his expression tightened, as he obviously tried to pretend he didn't have a clue who she might be.

"A lot of girls went to school there," he growled. "You can't expect me to remember them all."

Niko reached toward the handle. "Can we come inside?"

"No." Henri stepped back, his hand on the wooden door. He was ready and eager to slam it in their faces. "I'm busy."

"We just want to ask you a few questions," Rayne hastily assured him.

"About what?"

"My sister." Niko took control of the conversation. There was a hard glint in the bloodshot eyes that warned him this man could be a nasty enemy. "Natalie Scantlin."

"I don't know who you're talking about."

"She was found with her wrists slit," Niko said. "It's not something you could forget."

Henri licked his lips, his gaze darting from Niko to Rayne. "I didn't have anything to do with the students."

"That's a lie. You spent time with them every day," Rayne accused. "In fact, I remember that you personally taught a few of the beginner lessons for the students."

The face that was lined with bitterness twisted into an ugly expression. "They were in the stables to play. I was there to work." He spit out the words. "I wasn't born into money. I had to shovel shit and polish tack to put food on my table."

"You knew the students well enough to ask Brooke Orwell's father for a job," Niko smoothly pointed out.

"Yeah, well." The man hunched his shoulders. "She was always hanging around the horses."

"Along with Nat," Rayne added in sharp tones, pulling

out the picture to press it against the screen. "She took this picture. You were in the stall with the foal. See?"

"No. I don't remember her. I . . ." The words trailed away, an unmistakable tremor in his voice. "I can't. Leave me alone."

Without warning, he stepped back and slammed the door with enough force to make the entire house shudder. Both Niko and Rayne scurried off the porch. It was close to collapse. Neither of them wanted to be standing on the rotting structure when it succumbed to its inevitable fate.

Reluctantly heading back to the van, Rayne glanced in his direction with a grimace. "That could have gone better."

"No shit."

Rayne used the graveled roads to head back to the city. It would take longer to reach Chicago, but her thoughts were too jumbled to feel comfortable dealing with traffic on the highway.

When she'd started this journey, she'd simply hoped that Nat's best friend could explain the meaning of the note and the person responsible for writing it. Or, best of all, dismiss it as a hoax. As much as she'd been haunted by the thought of Nat killing herself over the years, it would be a thousand times worse to discover that she'd been murdered.

But both Brooke and Trent had only added to the mystery surrounding Nat's death. It was obvious they knew something. Just as it was obvious they were determined to keep it a secret. Then there'd been the shocking recognition when she'd seen the picture on the wall.

Henri Wagner had worked at the Orwell farm. That might have been a coincidence. He was a stable hand in Austria, after all, and he had no doubt spent a lot of time with Brooke. She could have convinced her dad to take a chance on him. But a few minutes questioning Henri had convinced Rayne that there was much more to his presence than a quirk of fate.

He'd been hiding something, too.

So the question was whether his secret was the same as Trent and Brooke Orwell's. Or a different secret.

Rayne slowed as they entered a small town with a four-way stop at the very center. That was the problem with taking the backroads. There was no straight shot to Chicago. The streets meandered through a dozen different communities. Pressing her foot on the brakes, Rayne glanced toward the silent man at her side. He hadn't said a word since they'd left Henri's property, but there was a deep frown furrowing his brow.

"I don't care what Henri claimed. He remembers Nat," she said, as much to draw Niko out of his brooding as to discuss the suspicions that were nagging at her. "Did you see his face before he slammed shut the door?"

"They all know something. The Orwells along with Henri Wagner." His voice was hard. He was obviously struggling to contain his anger toward his sister's supposed friends. "I can feel it."

"Me too." Rayne tapped her fingers on the steering wheel, a restless frustration seething inside her. "Unfortunately, we can't force them to tell us what they know."

"I could," he said in harsh tones. "But I might end up in jail."

Rayne swallowed a sigh. Niko should be in his elegant Kansas City office, concentrating on his future. Not ripping open old wounds. But it was too late to regret her impulsive phone call. Pandora's box had been well and truly opened.

"We can't have you getting hauled off by the cops," she teased, trying to lighten the dark mood that filled the van.

He turned his head to send her a wry smile. "Would you come visit me?"

"Maybe." She shrugged. "I've never been inside a prison. Nat told me that I needed to broaden my horizons."

His smile widened. "That sounds like something my sister would say."

"She—" Her words were cut short as something hit the side of the van.

What was that? There was another thump. Was someone throwing rocks at her? The thought barely had time to form before Niko grabbed her shoulder and yanked her down.

"Stay low!" he commanded, his hands fumbling with his seat belt. "Someone's shooting at us."

Rayne's brain refused to accept what he was saying. There had to be a mistake. People didn't shoot at random vehicles in the middle of the day. Especially not in a small town that probably hadn't seen a violent crime in years.

Then the side window, just above Niko's head, abruptly shattered, sending tiny shards of glass spraying through the van.

Rayne stifled a scream even as Niko finally managed to wrestle out of his seat belt and reached for the door handle.

"No, Niko!"

Rayne grabbed his arm, a sizzling fear clenching her heart. There was no way she was going to allow this man to be injured, maybe even killed. Not only because she would blame herself. But because . . . because it would destroy something inside her, she realized, with a jolt of surprise.

"I need to see who was shooting at us." He gently pulled out of her grasp, holding her gaze as he cautiously straightened in his seat. He turned his head to study the broken window, at the same time there was the sound of squealing tires.

"Damn," Niko growled. "It's too late."

Rayne sat upright, glancing around. On her side of the van was a row of brick buildings that were a combination of small businesses and empty shells. On Niko's side, however, there was a frozen park with an enclosed shelter that was next to a side road. A shooter could have parked behind the wooden building and remained out of sight of the locals as he—or she—tried to gun them down.

"Did you see anything?" Niko demanded. "A vehicle following us?"

"Nothing. But I wasn't really paying attention. Obviously a mistake." She muttered a curse. "I suspected that Brooke and Trent and even Henri Wagner were hiding something. But it never occurred to me that they would be desperate enough to try to get rid of us."

He grabbed his seat belt and pulled it across his body, his jaw set in a stubborn line. "Let's turn around."

"Turn around?" She blinked, certain she couldn't have heard him right. "Why?"

"Someone doesn't want us asking questions."

"Exactly." Rayne deliberately reached out to brush the shards of glass from his shoulders. It'd been so close. If Niko hadn't recognized that first thud that hit the van, they never would have bent down and the bullet would have gone through his head. Her stomach clenched and her mouth went dry. "Which is why we should go back to Chicago and call the cops."

"And tell them what?" he demanded. "That we found an old note in the attic and now we think two members of a highly respected, powerful family are trying to kill us?"

Put like that, it did sound like a wasted effort. For better or worse, the cops weren't going to investigate the Orwell family unless there was solid proof of a crime. And perhaps not even then. Old money was still a perfect barrier to avoid the bad things in life.

"It could have been Henri," she gave one last shot at convincing him to return to Chicago.

"You're right." A tight smile curved his lips. "We'll talk to him first."

"Niko . . ."

She heaved a harsh sigh. Niko wasn't going to be satisfied until they'd gone back and demanded explanations. Even if it meant facing a potential killer. And a part of her agreed with his grim resolve to discover the truth. Whoever had followed them was determined to keep the past buried. Neither she nor Niko would be safe until they'd uncovered what had really happened to Nat.

"Fine." She turned the corner to head back toward Henri's stables. "But if I get shot, I'm not going to be happy."

CHAPTER SIX

Somewhere in the back of Niko's mind was a tiny voice of sanity. It whispered that he was allowing his festering anger at Nat's death to cloud his thinking. It wasn't like he was a detective. He didn't even play one on TV. He was a businessman who didn't know a damn thing about deciphering clues or interviewing witnesses.

On the other hand, the fact that he didn't carry a badge meant that he didn't have to follow any rules.

Since Nat had been discovered on her bed with her wrists cut, Niko had been haunted by the need to know what had happened. And, more importantly, who was responsible.

At last he was certain that there were people who could give him answers. Even if they didn't know exact details, they must have information that would point him in the right direction. Why else would they be so reluctant to discuss Nat's death? And why try to keep Henri Wagner's presence in the neighborhood a secret?

The fact that someone had followed them with the intention of scaring them off, or even killing them, only solidified his belief they were protecting something that happened in the past. There was no way anyone would take such a risk unless they were scared what Rayne and he might reveal.

It wasn't until they were parked behind one of the dilapidated stables to avoid being seen by anyone in the nearby house that he realized he was putting Rayne in danger.

Niko unhooked his belt and turned in his seat. "I think you should stay here while I talk to Henri."

Rayne snorted, shutting off the engine and removing her seat belt. "Didn't you ever watch old horror flicks?"

Niko blinked in confusion. "Excuse me?"

"It's the person who's left alone who always gets taken out first," she explained.

His heart clenched at her light words. She was teasing him to ease the tension, but the mere thought of her being hurt was like salt being poured into his raw nerves.

Reaching out, he framed her face in his hands, his gaze drinking in each line and curve. "You're not getting taken, out, Rayne," he rasped. "I lost Nat, but I'm not going to lose you."

"Niko."

Her lips parted, as if inviting his kiss. Niko didn't hesitate. Lowering his head, he brushed his mouth over hers, deliberately keeping his touch light. It was a promise of pleasure to come.

Then, straightening, he released a harsh breath. "You're right. We started this together. We'll finish it together."

They exited the van, pausing at the edge of the stables to study the house. There wasn't much to see. The curtains were all pulled tight and there wasn't any smoke coming from the chimney. There wasn't even a vehicle in the driveway. From a distance it appeared to be empty. Niko, however, wasn't going to take the risk that Henri was inside, waiting for them with a gun.

"Maybe we should use the back door," he suggested.

Rayne nodded. "Good idea."

They circled through the paddock, hearing the soft snorts of the horses inside the stables before they approached the house from behind the garage. Cautiously, they climbed the steps that were as decrepit as those leading to the front porch. Niko reached out to grab the knob and shoved open the wooden door. Standing with his back against the side of the house, he peered through the opening.

A quick glance revealed a cramped kitchenette with one row of cabinets that were framed by a narrow fridge at one end and a stove at the other. Closer to the back door, there was a sink beneath a window that was piled with dirty dishes and countertops that were stacked with empty beer cans. And in the center of the tiled floor, Henri Wagner was staring at them with an incredulous expression.

"What the hell?"

Not willing to give the man the opportunity to react, Niko charged forward and shoved Henri against the wall.

"You should have killed me the first time, Wagner," he growled, the adrenaline still rushing through him. It was going to be a while before he fully recovered from someone taking a shot at his head. "You won't get a second chance."

"Kill you?" Henri frowned. "What are you talking about? I have never seen you before today."

Niko muttered a curse. "Do you think I won't beat the shit out of you?"

"Why? I have no idea what you're yammering about," Henri complained.

Niko narrowed his gaze. "I know you followed us after we left here and shot at us. Several times."

Henri blinked. "Are you on drugs?"

"Not yet," Niko said in dry tones.

Henri struggled against the arm Niko was using to press him against the wall. Niko leaned in, easily able to keep the man pinned in place.

"Let go of me."

"Not until you admit what you did."

"I didn't do anything." Henri's German accent was more pronounced as his narrow face flushed with anger.

"You were afraid of us digging into the past, so you followed us and—"

"Followed you?" Henri made a sound of disgust. "How? My truck won't start. It's been in the shop for over a week."

"Convenient story."

"There's nothing convenient about it." Henri's voice held an edge of genuine annoyance. "Go look for yourself."

"Niko." The sound of Rayne's voice had Niko glancing over his shoulder. He discovered her standing next to the stove with her hand over a pan that was sitting on the front burner. "There's soup in this. It's warm."

"Of course it's warm," Henri snapped. "You interrupted my lunch. I should call the cops."

"You can call them when we're done chatting." Niko turned his head back to glare down at Henri.

"I already told you, my truck is in the shop," Henri stubbornly insisted. "If someone took a shot at you, it wasn't me."

Was it possible he was telling the truth? Niko scowled. He didn't want to believe him. Henri Wagner was, after all, the most likely culprit. He'd been the last person they'd spoken to before they were attacked. And it'd been obvious during their conversation that he was hiding something from the past.

But there hadn't been a truck parked near the house when they'd returned here. And even though there were outbuildings where he could have parked it, would he have the sense to hide it on the off chance he might be followed back here? Most certainly he wouldn't have had the time to open a can of soup and have it warmed.

"Then it must have been one of your partners," Niko accused.

Henri shook his head. "What partners?"

"The Orwells."

"Orwells?" There was a shocked silence before Henri released a harsh bark of laughter. "You really must be on drugs if you think those . . ." His words trailed away as he glanced toward Rayne across the kitchen. He cleared his throat and continued. "Those people would be partners with me."

"You were a trainer for them," Niko reminded him.

"For a few months." Henri spat out the words. "As soon as they could find a reason to get rid of me, they kicked me out. It didn't matter to them that I was the best trainer they'd ever had."

"Why would they go to the trouble of bringing you

from Austria to America if they intended to get rid of you?"

"Ask them."

"Oh, I intend to." Niko pressed his forearm against Henri's bony chest hard enough to make him grunt in pain. "But first you're going to tell me everything you know about Nat's death."

"I don't know—"

"I'm getting the information, Wagner. I can beat it out of you." Niko watched the man's expression harden into stubborn lines. Henri Wagner wasn't the sort of person to be intimidated by physical violence. Always the savvy businessman, Niko swiftly altered his tactics. "Or . . ." Dropping his arm, Niko stepped away from Henri and headed toward the small dining room table near the cabinets. "We can all have a seat and stare at one another until you reveal the truth." Settling in one of the wooden chairs, Niko folded his arms over his chest and glanced toward the woman eyeing him with raised brows. "I have nothing but time on my hands. Rayne?"

Easily sensing his motives, Rayne smoothly settled in the chair next to him. "I can stay the next month. Everything I own is in my van."

Niko sent Henri a warning smile. "Seems like we're all set to become roommates. I hope you have extra soup."

Henri's lips parted, as if he was about to renew his threats to call the cops. Then, as if realizing that nothing was going to force Niko to leave without answers, a sly expression settled on his face.

"You want the truth? Fine." Strolling toward the fridge, Henri opened the door to pull out a beer before he joined them at the table. Once he was seated, he popped the tab and flashed Niko a mocking smile. "I'll even start at the beginning."

Niko shrugged, unimpressed by the man's bravado. "We're listening."

"I was sixteen when my parents' car slid off the road and ended up at the bottom of a ravine. I didn't have any family, so I started roaming the streets." Henri paused his story to take a deep drink of the beer. He burped loudly before he continued. "Eventually, I was arrested for shoplifting. The authorities gave me two options: I could go to jail or work for the nuns in their stables."

"Doesn't seem like a difficult choice," Niko said.

"It wasn't."

"But?"

"But their charity meant I was stuck in the stables shoveling shit while I watched spoiled little bitches prance around like they were some sort of princesses."

"Your gratitude is overwhelming," Niko drawled, even as he silently acknowledged it couldn't have been easy.

Not only had Henri been an orphan who'd been left without anyone to love or care about him, but he'd been tossed into a situation where he was in constant contact with kids who'd been blessed with the most privileged lives. Who wouldn't be bitter? The question was whether his bitterness had driven him to murder.

Henri took another drink. "I was grateful for the chance to learn to speak English, and the opportunity to work with the horses. They brought me a comfort I never expected. They still do." With a grimace, Henri glanced toward the dusty window that revealed a hazy outline of the stables. "At least when they're not draining my bank balance. But the students were a pain in the ass."

"So why stay?"

"At first I didn't have anywhere else to go."

"And then?"

Henri slouched in his seat, like a petulant child, not a grown man. Niko suspected that Henri had a chip on his shoulder that was slowly crushing him to death.

"I discovered that there were a few perks to working in the stables."

"What sort of perks?"

"The students began asking me to locate items they couldn't buy or have sent from home."

Niko frowned. What was the man implying? Then, realization hit, and he rolled his eyes. It'd been a long time since he'd been in high school.

"Alcohol?" he demanded.

"Alcohol." Henri gave a mocking toast with his beer can. "Cigarettes. Pot. Whatever they wanted."

Niko had his own source in school for getting him things his parents had forbidden. And it'd cost a sizable chunk of his allowance.

"And you would charge a finder's fee, I presume?"

"Of course." Henri stared at Niko as if it was a ridiculous question. "It started to add up, but it wasn't enough."

"Enough for what?"

"To give me the money I needed to immigrate to America and start my own stables."

"Ambitious."

"The rich aren't the only ones with dreams," Henri snapped.

Niko resisted the urge to glance around the decaying

house. It seemed doubtful that this had been his dream. At the moment he wasn't willing to risk distracting Henri from his story. Eventually he was going to get to the point. At least Niko fervently hoped so.

"Continue," he commanded.

Henri polished off the beer before he returned to his story. "I discovered over the years that I was more or less invisible."

"Hardly invisible," Rayne said in dry tones. "You were always hanging around when I visited the stables."

Henri sent her a sour frown. "I was there, but not as a person," he complained. "I was just another tool, like a pitchfork or a shovel. When someone wanted something they expected me to rush in and take care of it. Otherwise they ignored me." He returned his attention to Niko. "In the beginning it pissed me off. And then I realized I could use it to my advantage."

"What does that mean?" Niko asked.

"The stables were the one place the nuns rarely visited. It made it a favorite spot for the girls to gather so they could whisper and tell each other secrets. Sometimes I would overhear what they were saying."

"You were eavesdropping?" Rayne demanded in revulsion.

Henri's jaw tightened. "I was negotiating a business deal." He jerked his head toward Niko. "I'm sure Scantlin can appreciate that."

Niko attempted to disguise his distaste. He was an entrepreneur, not a petty criminal who extorted little girls.

"What did your negotiations involve?"

"It was simple," Henri said. "I promised that I would keep my mouth shut in return for a few bucks."

"Blackmail," Rayne insisted.

Henri shrugged. He obviously didn't feel any regret for squeezing money out of schoolchildren. "Most of the stuff they did was just bending the rules. Sneaking out after curfew. Or cheating on tests. I never charged more than fifty or a hundred dollars."

Niko silently wondered if the discounted amount was supposed to make it better. "Did you blackmail Brooke into giving you a job?"

A nasty smile curved the man's lips. "Ah, Brooke. She was my . . ." He paused, as if searching for an elusive word. "What is the saying? Pot of gold. Yes, that's it. She was my pot of gold."

Niko studied the man in confusion. The Orwells were wealthy, but they weren't in the same league as some of the families who sent their daughters to St. Cecilia's School for Girls. Including Rayne Taylor. Her father numbered his wealth in billions, not millions. It had to be because the Orwells owned a horse farm. Henri's childhood dream.

"I assume she broke some rule?" Niko asked. "Or did she cheat on a final?"

"Neither." The nasty smile remained. "I caught her in one of the stalls having sex a few weeks before she was supposed to graduate."

Ah. The pot of gold wasn't referring to Brooke's ability to pay more, but the potential worth of her offense.

"I can't imagine that would have made the nuns happy," Niko acknowledged in dry tones.

Henri shook his head. "She wasn't worried about the nuns. She was terrified of her parents."

Niko paused, trying to remember back to his senior

year in high school. His parents had made vague attempts to maintain control over him. Especially because he was destined to take over the family business. But they'd understood that he was no longer a child. He was becoming independent, with the need to make his own decisions. And his own mistakes.

"She had to be eighteen by then." He spoke his disbelief out loud. "Her parents might have been disappointed, but I can't imagine it was that big of a deal."

"It wasn't the sex she was concerned her parents might find out about." Henri deliberately paused. "It was the person she was with."

Niko made a sound of impatience. "One of the staff?"

Henri leaned forward, his eyes glowing with a wicked anticipation. "Natalie Scantlin."

CHAPTER SEVEN

Rayne had heard the phrase *the silence was deafening*, but she'd never truly understood what it meant. How could silence be deafening? Now she shifted in her seat, the thick air seeming to press against her.

She'd known that Nat and Brooke were close. Sometimes they seemed inseparable, but she'd never thought it was more than friendship. They'd obviously gone to a great deal of effort to hide their relationship. A fact she appreciated, but at the same time she couldn't deny a small sting of betrayal.

Rayne had assumed that she and Nat had shared everything when they'd huddled beneath the blanket together to keep warm on icy winter nights. They'd gossiped about the other girls, bitched about their parents, who didn't understand anything, and fantasized about the future that they were convinced was filled with an inevitable artistic success.

Surely Nat knew that Rayne would support her no matter who she fell in love with?

At last it was Niko who broke the silence.

"That's why Brooke convinced her father to give you a

job?" he demanded, his voice tight, as if he was struggling to leash his emotions.

And no doubt he was. He looked as blindsided as she had been by the revelation that Brooke and Nat were in an intimate relationship.

"Yes." Henri had a smug look on his face. He was pleased that he'd managed to shock them. Perhaps he hoped he'd wounded Niko with the truth. "The little bitch was desperate to keep her girlfriend a secret. No matter what the cost."

Niko's jaw tightened, and Rayne had a sudden fear he was going to reach across the table and punch the jerk in the face. Not that she would mind seeing the mocking smile knocked off his mouth, but she didn't want Niko to do something that might get him arrested.

"And what about Nat?" She directed Henri's attention to herself.

Henri grudgingly turned his head to send her an impatient frown. "What about her?"

"Did you blackmail her?"

"I . . ." The words faded as he licked his lips.

"No lies," Rayne snapped. "You owe Natalie the truth."

Rayne braced herself for some smart-ass comment. Henri Wagner had readily abused the trust of the nuns who'd taken him in as an orphan to blackmail young girls for a few bucks. Why would he have remorse because one of them was dead?

Surprisingly, however, Henri's gaze lowered, his jaw clenched, as if she'd managed to strike a nerve.

"Okay. Fine. I blackmailed her," he muttered. "I don't think she cared about people finding out, but she didn't want to hurt her lover."

Rayne leaned forward. She had no idea what this might have to do with Nat's death, but it couldn't be a coincidence, could it?

"What did you demand?"

"Five thousand American dollars."

"Five thousand?" Rayne blinked in disbelief. The Scantlins were a wealthy family, but Nat had only been eighteen at the time. There was no way her parents would have handed over that amount of money without asking questions.

Henri hunched his shoulders. "I knew she would do anything to protect Brooke. And I was becoming desperate. I'd been stuck in those damned stables for what felt like an eternity. If I didn't do something to get out of there, I'd be trapped until I became too old to work and I became another pensioner the nuns had to support."

Rayne ignored his peevish explanation. He clearly had a victim mentality. Everything was someone else's fault.

"You wrote the note threatening her," Rayne said, the words a statement not a question.

"She was trying to stall. She needed a little incentive to give me what I wanted."

"And when she refused, you killed her," Niko abruptly intruded into the conversation.

"No." Henri's fingers tightened around the empty beer can, nearly crushing it. "She didn't refuse."

"What?" Rayne breathed in disbelief.

"She gave me the money," Henri said.

"When?" Niko demanded.

Henri shot him a wary glance. Was he wondering if he'd pushed Niko too far? He should be. Rayne could feel the tension radiating from her companion.

"The day before the graduation," Henri said. "She walked into the stables with an envelope stuffed with cash."

"I don't believe you," Niko growled in harsh tones. "I think she threatened to expose your blackmail scam and you decided to silence her."

"No, no, no." Without warning, Henri jumped to his feet, as if preparing to flee. "I wasn't even there when she died."

"You weren't where?" Niko slid out of his seat, no doubt prepared to stop Henri from making his escape. "At the school?"

"I wasn't in Austria," Henri insisted. "I flew to Oslo the night before. From there I went to London, before heading to America. You can check my passport." Henri glanced around the kitchen, as if expecting the passport to magically appear. Then he pointed toward a drawer next to the back door. "It's in there."

Rayne was the last to climb to her feet. Her knees felt oddly weak, but she forced herself to cross to the drawer and pull it open. She grimaced at the messy piles of papers shoved inside, but at last she managed to locate the passport. It was out of date, but it held the information she needed. Rayne flicked to the front page, scanning the stamps that marked the dates of Henri's travel itinerary.

"He's telling the truth," she muttered, lifting her head to meet Niko's gaze. "He'd already left Austria by the time Nat died."

Henri scowled. "Why would I lie? I had the money I needed, along with a promise of a job with the Orwells.

I was eager to start my new life as soon as possible. I took the first flight I could buy out of Austria."

"So, what happened?" Rayne tossed the passport back in the drawer and closed it. "Why didn't you stay with the Orwells?"

"When Brooke came home it was obvious that she blamed me for what happened to Natalie."

Rayne narrowed her eyes. "How could she blame you? You have proof that you weren't there."

"She thought I drove her to suicide by threatening to expose her. And . . ." Henri released a harsh breath, his face flushing.

Rayne studied him. Something had changed. The brittle, smug expression was gone, and in its place was a darkness in his eyes that might have been regret.

"And what?" she prompted him to finish.

"And I couldn't disagree," he ground out. "Eventually Brooke found a way to drive me off and my life went into the crapper."

Stomping across the floor to yank open the door to the fridge, Henri pulled out another can of beer and swiveled to face them with a grim expression.

"That's it. That's all I know." He popped open the can and headed toward the opening that led to the front of the house. "I'm going to take a piss now. When I come back I want you gone." He paused to glare over his shoulder. "Or I really am calling the cops."

He disappeared from view, and with a wry glance, both Rayne and Niko made their way out the back door and down the steps. In silence, they circled the stables to climb into the van. Rayne grimaced as Niko carefully brushed away the shards of glass that were scattered over his seat before she started the engine. It was a visual reminder that this wasn't a game, she acknowledged as she pulled onto the gravel road, headed back toward the Orwell farm. There was someone out there who didn't want them to discover the truth.

Once they were out of sight of Henri's house, she glanced toward Niko, who was staring straight ahead with a deep frown pulling his brows together.

"Do you believe him?" she asked.

"The dates of his passport prove he wasn't there," Niko said. "And if he had somehow arranged to have Nat killed, I doubt he would have confessed to blackmailing her."

Rayne nodded. That had been her thought as well. Henri was a selfish, immoral jerk who'd used the hard knocks in his life to give him permission to abuse others. But while she didn't doubt he would have murdered Nat if she'd been a threat to his blackmail scheme, or even if there was a way to make money from her death, he'd been out of the country before she died.

Rayne forced her mind back to the morning of graduation. She could remember sharing breakfast with Nat before they'd gone back to their room. Rayne had taken a quick shower and then headed out to meet her mom to go shopping. Nat had definitely been alive then. Which meant that Henri couldn't be responsible.

She abruptly frowned. Erin had told her that she'd seen Nat going to the stables when she'd asked if anyone had seen her roommate. Why? Was she making sure that Henri wasn't going to cause trouble? Or was she going to meet with her lover?

"We need to talk to Brooke," Rayne said, pressing on

the gas pedal until they were bumping over the rough road at a jarring speed.

"Agreed."

Rayne sent her companion a worried glance. As traumatic as stirring up the past was for her, it had to be intensely more difficult for Niko. Nat had been his twin. That was a bond that went soul deep.

"Are you okay?" she asked.

He slowly shook his head. "I'm not sure."

She turned onto the road that led directly to the farm. "Does it bother you that Nat and Brooke were more than friends?"

He jerked his head toward her, as if startled by the question. "Of course not," he insisted. "It bothers me that she didn't trust me enough to tell me."

Rayne heaved a sigh. "Yeah, I get that. We shared everything when we were young. I mean . . . everything. She was the sister of my heart. I don't want to believe she couldn't reveal something so important in her life." She hesitated, trying to untangle her wounded emotions. "But now that I've had a chance to think about it, I'm not certain it was her choice."

Niko sent her a puzzled glance. "What do you mean?"

"Brooke obviously wanted to keep their relationship a secret," Rayne murmured, slowing as they reached the outbuildings that were spread across the Orwell property. "And knowing Nat, she would have done everything in her power to make Brooke happy. That's just the person she was."

Niko slowly nodded. "Yes."

"Eventually, however, she would have grown tired of hiding in the stables. She would have insisted they be open with their family and friends." Rayne reached the driveway to the main house, but she didn't pull in. Instead, she put the van in Park and turned toward Niko. "The question is, how far would Brooke go to prevent Nat from revealing the truth?"

Removing his seat belt, Niko shoved open his door. "Let's check out the stables first. I don't want anyone sneaking up on us from behind. If they're not there, we'll work our way toward the house."

Rayne shut off the engine and exited the van. She joined Niko as he crawled over the fence, easily dropping over the top and into the yard. They stayed away from the paddock where the horses were grazing and passed behind the barn. Then, rounding the corner, they angled across the muddy ground. Rayne kept her gaze turned toward the house. She couldn't see any movement, but it was lunchtime. That seemed the logical place for the Orwells to be.

It wasn't until they had reached the long, white stables that she realized she'd miscalculated.

The Orwells weren't in the house. At least Trent wasn't. He was currently standing in front of them with a shotgun pointed at her face.

"You're trespassing on private property," he warned. "Leave or die."

If Niko had the opportunity to consider what he was about to do, he would have warned himself not to be an idiot. Getting himself killed wasn't going to bring back

Nat. But as soon as he saw the shotgun pointed at Rayne, instinct had taken over.

With a curse of fury, Niko launched forward, tackling Trent to the ground with enough force to make the man grunt in pain. At the same time he wrenched the weapon from Trent's hands. Once he was sure the man was no longer a threat, he rose to his feet, keeping the gun pointed at his attacker, who remained sprawled on the ground.

"No, don't shoot him," Brooke commanded as she appeared around the corner of the stables.

"I wasn't the one who brought a gun to the party," Niko muttered. "Now all bets are off."

"We've had trouble with thieves and Trent was just—"

"Shut it," Niko snapped.

Brooke sucked in a shocked breath at the interruption. "How dare you?"

Niko sent her a jaundiced glare. "We spoke to Henri."

A flicker of fear darkened Brooke's eyes, but she stood her ground. "So?"

There was the sound of a muffled conversation and the smack of hooves against cement as a couple of trainers moved past them, leading the horses inside the stables.

"I don't think this is a conversation you want to have with an audience," Niko warned.

"We don't want a conversation with you at all," Trent growled, scrambling to his feet as his face flushed with anger. "Get the hell off our property."

Niko kept his attention on Brooke. She was far more dangerous than her brother. "Well?"

A muscle clenched in her jaw. "Let's go into the house."

"No." Niko didn't trust the Orwells as far as he could

throw them. "Let's go in there." He nodded toward the nearby barn. They would be close enough to the stables that he could call out for help if necessary.

"Fine." Spinning on her heel, Brooke crossed the narrow space to shove open the sliding door.

Niko waited for both Brooke and Trent to disappear into the shadows before walking next to Rayne as they entered the barn. The place was immaculate, of course. Whatever his opinion of the Orwells, it was obvious they took great pride in their horse farm.

They were standing in the tack room, with stairs on one side that led to the upper loft and stacks of hay on the other side. A quick glance was enough to assure Niko they were alone. Standing close to Rayne, Niko watched as Trent stretched out his hand.

"Give me my gun."

Niko made a sound of disbelief. "You've got to be joking."

Brooke clicked her tongue. "What do you want, Niko?"

"The truth." He narrowed his eyes. "Starting with your relationship with my sister."

"She was my friend."

"She was more than that," Niko insisted.

A blush stained her cheeks. "If that creep told you anything about Nat and me, I can assure you, he's lying."

Without warning, Rayne stepped forward, her expression troubled. "Why are you so ashamed of your love for Nat? She was glorious," she burst out. "I would never have found the courage to become an artist without her giving me the confidence I needed. And I'm not the only one she helped. She was always the first to reach out a hand to someone who was struggling."

Brooke's lips parted at the attack; then she hastily turned her head, as if to hide her tears. "I can't change the past. All I can do is concentrate on the future."

"That's a lie. You *can* change the past," Rayne insisted. "You can allow Nat to rest in peace."

"If you think you can play on my emotions, you're wasting your time," Brooke warned.

"Because they're buried with Nat?" Rayne asked, her voice soft.

There was the sound of a muffled sob, and Trent hurried to wrap an arm around his sister's shoulders. "Stop it."

Niko nodded toward Rayne. She'd managed to break through Brooke's brittle defiance, but he was done playing nice. It was time for answers.

"Henri told us that he found you together in the stables," he directly confronted the woman.

"That sleazy bastard." Brooke turned back to Niko, her features tightened with a smoldering anger. "He was always sneaking around, spying on us like some perv. Did he also tell you that he blackmailed us?"

"Yes." Niko nodded. "Which explains why he came here to work."

Brooke shuddered with a blatant loathing. "We certainly would never have willingly allowed him to step foot on our property."

"And why you so quickly drove him away," Niko added.

"Not nearly far enough," Trent muttered, proving they'd

known Henri's location despite what they'd told Niko earlier.

"If he was so awful, why not just tell the truth?" Rayne demanded. "Nat would have stood by your side."

Brooke waved her arms in a vague gesture. "Because of this."

Niko glanced around. "A barn?"

"Not just the barn. This entire farm. My inheritance."

Niko frowned, not sure what she was trying to say. "What does that have to do with Nat?"

Trent snorted. "You didn't know our parents. They weren't just conservative, they were . . ." He struggled to find the appropriate word.

"Bullies." Brooke came to the rescue. "They used our love for this land and the horses to control us. Any infraction of their strict rules and they threatened to cut us out of the will." Her lips twisted into a humorless smile. "And it wasn't an empty threat. They would have done it."

Niko felt a sharp burst of pain, the image of his beautiful sister lying in her coffin searing through his mind.

"You're saying this farm was more important to you than Nat?"

Brooke flinched, the color draining from her face. "I didn't think so in the beginning. Nat and I . . ." She was forced to stop and clear her throat. "We'd made a pack to tell our parents we were a couple when they came to graduation."

"What happened?"

"Henri." She spit out the name as if it was a curse. "After he caught us together he threatened to expose our relationship. Suddenly I panicked." Brooke wrapped her arms around her waist. "It was one thing to fantasize about a future with Nat and another to face the reality of what it would cost."

"Your inheritance?"

"Not just that. I would have lost my family and my friends and the only home I've ever known."

Niko didn't want to think about Brooke being a terrified girl who was facing the most difficult decision of her young life. His sister was dead and he'd waited endless years to make someone pay.

"Instead, you agreed to hire Henri," he said.

"Yes."

"And Nat agreed to pay him five thousand dollars."

"No." Brooke appeared confused by his words. "She couldn't pay. That's why she killed herself. And it was my fault."

CHAPTER EIGHT

Rayne studied Brooke's expression with a frown. She genuinely appeared to believe that Nat had refused to be blackmailed and instead killed herself to protect their secret. She also appeared to have suffered from the guilt that she'd carried all these years.

"Henri told us that Nat gave him the cash," she told her onetime friend. "That's what he used to buy his plane ticket to America."

Brooke shook her head. "That's impossible. She didn't have that sort of money. Besides, she told me that she wasn't going to let herself be extorted by a grubby stable hand."

"I told her to pay," Trent abruptly broke into the conversation.

They all glanced at him in surprise.

"What?" Brooke demanded.

"She called me the morning we were headed to Austria. She told me what happened, and that she was going to refuse Henri's blackmail," Trent admitted. "I begged her to reconsider. I didn't want Brooke to be hurt."

Rayne widened her eyes in surprise. "You knew about your sister and Nat?"

"Of course." Trent shrugged. "They wanted me to claim to be Nat's boyfriend. At least in the beginning. Later, Nat was frustrated with the act."

"I didn't know she'd called you," Brooke breathed, her expression troubled.

Trent sighed. "After Nat's suicide we never talked about what happened."

"How far were you willing to go to keep your sister from being hurt?" Niko asked, his voice hard with suspicion.

Trent sent him a wary glance. "What are you asking?"

"Did you kill my sister?"

"No one killed her," Brooke insisted. "She committed suicide because I broke her heart."

Niko stubbornly shook his head. "She didn't kill herself."

"That threatening note you found came from Henri," Brooke told him. "Nat showed it to me."

"Henri might have written the note, but if Nat had killed herself, someone wouldn't have taken a shot at us less than an hour ago," Rayne said.

Brooke jerked, as if shocked by Rayne's accusation. "What are you talking about?"

"Someone followed us after we left here and tried to kill us." Rayne carefully watched Trent's expression. He wasn't nearly as accomplished as his sister in hiding his emotions. "Why would they do that if they weren't trying to keep us from prying into the past?"

"Because you're a pain in the ass," Trent muttered, looking more like a sulky child than a potential killer.

Brooke abruptly stepped in front of Trent, as if protecting him from Rayne. "I don't know what you're talking about. Trent and I were meeting with a potential client for the past two hours."

Niko snorted as he glanced at the shotgun. "Now why don't I believe you?"

"If you need proof, there's video surveillance that covers the main house and all of the outbuildings, as well as the paddocks." Brooke pointed toward the rafters. Rayne tilted back her head to see the small camera that was angled downward to capture the barn on video. "There's no way either of us could have left the property without being seen."

"You could have sent one of your employees," Niko pointed out.

Trent rolled his eyes. "I can hardly get them to clean a stall, let alone kill someone."

"Besides, neither of us would have hurt Nat," Brooke hastily added. "We loved her."

Niko's expression remained hard. He clearly wasn't satisfied with the Orwells' pleas of innocence. "You thought she was going to destroy your life."

Brooke jutted out her chin, meeting Niko's glare with one of her own. "A part of me wanted her to. I didn't have the backbone to stand up to my parents. I wanted her to take away my choice. If she forced the issue, I would have to stay with her."

"Someone killed her," Niko grimly insisted.

"It had to have been Henri," Brooke said, her voice

edged with impatience. "He told us himself that he'd been a criminal before coming to St. Cecilia's."

"It couldn't have been him. He'd left the country before Nat died." Niko shifted his gaze from Brooke to Trent. "It had to have been one of you."

"Bullshit," Trent rasped. "We were with our parents the entire day."

Rayne couldn't see anything but genuine outrage on Trent's face. She turned her attention to Brooke.

"You never saw Nat?"

She paused, as if considering lying. Then she heaved a resigned sigh. "Yes, I saw Nat. I went to meet her that morning."

"Where?" Rayne asked.

"The stables."

Rayne nodded. That explained why Nat had gone there. "What did she say?"

"She told me not to worry." Brooke's voice broke, as if she was once again fighting back tears. "She said she'd taken care of everything."

"Taken care of what?" Rayne asked.

"She refused to tell me. To be honest, she was acting strange. If it hadn't been Nat, I would have thought she was drinking. Then the head groom ran us out. He said the stables were closed until the next term." Brooke grimaced. "I told Nat I would see her later and returned to my parents. That was the last time we spoke."

"What about you?" Niko demanded, his gaze locked on Trent.

"I was with my parents," Trent ground out. "Besides,

there was no way I was going to face the wrath of the nuns by trying to sneak into the dorms. They terrified me."

Rayne grimaced. It was true. The nuns were a daunting force. But a few of the girls had figured out ways to smuggle boys from Salzburg in and out of their rooms. Where there was a will there was a way, one of her friends had assured her.

Still, if the Orwells hadn't been the ones to take a shot at them, there had to be someone else out there trying to stop them from probing into the past.

But who?

Rayne glanced toward Niko, sensing his frustration vibrating around his tense body. He knew as well as she did that they'd hit a brick wall. It was time to regroup and consider their next move.

"Niko, I think it's time to leave."

His jaw tightened, but with a surprising expertise, he turned to the side, pointing the weapon toward the ground as he pressed a button near the trigger. There was a soft snap as the gun hinged open, allowing Niko to pull out the cartridge shells. Pushing them into his pocket, he held out the gun to Trent.

"You'd better put this up. If I find out you lied to me, I'm coming back, but I won't be alone. I'll be bringing the cops with me."

Niko sat next to Rayne as they headed back to Chicago. It was frigid with the window busted out, even when Rayne blasted the heater on high, but neither of them really noticed the cold. They were both struggling to accept that they were leaving without the answers to Nat's murder, plus the unnerving realization that they still didn't know who had shot at them.

Or when they might try again.

They had to discover the truth. And they had to do it quickly. But how?

It wasn't until they were driving through the suburbs of Chicago that he abruptly remembered what had led them to the Orwells in the first place.

"Where are the pictures?" he asked.

Rayne sent him a puzzled glance before realizing what he meant. "Oh." She waited until she was forced to halt at a stoplight before she dug into the pocket of her jacket to pull out the photos. "Here." She handed them to Niko. "Are you looking for something?"

"There had to be a reason why Nat kept them in her special box."

"We know she was in a secret relationship with Brooke," she reminded him. "And was being blackmailed by Henri."

"Good reasons to keep them hidden," he agreed, holding the third picture toward the window to catch the afternoon sunlight. "But why this one of the fountain?"

She pressed on the gas pedal as the light turned green. "I really have no idea."

"Maybe it was a meeting place for her."

Rayne was shaking her head before he finished his thought. "I don't think so. She went to our room or the stables when she wanted to talk in private. Besides, most of us avoided the area."

He sent her a surprised glance. He remembered seeing

the fountain when he'd visited St. Cecilia's. It was close to the gardens behind the cathedral. It was a beautiful spot.

"Why would you avoid it?"

"There were rumors a nun had jumped from the bell tower and landed in the fountain. Her ghost supposedly haunted the area," she explained. "I doubt the story was true, but when we were young it was easy to scare one another with ridiculous stories."

Niko narrowed his gaze. "There's someone in the background, but it's too fuzzy to make out who it is."

She pointed toward the dashboard. "There's a magnifying glass in the glove compartment."

He sent her a startled glance. "Seriously?"

"I use it when I paint."

Oh. That made sense. He'd seen the impossibly fine details in the landscapes he had hanging at his office and his condo. He'd even gotten out his own magnifying glass to admire them.

Leaning forward, Niko opened the glove compartment and pulled out the round glass that was set in a black frame. He held it over the photo, enlarging the blurry form.

"It's definitely a woman," he murmured, able to make out blond hair and a delicate profile.

"A student?" Rayne asked.

"I don't think so. She's not wearing a uniform."

"One of the nuns?"

Niko's gaze traced the slender body that was faithfully outlined by the skin-tight dress. Was that a leopard-skin print?

"Absolutely not," he muttered, his gaze returning to the woman's profile. Suddenly he sucked in a shocked breath, feeling as if he'd just taken a punch to the gut. "Shit."

"What's wrong?"

"I think I recognize the person."

"Who is it?"

He hesitated, reluctant to share what he'd discovered. Then, grimacing, he accepted that Rayne was going to insist on seeing this investigation to the end. No matter where the clues might lead.

"Your mother."

With a sharp jerk of the steering wheel, Rayne swerved into a gas station and put the van in Park.

"Let me see." She held out a hand that wasn't quite steady. He placed the picture on her palm and Rayne leaned forward. A second later her jaw tightened as she slowly lifted her head to meet his worried gaze. "Yes. That's her."

"Why would Nat have a picture of your mother?"

"I think this was taken the day she arrived in Austria for our graduation," she told him.

Niko arched a brow. "How can you know?"

"I remember the dress."

"It's . . . distinctive," Niko agreed.

"My mother has never been known for her modesty," Rayne said dryly.

"Why was she at the fountain?"

"She was probably headed back to her hotel in Salzburg." Rayne furrowed her brow, visibly trying to recall the events of the day. "She'd stopped by before breakfast, which was weird."

"Why would that be weird?"

"She hates getting up early." Rayne's expression was distracted. "But I assumed she hadn't gone to bed after the flight. She brought me my graduation present. And then . . . oh."

Niko leaned toward her. "What?"

"She brought Nat a gift as well. I remember being surprised." She grimaced as Niko sent her a confused frown. "To be honest, my mother and your sister never really liked each other. Nat thought my mom was a selfish bitch, and my mom thought Nat was too opinionated." She shrugged. "They were both right."

Niko couldn't argue about Nat being overly opinionated. Their mother said she'd started arguing the minute she came out of the womb.

"What was the gift?" he asked.

"I don't know. Nat took the package and put it in her desk. She had a strange smile on her face. It was . . ." Rayne struggled for the right word. "Triumphant," she finally said. "I meant to ask her about the gift later, but there was so much going on, it slipped my mind."

Niko tried to imagine why Tami Taylor Jefferson would bring his sister a present. A girl she didn't even like. And why had his sister hurried to take a photo of Tami as she left the school grounds?

There was one explanation that would answer both questions.

"Do you think the gift was the five thousand dollars that my sister gave to Henri?"

Rayne's face was pale, but with a grim determination she put the van into Drive and squealed out of the gas station.

"Let's find out."

CHAPTER NINE

Rayne parked across from her mother's mansion and drew in a deep breath. She'd hoped it would steady her nerves. It was a wasted effort. Coming to this place was always stressful. And that was when she wasn't about to confront her mother.

Even worse, her mind was in a tangle of confusion. On one hand, she knew that Niko was right. Everything pointed toward Tami Taylor Jefferson somehow being involved in the events leading to Nat's death. On the other, she couldn't imagine how the two could possibly be connected.

It wasn't like Nat ever came to stay with her in Chicago. And Tami wasn't friendly with the Scantlin family. How could their paths have crossed?

Rayne was jerked out of her thoughts as Niko unhooked his seat belt, obviously preparing to join her. She reached out to grab his arm.

"Wait."

He sent her a puzzled glance. "What's wrong?"

She grimaced. He wasn't going to like this. "I think I should speak to Tami alone."

"Why?"

"My mother and I have a long, steadfast tradition of doing everything in our power to avoid actually talking to each other," she informed him. "We've gone years without exchanging a word. I'm not sure I can make her tell me why she gave Nat a present, but I can guarantee she won't say a word if you're there."

He scowled. "I don't like the thought of you facing her on your own."

There was a fierceness in his tone that sent tingles of heat swirling through her body. It'd been a very long time since anyone had been worried about her. Certainly not since Nat died.

"I'll be fine." Her voice was oddly husky.

He reached out to brush his fingers down the length of her jaw. "You have fifteen minutes and then I'm coming in."

"Niko—"

"If you haven't managed to get her to talk in that amount of time, she's not going to," he interrupted in a tone that defied argument.

Rayne clicked her tongue, pretending to be annoyed. The truth was that she savored his concern.

"You're very pushy."

He offered a wry smile. "It's part of my charm."

"Is that what you call it?"

"If I don't, who will?" Swooping his head down, he brushed a light kiss over her lips. "Be careful."

A shiver of pleasure raced through her. Or maybe it

was the icy breeze that was making her shake. Shoving open her door, she sent Niko a stern glance.

"Keep the van running. I don't want you to freeze."

His glance was equally stern. "Fifteen minutes, Rayne. The clock has started."

Jumping out of the van, Rayne crossed the street and climbed the steps. For the first time in years she used the old key she'd kept for emergencies to let herself in the front door. She paused in the foyer, not sure which direction to take. During the late afternoon her mother was usually preparing for some event to take place that night. Or being pampered at her favorite spa.

It was at last the clink of ice in a glass that led her into the sitting room. Stepping through the opening, she blinked as she was swallowed into the white space. As an artist, she could appreciate the simplicity of monochrome. But this was just . . . blinding.

"Mark?"

Rayne turned toward her mother's voice, discovering the older woman in the corner, pouring herself a large glass of whiskey. Obviously, Tami was of the opinion it was five o'clock somewhere.

"No," Rayne said. "It's me."

"Rayne?" Tami whirled around, her eyes wide with surprise. She was wearing a long, satin robe that was tied around her waist, as if she'd just stepped out of the shower. "What are you doing here? Did you forget something?"

Rayne left on her coat. She didn't doubt for a second if this conversation wasn't done in fifteen minutes, Niko would come charging to the rescue.

"I have a few questions for you," she said.

"Now?" Tami gave a sharp shake of her head. "I'm expecting guests tonight and I still have to change."

"Now."

Her mother made a sound of impatience. "You'll have to hurry."

Rayne had spent the drive to this house trying to decide the best way to approach her mother. It wasn't going to be easy. Tami was a master at avoiding anything she considered unpleasant. If she didn't want to discuss a subject, she would come up with a dozen excuses why she needed to leave the room. Rayne couldn't count the number of times she was speaking only to have her mother turn her back and walk away.

Her only hope was to go straight for the jugular and try to shock the truth out of the older woman.

Stiffening her spine, she spoke the words that had been hovering on her lips since Niko had recognized her mother in the picture.

"Why did you give Natalie Scantlin five thousand dollars when you came to Austria for our graduation?"

It felt as if the air was sucked from the room as Tami's face paled to a white that matched the carpet.

"What?"

Rayne's stomach twisted with a cold dread. She could see the truth etched in Tami's expression. Her reaction to the question should have been confusion, not shock.

"You heard me." She studied the older woman with an accusing gaze. "Why did you give Nat five thousand dollars?"

With jerky motions, Tami drained her whiskey and set down the glass hard enough to make the ice cubes rattle.

Then she reached for her cigarettes, lighting one to suck in a deep lungful of smoke and nicotine.

"I don't know what you're talking about." She at last spoke the words Rayne had been expecting.

"I'm too tired for games, Mother."

"So am I." Tami waved a too-slender hand toward the door. "I think you should leave. As I said, I have guests coming."

Rayne shook her head. "Not until I have the truth."

"The truth about what?"

"How Nat managed to get such a large sum of money from you." Rayne held up her hand as her mother's lips parted. "Don't try to deny it. I spoke to Brooke Orwell, Nat's best friend. She admitted that Nat was in desperate need of the cash." Rayne was careful to gloss over the fact that Brooke didn't know anything about Nat paying off Henri. She wanted her mother to think that she had concrete evidence. "I just don't understand why you would agree to give it to her."

"It was a long time ago." Her mother continued to puff on her cigarette. "I don't remember."

Rayne felt her eyes sting. The smoke was more annoying than usual. Probably because she was so on edge.

"You don't forget giving an eighteen-year-old girl five thousand dollars," she tartly retorted.

"Enough, Rayne."

"No, I'm not going to stop asking questions until I'm satisfied that I know what happened." Rayne held her mother's gaze, silently warning her that this wasn't a bluff. "I don't care if I have to ask everyone you know in Chicago. Starting with the neighbors. Someone has to know what you were willing to pay five thousand dollars to keep hidden."

Rayne didn't truly believe the neighbors knew anything, but the older woman would be horrified by the thought of people gossiping behind her back.

There was a tense pause, as Tami considered her options. Rayne watched in silence. The late afternoon sunlight slanted through the window, pooling over the older woman. She didn't appear quite real, Rayne silently acknowledged. She looked like a mannequin. A pale, perfect mannequin.

"It wasn't me," Tami finally said through clenched teeth. "It was Mark."

"Mark gave Nat the money?"

"No." Tami made a sound of angry impatience. "It was because of him that I was forced to hand over the cash."

Something clicked inside Rayne's mind. Like a puzzle suddenly fitting together. She'd been baffled by what her mother could have done that would have been awful enough for Nat to be able to demand such a large sum of money from her. It took zero effort to imagine Mark committing some despicable sin.

"What did he do?"

Tami wrapped her arms around her narrow waist, a bitter expression twisting her features. "What he always does," she rasped. "He fell into bed with the first willing woman who crossed his path. Only this one was more a girl than a woman."

It took a second for Rayne to be able to accept what her mother was saying. She'd known Mark was a sleaze. He lied, he cheated, and he manipulated the vulnerable.

But she'd never considered the possibility he was a pedophile.

"He had sex with one of the students?" she breathed in disbelief.

"Yes." Tami shrugged in a restless gesture. "When we'd visited during your spring break, he'd snuck into a dorm room." She sent Rayne an accusing glare, as if it was somehow her fault that Mark couldn't keep his pants zipped. "And your nasty little roommate had the receipts."

Receipts? Rayne frowned, until she understood what Tami was telling her. "Nat took photos."

"Very revealing ones." Tami tossed her hair, the blond locks tumbling around her shoulders. "She sent me an email shortly before we left for Austria with copies of the pictures and a warning that she was going to send them to the police if I didn't bring her five thousand dollars."

Rayne grimaced. She loved Nat, but the fact that her friend had used the photos to extract money from her mother rather than sending them to the authorities made her sick to her stomach. Even if Nat was desperate to protect Brooke, it was . . . disappointing.

Was love always so twisted? Her father had struggled to show any affection. Her mother was willing to sacrifice her pride, her money, and her heart for a man who barely tolerated her. And now she discovered Nat had lost her moral compass for a girl who was ashamed of their relationship.

Without warning, the image of Niko's perfectly sculpted face and piercing blue eyes seared through her mind. There was something refreshingly solid and dependable about him. He would always be loyal to those he loved, but he wouldn't allow his ethics to be compromised.

With a shake of her head, Rayne forced herself to concentrate on her mother. "And you agreed to pay to keep her silent."

"Obviously," Tami snapped, as if it was an unbearably stupid question.

"And what about Mark?"

"What about him?"

"Did he know you were being blackmailed?"

Tami's lips tightened, but she forced herself to answer. "Yes. I confronted him. Of course he promised it would never happen again."

Rayne parted her lips, unable to believe her mother hadn't been horrified to discover that her husband was preying on young girls. Then she snapped them shut. What was the point? Her mother was blind to Mark's numerous faults. No. Not blind, she corrected herself. Just too besotted or obsessed to accept he was a pig.

"Was he okay with handing over the money to Nat?" Rayne demanded.

"Not really. He was convinced the little bitch would keep asking for more money."

"What did he suggest?"

Tami turned to snub out the cigarette. Not that it helped. The stench of smoke still hung thick in the air. "He wanted to ignore her."

Ignore her? That didn't sound right. "He was willing to be arrested for having sex with a minor?"

"The girl was eighteen," her mother snapped.

"Even if she was eighteen, which I doubt, he still seduced a schoolgirl."

Tami waved aside the accusation. "As I said, it was all in the past."

"No longer."

"What do you mean?"

"She means that she intends to ruin my life, my dear," a male voice drawled as Mark stepped through a side door and strolled toward his wife.

He was dressed in casual jeans and a cashmere sweater and his hair was ruffled, as if he'd been out in the wind.

Her mother held out her hand, looking like a pathetic child in need of comfort. "Mark."

Mark paused next to the fireplace, grabbing the iron poker before he continued toward his wife. "A shame, really, but I've expected this day to finally come."

With a casual motion, Mark lifted the poker, and before Rayne could absorb what she was seeing, he was slicing it through the air to hit her mother on the side of her head. Rayne gasped, watching in shocked disbelief as the older woman crumpled to the ground, blood dripping from the wound at her temple to stain the white carpeting.

"What are you doing?" she rasped, backing away from the man who'd been a blight on her life since she was just a child.

He twirled the poker, something that might be anticipation shimmering in his eyes. He was looking forward to hurting her. No doubt he'd been wanting to bash in her brain for years.

"Bringing an end to what you started," he taunted.

She licked her dry lips. She didn't know how much time had passed, but soon Niko was going to come crashing through the door. She just had to stay alive until then.

"I didn't start anything."

"You stuck your nose into the past, stirring up things that were best left buried."

"Like Nat?" she demanded, trying to keep him talking.

His smile widened. "Exactly."

Rayne's hands clenched into fists. She'd never hated this man as much as she did in this moment. "You killed her."

"The bitch had it coming."

Rayne curled her lips in revulsion. "Because she caught you having sex with a child?"

"Because she thought she could outsmart me," Mark snapped. "And now you've done the same. A deadly mistake."

Rayne ignored the word *deadly*. She just had to keep Mark bragging about his accomplishment of murdering a defenseless teenage girl. Something that should be easy enough. He'd always been a blowhard.

"How?"

"What?"

"How did you kill her?"

"I had my . . ." He hesitated, as if debating whether or not to confess his sins. Then he gave a small shrug. "My friend slipped a few painkillers into Natalie's water bottle, which she always took on her morning run, while she was at breakfast. Then I climbed through an open window and snuck into the dorms while everyone was busy."

"I assume your friend was the child you seduced?"

His jaw hardened as he ignored her question. Clearly, he didn't like being reminded he'd had sex with a school-girl.

"I had to hide in the janitor's closet. Those damned nuns were everywhere. But eventually Natalie returned to her room. I came in behind her. She was already struggling to stay awake, so she didn't even put up a fight. Once she was unconscious, I placed her on the bed and slit her wrists. It was remarkably easy."

Rayne shook her head; later she would grieve for her friend. She couldn't let herself be distracted.

"I wasn't so easy to kill, was I?" she demanded, suddenly realizing who had shot at her van. "How did you find me?"

"After your mother told me that you'd been nosing around in your old school things I had a sleepless night. I didn't think there was any incriminating evidence hanging around, but I couldn't be sure."

"Nat left me pictures," Rayne said with a cold smile, careful to avoid admitting that they didn't have any actual proof of his guilt. "She reached out from the grave to have her vengeance."

Mark breathed a curse, but he didn't give into the panic that briefly flared in his eyes. "It doesn't matter. Not now," he muttered, speaking more to himself than to her.

Rayne didn't like the sound of that. "I still don't understand how you knew where to find me."

"This morning I got up and went to the hotel you usually stay at when you're in Chicago. You were just taking off in your van, so I followed you. It was more an impulse than genuine fear of being exposed." He grimaced. "It wasn't until you pulled into the Orwell farm that I really started to worry. I wasn't sure what you'd discovered, but I was determined to stop you from getting to the truth."

Rayne forced her smile to remain glued to her lips. "Too late."

"It's never too late," he retorted, his tone edged with a smug confidence. "Not for me. I am the ultimate survivor."

Just like a rat scurrying through the gutters, she silently acknowledged.

"What do you intend to do to me?"

Mark shrugged. "You and your mother are about to have a tragic accident."

Accident? It was the acrid stench of smoke that forced Rayne to accept what Mark was implying. That wasn't coming from her mother's cigarette. This lunatic had set a fire in the house. And he intended to knock her out and leave her and her mother to die in the flames.

She couldn't wait for Niko to rescue her, she grimly acknowledged. She had to get out of there. With a burst of speed, she made a mad dash toward the doorway. Mark, however, had anticipated her attempt at escape. Leaping to the side, he blocked her path. At the same time he sliced the poker through the air, aiming at the side of her head.

Rayne stumbled backward, knowing she couldn't risk a direct confrontation. He was not only larger and stronger than her, he had a weapon. She continued to put space between her and the advancing monster. It wasn't until she heard the rattle of ice as her back rammed into a hard object that she realized she'd crossed the entire length of the room. She was at the bar where her mom had been making a drink when she first arrived.

Keeping her gaze locked on Mark, Rayne reached behind her. She ignored the bottles of booze as well as the glass tumblers. She was searching for something specific. At last her fingers curled around the wooden handle of the small ice pick her mother always kept next to the silver bucket.

It wasn't large, but it would put out Mark's eye. And that's exactly what she intended to do with it.

CHAPTER TEN

Less than ten minutes had passed before Niko reached over to switch off the van's engine. He should never have allowed Rayne to go inside by herself. Then again, he suspected she was right that her mother wouldn't talk in front of him. Not if she was guilty . . .

Wait. Niko frowned as he was struck by a sudden memory. Tami couldn't be guilty. Rayne had told him that she'd spent the morning with her mother shopping in Salzburg, right? Besides, why would Tami hand over the money if she intended to kill Nat?

She wouldn't. Not unless she was working with someone else.

Someone like her husband, Mark Jefferson.

Damn. Leaping out of the van, Niko charged across the street and up the steps. He didn't bother to knock as he shoved open the door. He had no idea why he was suddenly so certain that Mark was the killer.

He'd been wrong about Brooke and Trent Orwell, about Henri Wagner, and now Tami. But in that moment, he couldn't think of anything but getting Rayne away from the house before Mark found out what they'd discovered.

Entering the foyer, Niko came to a sharp halt as he was met by a wall of smoke. He coughed, lifting his arm to cover his mouth and nose. There was a fire at the back of the house that was rapidly spreading.

"Rayne!" he called out, coughing as the smoke threatened to choke him.

"Niko, I'm in here."

Barely able to see, Niko followed the sound of Rayne's frantic voice, ramming into the wall twice before he found the opening into a long sitting room.

The smoke wasn't as thick in there, and he could make out Rayne, along with an unconscious woman lying on the white carpet. His attention, however, was captured by the man who whirled around at his entrance holding a steel poker.

Mark Jefferson.

Niko had only seen him a couple of times, but there was no forgetting the smug expression on the too-pretty face. Niko had wanted to punch the cocky grin off the man's lips when he'd visited St. Cecilia's School years ago. Now he was going to get the opportunity, he grimly promised himself.

"Rayne, get out of here," he commanded, his gaze never leaving Mark. "The house is on fire."

She stubbornly shook her head. "Mark killed Nat. She had pictures of him sleeping with one of the students at St. Cecilia's."

Niko felt a surge of revulsion, but now wasn't the time

to be distracted. Later he'd mourn his sister. Right now all that mattered was protecting Rayne.

"I've got this," he assured her. "Please just get out of here."

He thought he heard her mutter something, but out of the corner of his eye he caught the flash of movement. Assuming that Rayne had accepted it was too dangerous to stay and was headed toward the nearest exit, Niko stepped toward Mark.

The man might hold a weapon, but he was fifteen years older and devoted his days to lying next to the pool sipping martinis. Niko was confident he could overpower him.

"I don't know who you are, but you shouldn't have come in here," Mark snarled, waving the poker in a threatening gesture.

"I'm Niko Scantlin. Natalie's brother." Niko wanted the man to know who was about to beat the shit out of him.

Mark jerked, as if shocked to discover his identity, then that smug smile curved his lips. "Your sister should never have messed with me. I always win."

Niko made a sound of disgust. "You're a failed, wannabe actor whose only claim to fame is going to be spending the rest of your life in jail. Pathetic."

"I killed one Scantlin, I'll kill another." Mark twirled the poker, obviously trying to provoke Niko into a fury.

Niko shrugged, refusing to take the bait. Instead, he lifted his hand, giving a come-here motion with his fingers.

"Bring it on."

With a low growl, Mark sprung forward, slashing the poker at Niko's head. Niko waited until he could hear the swoosh of air before he ducked beneath the weapon. Once it was past he surged upward, using his momentum to power the punch he aimed directly at Mark's chin. As if realizing he'd left himself dangerously open to attack, the older man jerked back. Niko managed a glancing blow, but not enough to disable his opponent.

Swinging the poker in a wild pattern, Mark managed to drive Niko back several steps as he was forced to wait for another opening. His eyes burned and his lungs felt as if they were on fire, but he never let his attention waver. All he needed was one small opportunity . . .

The thought was drifting through his mind when there was a sudden blur of movement and Rayne appeared directly behind Mark. She held her hand over her head and was clutching something in her fingers. Was that an ice pick? He had only a brief glance at the weapon before she was jerking her arm down with all her strength, slamming the weapon into Mark's back.

The man grunted in shock, his eyes widening even as he arched his back in a futile attempt to escape the pain. Niko allowed a humorless smile to twist his lips as he stepped forward and, with one crushing punch to the jaw, knocked him out cold. Mark dropped to the floor, landing flat on his face with the handle of the pick sticking out of his back.

Niko took a second to savor the sight. He wished he'd gotten in a few more blows, but just seeing him crumpled and bloody soothed part of his hunger for justice.

"Niko." Rayne grabbed his arm, giving him a small shake. "We have to get out of here."

He blinked, belatedly realizing the room was swiftly filling with smoke. He turned, intending to head toward the opening only to realize that the flames were already consuming the foyer. Swiveling back, his gaze landed on the large front window. That was their only hope of escape.

"Stand back," he urged Rayne, grabbing a small coffee table and rushing forward.

Once he was next to the window, Niko turned his head and smashed the table through the fragile pane. The window easily shattered, spraying shards over the front porch. Turning back to inspect the opening, he nodded toward Rayne. There were still jagged bits of glass, but her heavy jacket should protect her.

"You go first," he insisted.

She hesitated, glancing over her shoulder. "My mother."

"I'll hand her out to you," he promised, urgently gesturing her toward the window. He had no idea how much damage the fire had already done. He wasn't eager to have the house collapse on top of them.

"Okay."

Rayne climbed onto the sofa and through the opening, turning once she was standing on the porch. Niko moved to scoop the unconscious Tami from the carpet and carried her to the window, pushing her out of the house headfirst. Thankfully the older woman barely weighed anything, and Rayne hooked her hands under her mother's arms and tugged her toward the nearby stairs.

Niko started to climb out to join them, only to hesitate.

His first instinct was to let Mark Jefferson burn to death. What better way to purge his bitterness at his sister's death than to know the killer was reduced to ashes? But another part of him wanted the bastard to suffer. Day after day. Year after year. For a man like Mark, losing his pride would be worse than losing his life.

With a muttered curse, Niko turned back, hissing at the heat that was becoming unbearable. Then, with a grim determination, he crossed to grab Mark's foot and dragged him to the window.

He didn't want revenge for Nat's death. He wanted justice.

Two days later Rayne headed out of the hospital where her mother was being pampered by a bevy of doctors and nurses in her private room. She'd just received a text from the auto repair shop that her van was waiting in the parking lot with a new window and the interior freshly cleaned. Her bags were packed and she was ready to go.

Stepping out of the glass doors, Rayne crossed toward the van that was parked next to the sidewalk. It was Chicago, so the winter air was cold enough to bite into her flesh, but the sky was a brilliant blue and there wasn't a hint of snow in the forecast. A perfect day for a drive.

Nearly blinded by the early morning sunlight, it took Rayne a second to spot the dark form leaning against the side of her vehicle. Not until he straightened and stepped toward her.

"Niko." Her heart took a funny dive as she allowed her gaze to absorb his sculpted face and the eyes that rivaled the blue sky for brilliance. He was wearing black slacks and a long trench coat that gave him a hint of elegant power. She hadn't seen him since she'd been whisked off to the hospital with her mother, but she'd assumed he'd returned home to share with his parents what had happened to Nat before they heard it on the television. "I didn't expect to see you."

"I wanted to find out how your mother was," he murmured.

She wrinkled her nose. "Physically she's fine. In fact, she's going to be discharged later today. But emotionally . . ." She heaved a sigh. Tami had been crying and wailing nonstop, playing her tragic role as victim for all it was worth.

Mark sent her a sympathetic smile. "I heard Mark was still in jail."

"Yes." Rayne had spoken to the prosecutor earlier that morning. It would be months, maybe even years, before Mark's actual trial, but he was confident he had a solid case to ensure that he could get a life sentence. "He's being charged with murder, three attempted murders, arson, and sex with an underaged victim. Plus, my mother refuses to pay for his bail."

"Good for her," he said, his voice hard with satisfaction. No one had a greater desire to see Mark Jefferson punished than this man.

"I think she's finally seen the light. She's even talking

about joining my dad in Singapore. At least until the trial."

There was a brief silence as Niko stared down at her, his golden hair ruffled by the breeze. Heaven almighty, he was gorgeous. Her heart took another one of those crazy dips.

"And what about you?" he asked.

"What about me?"

He glanced at her refurbished van. "Are you going to hit the road?"

"Eventually. First, I think I might stop by Nat's grave," she told him, lifting her hand to touch the paintbrush charm that Lucy had sent to her all those years ago. She'd placed it on a silver necklace as a reminder that not all her memories were bad. In fact, some of them were wonderful. "I never did get the chance to say goodbye. It would be nice to have . . ." She shrugged. "Not closure. I'll never accept her death or forgive Mark for what he did. But the ability to remember how much she touched my life."

Niko's lips curved in a slow smile. "If you need a place to stay while you're in Kansas City, I have a suggestion."

She met his steady gaze. "Your office?"

"Or my condo." He stepped toward her, surrounding her in his fresh male scent. "I can show you my paintings."

"True." She chuckled as he turned the old, clichéd line into a genuine temptation. It would genuinely be nice to view her paintings in his home. "I haven't seen them for a while."

"They missed you." He brushed his fingers down her cheek in a soft caress. "And so did I."

"I suppose I could stay for a few days," she murmured.

"Or longer," he added.

She shook her head in resignation. "Pushy."

He leaned down to press his lips against her mouth. "Always."

ALONE

❦

BY
LISA CHILDS

CHAPTER ONE

Twenty-five years ago

The house hummed and vibrated with all the sounds of the party. The music. The laughter. The raised voices. The clink of glasses. The rumble of cars driving up or away.

Erin MacDonald had slipped away from the party hours ago. Not that anyone had noticed. . . .

Not that anyone ever noticed Erin. But that was fine with her. At seven she liked being invisible; it was so much better than being like her sister, Anna Beth. Everybody stared at fourteen-year-old Anna Beth. She was already more beautiful than Mother was. That was what everybody said: the photographers, the reporters, the magazines, the guests . . .

Erin had heard them saying it tonight. Mother had heard, too, and her lips had gotten all tight and thin and her pale-blue eyes had gotten cold—so cold that Erin shivered even now and tugged up the blankets to her chin.

Mother didn't like anyone being prettier than she was. Not even Anna Beth . . .

Where was Anna Beth?

Erin was in her sister's bed, which was where she usually ended up every night. She didn't like sleeping alone. She didn't like being alone. She didn't like the dark either.

The crystal lamp beside the bed was on, reflecting glittery prisms of light on the pink walls and ceiling of Anna Beth's room. It was so pretty. Everything about or around Anna Beth was pretty, except for Erin.

Erin, with all her freckles and her dark red hair, wasn't pretty like Anna Beth, with her pale-blond hair and blue eyes. Nobody even noticed that Erin had the same blue eyes—pale in the middle, with a dark blue circle around them. Nobody noticed anything about Erin but her freckles and her wild hair. Anna Beth was the only one who noticed her; the only one who thought she was pretty. She told her all the time. And she told her how much she loved her.

She was the only one who said that. Mother and Daddy never told her that they did, but they probably loved her, too. Just not like Anna Beth . . .

Where was she?

Erin's lids got heavy, so heavy she struggled to keep them up, struggled to see the light. The effort proved too much for her and she closed her eyes. A murmur of voices woke her up maybe minutes later, maybe hours. When she opened her eyes the room was dark, but the bed was warm. Anna Beth was beside her, but she wasn't sleeping. She was talking to someone.

"Who's there?" Erin asked.

"Don't hurt—" Anna Beth began.

Whatever she'd been about to say, Erin didn't hear . . . because something struck her hard on the head, and with an agonizing flash of pain she was plunged back into the darkness. Into oblivion . . .

When she awoke much, much later, she was alone.

All alone . . .

Now . . .

"Dying is probably the only way I'll get you to come home, girlie."

When he'd said that to her—during every one of their conversations—Erin hadn't been sure if her father had meant his death or hers was what would bring her home. It was his, and her heart ached with the loss.

And with the fear of coming back, a fear that increased with every mile the rental vehicle drew closer . . .

She would have rather returned to St. Cecilia's School for Girls in Austria than to her family estate just a couple of hours north of New York City. Despite the strictness of the nuns and some of the tragic things that had happened at the boarding school, she had better memories of that place than she had of home.

Home . . .

It hadn't been her home since that night so many years ago. The night two young sisters had gone missing and, despite a ransom being paid for both of them, only one had returned.

Erin.

She wasn't sure how she'd made it back then—so many hours after she and Anna Beth had disappeared from Anna Beth's bedroom. This time she was driving back, her hands tightly gripping the steering wheel of the SUV she'd rented from the airport. She steered the vehicle around the sharp turns of the winding, tree-lined road that led to the estate. The MacDonald estate was one of many on that street, set far back on manicured lawns, protected by wrought-iron fences and gates.

St. Cecilia's had been like that as well, set far back from the road behind a high fence. They'd claimed their security had been to protect the girls from reporters or would-be kidnappers because so many of them had come from wealthy, famous families. They hadn't been able to protect everyone, though, just as the fence and the gate at home hadn't kept out Anna Beth and Erin's kidnappers.

Her pulse quickened as she slowed the vehicle's approach to the end of the cul-de-sac. The road ended at the tallest of the wrought-iron gates on the street, at the tallest of the fences. She braked next to the security panel and lowered the driver's window. Instead of pressing the intercom button, she punched in the code that her father had never bothered to change, not even after the divorce.

Her mother's birthday.

Maybe he'd kept it all these years because he'd hoped *she* would return someday. Not her mother.

He and Sylvia Sloan had never had an easy relationship, and their divorce had been particularly acrimonious—with Mother learning just how ironclad that prenup she'd signed had been. No. He hadn't wanted his ex-wife to come back to the estate she'd fought so hard for in their divorce.

And despite his calls and visits to her over the years, Erin hadn't believed she was the one he'd really wanted to come back. He'd looked the same way Mother had that day he'd found her: disappointed. Like she wasn't the daughter they'd wished the kidnapper had returned.

No. Gregor MacDonald had kept the code the same for Anna Beth. So she could finally come home.

But in twenty-five years she hadn't come back. Would she now, as Erin had, for their father's funeral?

Tears stung her eyes, but she blinked them away and peered through the windshield as the gates rattled and shuddered open. Even though the SUV was stopped, Erin pressed harder on the brake, all the muscles in her right leg straining with the effort, as if the SUV was trying to move forward and she was all that held it back.

As if some force within the estate was pulling her toward it, toward the place she'd once called home . . .

But that force was gone now. Dead . . .

One of the tears escaped her eyes and trailed down her cheek. She unclasped her right hand from the steering wheel to dash it away. Then she eased her foot from the brake and started forward, down the long drive that circled around a big, gurgling fountain before stopping in front of the house.

Hell, it was more than a house. More like a mausoleum, or the old convent where Daddy and Mother had sent Erin after she'd come back twenty-five years ago. *Home* was three floors of stone and sparkling windows with a deep green slate roof topping it off. The faint sunshine of the early spring day gleamed in those windows, reflecting back the driveway and the fountain and revealing nothing of what was inside.

She parked in the middle of the drive, right in front of the imposing double doors of the entry. Then she turned off the ignition and reached onto the passenger seat for her duffel, which held her camera equipment and a few changes of clothes.

She wouldn't be here long. Just for the funeral.

More tears threatened, but she blinked them all back this time.

She shouldn't have been surprised that Daddy was gone. He'd already been in his late forties when he'd married Sylvia Sloan, when they'd had Anna Beth, and older yet when, seven years later, they'd had Erin. He'd always smoked too many cigars and drunk too much scotch and ate only red meat, so it was a wonder he'd lasted as long as he had, especially after the kidnapping. That had seemed to age him more than any of his vices.

After walking up the wide stone steps to those imposing doors, Erin punched in the same code she had at the gate. They drew open just as the gates had, with a rattle of hinges and a shudder, and she stepped into the dimly lit foyer. The floor here was stone, like the steps, like the floor of a castle.

That was what Daddy had liked to think the place had once been, a castle like the ones he'd admired and coveted in Scotland. A fortress.

But it wasn't a fortress. It hadn't protected any of them from loss or pain.

That pain gripped her now as the doors closed behind her, and she drew in a deep breath that carried the lingering odor of his cigars. It was like Gregor MacDonald was still here, as if he was smoking one in his study—the cigar in one hand, a glass of scotch in the other. She walked toward his study now and peeked inside, but nobody sat behind his massive, carved oak desk. The worn burgundy leather chair was empty, as was the darkly paneled room.

Only that sweet scent of cigars remained.

Given his age and his vices, she shouldn't have been surprised that he'd died, but she was . . . surprised and devastated.

"Daddy . . ." she murmured through the tears clogging her throat.

Poor Daddy.

Despite all his success and wealth, he'd lost so much, even before he'd lost his life. He'd lost his daughter, then his wife, but, probably the most painful thing for him, he'd also lost his reputation.

Because people had always wondered . . .

There had been so much speculation. So many accusations and suspicions for so many years that he'd been responsible for Anna Beth's disappearance. That the kidnapping, the subsequent sightings years later, had all been staged to hide his guilt. To escape it, Daddy could have done what she'd done. He could have moved away from it all.

But he'd stayed here all these years.

Waiting for *her*?

Rafe Montego sat alone in the interview room of the Lake George, New York, Police Department. A box, with a number scribbled on the end of it, sat on the table in front of him. He didn't need to take off the lid of the box to know what was inside; he was well aware of the evidence in this kidnapping case, and that there was pathetically little of it.

Instead of reaching for the box, Rafe reached for his tie, jerking at the knot to loosen it. His suit jacket was already thrown across the back of one of the hard, metal chairs in the windowless room. Rafe sat at the edge of the table, next to the box. He plopped his laptop on the lid of it, the screen showing the online version of the case file. Everything in that box had been photographed and cataloged, as well as all the notes scanned into it.

But as there wasn't much evidence, there weren't many notes either from the detective who'd investigated the case twenty-five years ago. Who had Detective Voller talked to? Who had he considered a suspect?

Rafe considered everyone suspect. Every family member. Every guest at that party.

Every person who'd worked that party, from the valets to the waitstaff to the cleanup crew.

Since he made detective five years ago, Rafe had tried to talk to them all. Tried to get more information to add to the notes and more evidence for the case file box. But despite all the people he'd talked to, he'd never been able to talk to the most important person: to the only one who'd returned from the abduction despite the ransom being paid for both of them.

Only Erin MacDonald had returned . . .

A full night after the abduction; at least twenty-four hours after she and her sister were last seen. But shortly after her return, the little girl had been shipped off to some boarding school in Austria, and since Rafe had reopened the investigation, she had not been back in the country.

He glanced at the *Lake George Tribune* newspaper sitting on the table next to the box. The headline speculated in bold print what Rafe had been privately speculating:

WILL THE DEATH OF BILLIONAIRE GREGOR MACDONALD FINALLY BRING BOTH HIS DAUGHTERS HOME?

He reached up and pushed one of his hands through his thick, dark hair. His fingers shook a little—with excitement. Would they both return for the funeral? Was it even possible?

Or had, as so many suspected, Anna Beth MacDonald died twenty-five years ago? Was that why only the little girl had been found? Because her beautiful older sister was dead?

If she was alive, Anna Beth would be thirty-nine now. A year older than Rafe was. He'd been thirteen when she'd disappeared, and he'd had a poster of her—from one of her modeling jobs—on his bedroom wall. To his thirteen-year-old self, she'd been so beautiful.

Was she still that beautiful? Was she alive? And if she was, where was she?

For twenty-five years every reporter and armchair detective had floated theories about the case. Some speculated that Anna Beth hadn't survived the abduction. Others theorized that she'd staged the entire thing, that she'd taken the million-dollar ransom paid for her and her sister and taken off with some older boyfriend she must have been seeing secretly.

What had happened that night she and her little sister had disappeared from her bedroom? Where had they been that full twenty-four hours they'd been missing? And why had only one of them returned?

Had anybody even asked the seven-year-old those

questions? If so, Rafe hadn't found any notes in the case file about that interview. And he hadn't had the chance to interview her himself.

Since being sent away to a boarding school in Austria, she'd rarely—if ever—returned home. At least he hadn't found any record of her return. He had found a record of what she'd been doing since she'd graduated from that boarding school and the small art school she'd attended after it.

She had a blog where she posted photos and reviews from her world travels. It was open on another tab on his laptop screen; he'd bookmarked it and looked at it often. He'd expected it to be as narcissistic as other blogs he'd glanced at since social media had become such a way of life for people. He'd expected it to be full of selfies and overly personal information. But there were no photos of her anywhere on the site. Nothing personal at all.

Just pictures of the places she'd seen: beautiful photographs of architecture and sunsets and food. She was a talented photographer and writer; her reviews made him want to visit all the places she'd been, to eat the food she'd eaten, to see what she'd seen instead of things he had when he'd done his traveling as a marine. After his last tour of duty had ended, he'd wanted nothing more than to come home and never leave again.

Would she return for her father's funeral? And if she did, would she stay, or would she jaunt off again on her next adventure?

Rafe could think of only one way to find out: to attend the funeral himself. He hadn't known Gregor MacDonald; the man's lawyer had thwarted all Rafe's attempts to reinterview him. Would the lawyer thwart his efforts to attend the funeral as well?

Or would Rafe be able to crash the ceremony and finally speak to one of the few people who knew what had happened that night?

CHAPTER TWO

Twenty-two years ago . . .

"Your sister is alive!" Beatrix Chevalier announced as she pushed open the door and burst into Erin's room. It was the smallest room in the boarding school and had probably once been a closet. But Erin preferred it to sharing with anyone else.

Usually she kept to herself, except for some infrequent conversations with Rayne Taylor and Lucy McKenna. They weren't pushy like Beatrix. Lucy was a little weird, though. And Rayne . . .

She and Rayne shared a love for old movies. Erin liked watching them and escaping into those make-believe worlds.

"Aren't you excited?" Beatrix asked as she dropped onto the narrow bed next to Erin.

Erin peered up at her through half-open eyes. She'd been sleeping when Beatrix had awakened her. Maybe that was why she hadn't reacted until now to what the other girl had said.

Maybe that was why her pulse hadn't started pounding

right away, why it hadn't been hard to breathe . . . until now. Or maybe Erin was just reacting to the overpowering, heavy fragrance wafting from the other girl. As usual, Beatrix had sprayed too much of her fancy French perfume on herself. That scent reminded Erin of Mother, though Sylvia Sloan had never worn this much. She only wore just a trace, so that people had to lean closer to her to actually smell her perfume. Not that Mother had ever allowed anyone that close to her.

Especially not Erin. Not even before Anna Beth had disappeared.

And after . . . Sylvia had wanted nothing to do with Erin.

Beatrix was too close now. So close that Erin rolled off the other side of the narrow bed to get away from her. Or maybe it wasn't just her she was trying to escape, but the magazine the girl waved around.

"Look!" Beatrix ordered. "It's her. It's really her!"

But was it?

Erin hesitated for a long moment before she reached for and took the magazine from Beatrix. She'd folded back the page of a series of photographs of a girl with long blond hair. The images were grainy, as if the photos had been taken from a distance. The girl wound through other people walking along a busy sidewalk in front of a row of brownstones.

It was New York City.

And the girl was tall and thin, almost painfully thin. It could have been Anna Beth, just like the photos that had been printed in another magazine the year before could have been her.

But were they? Erin felt no recognition, no connection, with the person in those photographs.

"Er—" Rayne Taylor began only to stop when she saw that it was Beatrix, not Erin, flopped across her bed. Disgusted, she shook her head, her black hair tumbled around her shoulders. "Of course you would go straight to her with those stupid pictures."

"Stupid?" Beatrix asked. "That's her sister. She's happy to see her—to see that she's alive."

But Erin wasn't happy. She hadn't been truly happy since she'd seen Anna Beth last—in person. Not in grainy photographs . . .

Maybe she should have been relieved that there were sightings of Anna Beth, that there was hope that she was alive. But all Erin felt was sadness that she had left, and that she hadn't taken Erin with her.

Maybe she hadn't loved her as she'd claimed.

Now . . .

The scent of the flowers reminded Erin of Beatrix Chevalier's overpowering perfume. Maybe she'd had some sprayed on the floral arrangement she'd sent. Hers wasn't the only arrangement from former boarders of St. Cecilia's School for Girls. Lucy and Rayne had sent flowers, too, with cards apologizing for not being able to make it to the funeral.

Erin hadn't expected them to make it, not after the ordeals they had each recently survived. Knowing them, they'd probably stayed away so they wouldn't draw more media attention to the funeral, to Erin. They both knew how much she preferred to stay invisible.

She wasn't now. Everybody was staring at her. Not just

the reporters she'd had to pass through to enter the funeral home, but also all of the mourners who'd gathered for the showing prior to the funeral. Were they actually mourning, though?

She heard no sobs. Saw no tears.

Only curiosity from some, like the reporters, and resentment and anger from others. From her *family* . . .

But her older half siblings had made it clear to her years ago, when she'd been just a child, that they didn't consider her family. She was just one of the unfortunate results of their father's midlife crisis with the young, former supermodel her mother had once been. Seeing her now at the funeral, Erin could tell that Sylvia Sloan wasn't young anymore. Despite the procedures she'd had to try to erase the wrinkles and the years, she looked old despite the tightness of her face, or maybe because of it. And she was thin, so thin that she looked almost frail. Her hair, once so thick and beautiful, was thin now, too, and brittle-looking. And the strands, once such a pale blond, looked more silver now.

And she was no less resentful or angry than the rest of them were.

Her pale-blue eyes were cold and hard, even as she leaned down to press her cheek to Erin's. That perfume wafted from her. She must use more than a dab now, perhaps to cover up the scent of alcohol that slipped through her lips with her sigh. "How sad that this is the only reason you've come home, Erin," she said, her voice sharp with disappointment.

Erin was used to her mother's disappointment in her. Usually she only had to hear it during their infrequent phone conversations, and on the rare holidays they'd met up in Paris or London or Milan.

Erin had spent most of the holidays with her father, usually in Scotland, in some castle he'd rented out for a week. If she'd known this past Christmas would be his last, she might have stayed the entire week, but she'd had a deadline. . . .

In addition to her blog, she contributed to several travel magazines. It was easier for her to focus on places than people. Unfortunately there wasn't much to the funeral home beyond silk wallpaper and soft carpet and dim lighting and the director who, with his size and demeanor, looked more like a bouncer. And he hovered around like one, as if ready to toss out any reporter who dared to sneak inside. He wasn't the only one who hovered. Daddy's lawyer stood nearby, too.

With his white hair and heavily lined face, Ethan O'Neill was probably nearly as old as her father was, but he was still practicing law. Like Daddy, he hadn't retired. He would probably die in his office, as her father had died in his den. Mr. O'Neill had already offered her his condolences, as well as the promise that he would make sure her father's wishes were carried out. He had already handled the funeral arrangements as Daddy had directed.

Bagpipe music wafted around the room as Daddy lay in the open casket. He wore a plaid suit, as he often had, and his white hair was long and a little unkempt, as it had often been, and a half grin played across his lips as if he was the only one in on the joke. But it wasn't a joke; he was really dead.

Erin kept staring at him, though, half-expecting him to open his brown eyes and wink at her. Her mother must have expected the same because she stared as well, and the expression on her face was even colder than it had been for Erin.

"That son of a bitch," she remarked. "He looks like he's having the last laugh, as usual."

Daddy had had a big, booming laugh. But after Anna Beth had disappeared, Erin hadn't heard it that often. Not that she'd seen him that often. And she'd seen her mother even less.

"What are you doing here?" Magnus asked Sylvia. He was the oldest of Daddy's children. Only a few wisps of gray hair remained on his head, and his belly strained the buttons of his worn suit. He was older than Erin's mother. Sally, Erin's half sister, was the same age as Sylvia, but now she looked younger. And heavier even than she used to be, her face full and red, whereas Mother's was thin and pale. So very pale.

Sally shoved her way into the conversation as well. "Yes, what are you doing here? Looking to twist the knife even deeper?"

But she wasn't looking at Sylvia; she addressed Erin with her venomous words and her dark, angry gaze. Erin wasn't used to them looking at her, much less speaking to her. They had never joined her and Daddy for those holidays. In fact, one of the last times she remembered seeing them was at the party that night so long ago.

Ethan O'Neill stepped forward. "Let's not do this here," he advised. "This isn't what your father wanted."

Sally snorted. "And you would know. You and her— you're probably the only ones who know the truth. It's clear that doesn't matter to either of you. All that matters is money."

Erin's head began to pound, the angry words like fists against her skull. "What's she talking about?" she asked Ethan.

Magnus snorted now. "Like you don't know, like *Daddy* didn't tell you exactly what he intended to do." He turned back toward her mother now. "That's why you're here, huh? Hoping to use her to get around the prenup? To get what you tried to get in the divorce?"

Her mother's pale skin flushed now with fiery color. She was more angry than embarrassed as she lashed out, "You're drunk!"

Magnus shook his head. "I'm not the drunk here."

Since when was her mother? Though when Erin thought back, Mother had always had a glass in her hand—a flute, actually. Sylvia had once claimed in an interview that she'd been born with champagne taste; it was why she'd started modeling at such a young age. She'd wanted the finer things in life. Maybe that was why, when fewer and fewer modeling jobs had been offered her, she'd married a man so much older than she was.

Erin's face heated—with embarrassment, not anger. Everybody was staring at them. Her father's extended family. His friends. The neighbors.

Michael Andover was here with his father. He had to be forty-one or -two now, but he still possessed the golden good looks of his teens. His blond hair was thick, his skin tanned.

Her face heated even more with embarrassment over the little-girl crush she'd always had on him. He offered her a small smile of pity. Probably more over the scene with her family than her father's passing. Daddy had never been that friendly with him or with his father, Peter

Andover. He'd considered them lazy and lacking in ambition because they'd inherited their money instead of working for it as he had. And yet he'd invited them to every party—even that last one. Maybe that was more to rub their faces in his wealth than to be friendly with them.

They hadn't been the only ones he'd done that to; there were other neighbors and acquaintances here that her father had openly disdained as well. Maybe that was actually why they were here. That despite the little grin on his face, Daddy hadn't gotten the last laugh. They had.

There was another man standing nearby. He was even better-looking than Michael: dark whereas he was light. His hair was thick and black, his eyes dark and watchful. His jaw square and rigid. Who was he?

She didn't recognize him. Maybe he was a newer neighbor or employee of her father's. Or . . .

Perhaps a reporter had slipped past the funeral director after all. This man certainly seemed interested in the conversation happening around the casket, and in her. He stared even more openly than the others.

"Please," Erin murmured to her family. "Let's not fight here." Or ever, but she knew that was too much to ask of them.

"There will be a fight," Magnus said, and this time he addressed her as his sister had. "You're not getting away with it."

"With what?" she asked.

Ethan O'Neill uttered a groan before turning to her. "I was going to come by the house to tell you later. . . ."

"What?" she asked again.

"Like she doesn't know," Sally said. "Like she didn't manipulate *Daddy* into leaving everything to her!"

Magnus glared at her. "Carrying his secrets to his grave for him? Is that why the big payoff, Erin?" he asked.

She was surprised that her brother actually knew her name because he had never addressed her by it. Instead, he'd always called her what her father had: girlie. But he hadn't said it the way Daddy had; he'd said it mockingly. Not like Daddy had, with affection, or so she'd thought. She glanced at the casket now, where her father was perpetually grinning that little grin. And she knew—by leaving everything to her—he had gotten the last laugh. But was he laughing at her, too?

Because she felt like he'd played the biggest—*cruelest*—joke on her, because if he'd left her everything, he'd left her the estate that was where all her nightmares took place.

Secrets? What secrets was Erin MacDonald carrying with her? Was that why she traveled so much? Because she was trying to outrun those secrets?

Rafe stood close enough to the arguing family that he'd heard every spiteful word they'd hurled at one another. She was the only one who'd noticed him watching and who actually seemed to care. Her face was flushed nearly as red as her hair with her embarrassment—though with her proliferation of freckles, it was hard to tell just how much she was blushing. She had so many freckles they blended together, making her skin look darker, which made her eyes look even paler. They were an arresting shade of silvery blue, except for a darker circle around the irises.

What was also arresting about her eyes was the expression in them: the fear and vulnerability. All his protective instincts kicking in, Rafe stepped closer to the people crowded around the open casket and pulled out his badge. "Some of you already know who I am, but I haven't had the pleasure of meeting you yet, Ms. MacDonald," he said. "I'm Detective Rafe Montego."

She nodded, as if he'd answered a question she'd had but hadn't uttered.

The lawyer had no qualms about asking *his* question. "How the hell did you get in here?" O'Neill demanded to know.

Apparently he had given orders to keep out Rafe, just as he had the reporters. Fortunately for Rafe, the funeral director knew him and appreciated his service—more as a marine than a lawman, though.

"I've come to pay my respects," he said. "And to offer my condolences, Ms. MacDonald."

She was the only one who truly looked the part of the mourner, with the skin around her pale eyes slightly swollen, as if from crying. And she wore black—a dress of some stretchy fabric that clung to her curves, drawing Rafe's attention to them, to her. Except for her eyes, she didn't look anything like her sister or her mother. Though she wasn't petite, at probably five foot six or seven, she wasn't tall and thin like them.

"Montego," O'Neill said, drawing Rafe's attention back to him. "That's not what I asked you. And we all know why you're here. You can't leave well enough alone."

"So they're right?" Rafe asked him with a jerk of his head toward the older MacDonald siblings. "You and Ms. MacDonald do have something to hide?"

"I don't have anything to hide," Erin said, but he

suspected she was addressing her siblings more than she was him.

"So you're willing to answer all the questions I have for you," he boldly stated as a matter of fact. He'd had these questions for the past five years—longer, actually— because that infamous kidnapping so close to his home and of someone he'd felt as if he'd known—had first piqued his interest in crime investigation.

Those stunning eyes of hers narrowed in a slight glare. "As I don't have anything to hide, I also don't have anything to tell you," she said. "Except . . ."

His pulse quickened with excitement. There was something. Something she'd remembered.

"That this is my father's funeral," she continued. "The only thing I'm doing today is laying him to rest." The last part she'd addressed to everyone; she obviously had no intention of fighting with them or with him. She turned toward the funeral director, then, and motioned for him to begin.

"Ladies and gentlemen," he announced. "Please take your seats and we will begin the service for Gregor Simon MacDon—"

"She's here!" someone shouted from the foyer of the funeral home.

"Anna Beth is outside!"

Was it possible?

Was Erin not the only daughter who'd returned for her father's funeral?

Anxious to see her, to question her, Rafe whirled away and pushed through the crowd, shouldering them aside until he burst through the exterior doors. The reporters must have seen the woman, too, because they were running toward the grounds of the cemetery.

"There she is!" one of them shouted.

And in the distance, a slim figure ran between the headstones and the statues, her long, pale blond hair flowing behind her. Was that Anna Beth?

From this distance he couldn't tell. Hell, even up close he probably wouldn't be able to tell with all the years that had passed. Except for the eyes . . .

He would recognize her eyes, which were exactly like her younger sister's. He turned back toward the funeral home to find her standing at the top of the steps outside, staring down at him with those very eyes.

"Was that her, Ms. MacDonald?" he asked.

She shrugged her slim shoulders. "I don't know." Despite her claim of knowing nothing, there was some kind of knowledge in her eyes—some awareness or realization.

"What?" he asked her.

She shrugged again. "I find myself wondering if you really want to solve that kidnapping case from so long ago, or if you just want to find my sister."

Had she guessed about his old crush? Had she realized that he'd once admired her sister as so many other men his age probably had done when they'd been just boys? Heat rushed to his face now that he might have been caught out about that old crush. But that crush had ended long ago, even though his fascination had continued—not with Anna Beth, but with the mystery of what had happened to her—to *them*.

"She's been missing for twenty-five years," Rafe said. "Don't you want to find her?"

"I don't know." She shrugged again. "If she's just been missing all these years, she must really not want to be found."

Rafe found himself nodding in agreement. If Anna Beth had been complicit in the kidnapping, it made sense that she wouldn't want to be found. But then, why show up here, or in any of those old photographs that had reported sightings of her? Why hadn't she managed to stay out of the public as Erin had all these years?

The day had already been overcast, clouds blocking the sun, but now the sky got darker and a cold wind kicked up. And Rafe shivered.

If Anna Beth hadn't been missing, she had to be dead. Did Erin think that she was, or did she know it? Had she witnessed her sister's murder?

Before he could ask, she turned away from him and stepped back inside the funeral home. And he noticed that, of the family, she was the only one who'd come outside, who'd come to see if Anna Beth had truly shown up at their father's funeral.

Why hadn't the others come out?

Because they didn't care if she was here, or because they knew it couldn't be Anna Beth—that she was dead? And the only way they'd know that for certain would be if one of them had killed her.

He ran back up the steps to the funeral home, but when he reached for the doors, he found them locked. Had the funeral director locked him out on the lawyer's orders, or had Erin locked him out?

Would he ever get a chance to ask her all those questions he had for her?

CHAPTER THREE

Twenty-five years ago . . .

Her head pounded, like her heart was beating inside it—like it was trying to bust out right through her skull. Erin lifted her hands to it and groaned. The sound of her own voice startled her, and she jerked open her eyes . . . to darkness. A whimper slipped out of her lips now—one of pain and fear.

She hated the dark. And it was so dark, she didn't even know where she was. Where was she?

She peered around, and as her vision cleared, she could see the walls surrounding her. Walls that moved, that rustled . . .

She was in the maze in the garden, way in back of the house. She shuddered with fear and cold. She hated the maze. She'd gotten lost in it so many times, playing hide and seek with Anna Beth.

"You're little, Erin, you can slip through the branches," Anna Beth always told her. "You'll never get trapped in here."

But she was trapped, and so very afraid and so very alone . . .

Now . . .

The maze was even bigger now, the walls of shrubs higher and denser. There was no way Erin could slip through any of these branches now. If she went any deeper into the maze, she would be lost, just as she'd been that night. And with her head pounding as it had been, she hadn't been able to remember the directions Anna Beth used to give her, the turns she was supposed to make when she entered or when she exited. She hadn't had any idea where she'd been inside it, or how she'd gotten into it.

How long had she wandered around it before someone had heard her crying?

Daddy. He was the one who'd rescued her that night. Who'd heard her sobs and rushed out to find her. "Oh, girlie, thank God . . . " he'd murmured as he'd picked her up in his arms. Then, seconds later, he'd asked, "Where's your sister?"

"I don't know," Erin had said, just as she'd told the detective that afternoon. She had no idea about Anna Beth. Was she alive? And if she was, why had she stayed away all those years?

Had that been her at Daddy's funeral this afternoon? She'd caught only that glimpse of pale-blond hair as the woman had disappeared into the cemetery. Just as Anna Beth had disappeared so many years ago . . .

Erin peered around the garden, wondering . . .

Could Anna Beth still be out here—somewhere?

Branches rustled, startling Erin so much that a cry slipped out.

"Erin!" a man's booming voice called out. It wasn't her father—just his friend, his lawyer.

Ethan had been both, right? He had liked her father, even though so few other people had. Even his family . . .

Daddy hadn't liked many people himself. Not even his family . . .

Had he really loved Erin? Was that why he'd left her everything—because even though he hadn't been able to show his love while he was alive, he was showing it to her now?

Or was he showing everyone else his hatred?

They were here now—all of them. The lawyer, her family, her father's friends and associates, and the neighbors. Just as they'd been that night for the party. The night she and Anna Beth had disappeared . . .

But this wasn't a party. It was a funeral. Erin felt as if it was more hers than her father's. Dread making her limbs feel heavy, she turned and walked slowly back toward the house.

Ethan stood on the stone patio that stretched along the entire back of the mammoth house. He peered into the darkness and called out to her. "Erin?"

"I'm here," she assured him.

"I figured you probably had enough for this day," he said, "so I sent some of the guests home. Some, however, refused to leave."

Through the open patio doors, voices drifted out, nearly repeating everything from the funeral home. Her mother and Magnus and Sally hurled insults and accusations at one another. She flinched at the depths of the hatred and resentment they all held for one another. And for her . . .

"She's not going to get away with this!" Sally vowed. "That little bitch isn't getting everything!"

"I don't care what she had on the old man," Magnus said. "He already paid a million for her and that was too damn much!"

"He would have paid more," Ethan murmured.

Erin turned to find the lawyer staring at her, his eyes soft with sympathy. "He would have paid more."

Daddy had paid that money for both of them, but only she had come home. Magnus was right; he had paid too much. Way too much.

He'd paid with his reputation, too, after all the rumors and speculation had started. That he'd been abusing Anna Beth . . .

That he'd killed her because she was going to talk. He'd just staged the kidnapping.

The photos of Anna Beth hadn't started turning up until a couple of years after the kidnapping. And even those hadn't quelled the rumors, the speculation . . . hadn't cleared her father of the cloud of suspicion that had hung over him. Some people had accused him of hiring that girl, of staging those pictures, to clear his name.

Erin hadn't known what to believe. Then or now.

"Why?" she asked the lawyer. Ethan O'Neill had known him best—even more than Erin had, and certainly better than his wife had. Maybe it had been a ploy during their divorce, or maybe it had been the reason for their divorce, but Sylvia Sloan had made accusations in the press, had accused him of killing "my *beautiful* daughter." That was how she'd referred to Anna Beth, as if that had differentiated her from Erin, because she hadn't been, and still wasn't, beautiful.

"He loved you," O'Neill said.

"Then why leave me everything?" she asked. "Why make me a target for them?" She gestured at the house.

O'Neill smiled—a half smile like the one her father had worn in the casket. "Because he knew you could handle it. That you're strong—so very strong."

Erin wasn't sure about that. But she did know that she was a survivor. She'd survived the kidnapping all those years ago. She'd survived St. Cecilia's School for Girls. And she would survive this, too.

Her father's funeral.

She drew in a deep breath and stepped inside the house. As well as her mother and siblings, some members of the catering company remained, flitting around, refilling glasses.

And Mrs. Markham. The housekeeper was semiretired now, coming in only a few days a week. But she'd attended the funeral today and had offered to stay with Erin until she left. Even Mrs. Markham knew she would leave again. . . .

Had Daddy known? Was that why he'd given her the house—because he'd thought it would make her stay?

"There's someone at the gate," Mrs. Markham told Erin before uttering a heavy sigh. "That detective."

"Montego's here?" Ethan asked, and he started toward the kitchen, where there was a link to the intercom at the gate. "I'll get rid of—"

"No," Erin said. "I'll talk to him."

"No!" Magnus shouted. "You're not going to let him in here!"

Her mother shook her head. "You can't, Erin."

"It's a bad idea," O'Neill said.

"This is my house now," Erin reminded them all, as if they needed to be reminded. "I can let whoever I want inside." It was getting rid of the ones she didn't want that she was finding harder.

"I'm leaving, then," her mother said, as if threatening her.

"Me too," Sally said.

Magnus just stared at her, as if waiting for her to change her mind.

Instead she walked toward the same doorway where O'Neill stood. As she passed him, he warned her, "Erin, you shouldn't talk to him. . . ."

"I have nothing to hide," she said. And nothing to share, which the detective would learn soon enough, as she stalked past O'Neill and pressed the button that released the gates.

She suspected, from their reluctance to speak to the detective, that she was the only one in her family with nothing to hide. With no secrets . . .

What did they know? Or better yet, what didn't they want the detective to know?

Rafe hadn't expected the gates to open for him. He wasn't sure if it had been done on purpose, or if they'd started opening for the guests who were leaving. As he parked his vehicle near the huge fountain and stepped out, he passed Erin's mother on her way to her car. Alcohol wafted from her.

"Mrs. Mac—"

"Ms. Sloan," she corrected him. "I haven't been Mrs. MacDonald for years."

"Ms. Sloan, I don't think you should be driving—"

She glared at him with those same eyes her daughters had. But hers were so much colder than Erin's. "I have a chauffeur," she said.

"I'd appreciate it if you stayed, though," he said. He glanced at the others who'd walked out of the house—the son, the older daughter, the lawyer. "I'd appreciate it if you all stayed to answer my questions."

"If you want to talk to me, you're going to need a fucking warrant," Magnus MacDonald warned him, and he shoved past on his way to his car. There was no driver waiting for him, though, and he reeked of alcohol, too. He even staggered as he walked.

"I'm not going to need that warrant," Rafe pointed out, "if I wind up arresting you right now for an operating under the influence cha—"

"No, I'm driving," the sister said, and she rushed after him, steering him toward the passenger's side. She looked sober enough—more sober than him and her ex-stepmother. In fact, her eyes, though dark, were cold and hard with her sobriety and her hatred. She wasn't looking at him, though, but at the woman who stood in the open doors to the foyer of the three-story mansion.

The lawyer didn't hurry to his vehicle like the others. He stood on the stone steps—between Rafe and Erin MacDonald. "I advised her not to speak to you," he said. But from the annoyance in his voice, it was clear Erin hadn't listened to him.

She must have been the one who'd opened the gates for him. Who'd let him inside. But had she done that because she wanted to talk to him or because she'd wanted to get rid of her guests? He suspected it was the latter, especially when he stepped around the lawyer and joined her at the door.

She didn't move aside to let him in; she acted as if she was blocking him instead as she leaned against the jamb. "Detective . . ."

"Montego," he said. Had she forgotten his name?

Maybe she still suffered from that concussion she'd sustained so many years ago. Her injuries had been listed in the previous detective's report. The blood on her night-gown and in her matted hair. The head wound. Was that why the investigating detective hadn't really questioned her? Because she'd been so wounded, so damaged?

She raised a hand to her hair, which curled wildly around her face, and pushed a few tendrils behind her ear.

His fingers twitched, as if he was tempted to touch her hair, too. To touch her. There was something about Erin MacDonald—that vulnerability that called out his every protective instinct, that made him want to save her. But she didn't need saving. Although she'd been wounded, she had survived the kidnapping that night. Had her sister?

"You let me through the gates," he reminded her. "Are you going to let me inside?"

She shrugged. "You're wasting your time, Detective . . ."

He stopped himself from supplying his name again. She knew it; she just didn't seem to want to address him personally—to make this personal. And it wasn't.

It was just a case to him.

That was all it was—all *she* was—to him.

Finally she stepped back and walked away from the

doors, leaving him to follow. He hadn't been inside the house before, hadn't even made it onto the grounds before. Gregor MacDonald had had his lawyer block his every attempt to investigate the crime scene or the man who'd once been considered the main suspect.

At least by the media.

Eventually—with the sporadic sightings of Anna Beth over the years—that speculation had changed. Anna Beth and a mystery man had become the primary suspects then.

Rafe stepped inside the foyer and turned back to close the doors. The lawyer stood outside still, as if reluctant to leave her. Had that vulnerability in her drawn out this man's protectiveness, too? Or did his loyalties lie yet with his dead employer? Or with himself?

O'Neill had been here that night—at the party. It had been an eclectic group of guests. MacDonald's business associates and high-class neighbors and the former super-model's friends and photographers from the entertainment industry. And all of them had claimed to notice nothing amiss that night. Hadn't even noticed when Erin had disappeared from the party, or when Anna Beth had, too.

At least one of them had to be lying.

And did Erin have any idea who?

He followed her down the hall toward a room at the back of the house. Waitstaff cleared away empty plates and glasses. "Was there another party here?" he asked.

She sighed. "For some it might have been a party . . ." But tears glistened in those arresting eyes of hers.

"I am sorry about your father," he said.

She tilted her head and studied his face, as if gauging his sincerity. "Did you know him?"

He shook his head. "But I know it's hard to lose a parent. My dad died when I was a teenager."

Around the same time her sister had disappeared. Maybe that was why he'd focused so much on the case; it had taken his mind from the loss of his father.

"I'm sorry," she said now. "That must have been hard for you, and for your mother."

"She was devastated," he admitted.

And they'd nearly been destitute from all the hospital bills from his father's long illness, so she'd had to work as many jobs as she could get. It was no wonder she'd died five years after he had. She'd worked herself to death.

"Was?" Erin asked. "Do you ever really get over a loss like that? The devastation?"

"She died a while ago," he admitted, his heart heavy with the loss. But he reminded himself, "They're together now."

"That's a sweet sentiment," she said wistfully, as if she longed to believe in an afterlife. For herself? Or for her father and her sister?

Or was Anna Beth still alive?

"Why am I answering your questions instead of asking my own?" he wondered aloud. She was good at deflecting from herself, from turning the focus to others. She did it on her blog, focusing on the places instead of anything personal.

She smiled then, a genuine smile that cleared the tears from her eyes and lit them up. She was beautiful—so much so that he lost himself for a moment in her gaze. He had to shake his head to clear it, to focus.

"Will you answer my questions now?" he asked.

"You're wasting your time," she told him again. "I don't remember anything about that night."

"Because of the concussion?"

She shrugged. "I have no idea."

"What's the last thing you remember?" he asked.

She sighed—almost wistfully. "Lying in Anna Beth's bed, waiting for her."

"So you left the party before she did?"

She nodded. "It was loud and there were too many people . . ." she murmured as she gazed around the room that was nearly empty now, but for the two of them. The staff had cleared away everything. "They weren't going to leave anytime soon, so I left."

"Where did you go?" he asked, and he glanced around the room, wondering how she'd left, how no one had noticed.

But what had a child been doing at the party in the first place? She'd only been seven, and he felt as protective of the little girl she'd been then as he was now of the woman. Maybe more so because he knew what had happened to her.

Someone had hurt her. Could have killed her . . .

Would her sister have done that to her?

"I went upstairs," she said.

He gestured toward the foyer, where the split staircase had wound up from both sides of it to the second-story landing.

But she shook her head and moved instead toward another doorway, to the kitchen and the stairwell in it.

"Miss MacDonald," an older woman called out to her. "Are you okay? Do you need anything?"

Erin smiled at her, but it was obviously forced now, her face tense. "I'm fine, Mrs. Markham. You can leave once you've seen out the catering staff."

The older woman glanced at him now.

"I'm with the Lake George Police Department," he said, to assure her that her employer would be safe with him.

"I know who you are, Detective," the woman replied, and it was clear she didn't think that made him safe for Erin.

"He won't be staying long either," Erin assured the older woman. "I don't have anything to tell him that he doesn't already know."

"I'm not so sure about that," Rafe said.

"This all must be in the police report from that night," Erin said.

He didn't want to admit how little was in that report, so he gestured toward that back stairwell again. "You went up this way?"

She nodded, and then she proceeded to do just that, moving quietly up the stairs to the second story. There was a door at the top that opened onto a wide corridor. There were several more doors off it. She passed quite a few of them before opening one. "I went into my room," she said. "And put on my nightgown."

He glanced over her shoulder into the room. With boxes sitting on the floor and on the small bed, it looked more like a storage closet than a bedroom. The walls were white, as were the curtains at the window. It was bland. Totally unlike the woman herself.

"This was your bedroom?" he asked, skeptically.

She smiled. "Mother called it a blank palate for my toys and blankets. Those are what's packed in the boxes now. They packed them up when they sent me to boarding school."

"St. Cecilia's School for Girls."

It wasn't a question as it was common knowledge, but she nodded, as if he'd asked. And that tension was back in her face, in her curvy body.

"You didn't like it there?"

She shrugged again. "I got used to it."

He wanted to ask her about that place, about her time there, but while he had her here, in the past, he had to focus on the case. So he drew in a deep breath and asked, "What did you do after you put on your nightgown?"

She stepped back from her bedroom door and bumped into his body. He didn't move right away, just let himself enjoy that moment of closeness. Of the softness and heat of her.

"Detective?"

He stepped back then and murmured, "Sorry . . ." But he really wasn't. He'd enjoyed that moment—too much. Maybe he needed to start dating again. Not that dating had ever led to anything serious for him. He tended to hold back so much, to not share anything too personal, as she seemed to do, at least on her blog. Hell, he'd already told her more tonight than he'd told other women he'd dated for weeks.

"Detective," she said again. And he glanced up to find her standing outside another door—one across that wide hall from hers. She hesitated with her hand clasped tightly around the knob.

This was it. The scene of the crime—where the blood and broken glass had been found. Where the note had been left on the pillow . . .

Leave a million dollars at the memorial bench in the park . . . or you will bury your daughters.

Neither of them had been buried, but only one had been returned. Where was the other one?

Not in that room.

But still he found himself at the door, his hand sliding over hers as he turned the knob. As he opened the door . . .

To a time capsule to the past. Nothing in it had been boxed up. Everything had been left as it had been . . . the pictures on the wall. Not of Anna Beth, except for the ones in which she'd been with Erin. Most of the pictures were of a little, red-haired girl. There were also posters of kittens and dogs taped to the pink paint. Pink curtains covered the windows, matching the blankets on the bed. The ones from that night were in the evidence box, so someone must have put clean ones on the bed, as if they'd expected Anna Beth to return.

"Was it always like this?" he asked.

Erin shrugged. "I don't know. I haven't been in here since that night." Then she shuddered.

And he found himself stepping forward, reaching for her.

She ducked under his arm, though, and stepped back

into the hall. And she drew in deep breaths now, as if trying to calm herself.

"Are you okay?" he asked. "Did you remember something?"

She shook her head. "No. This isn't going to work. You're not going to jog my memory," she warned him. "Too many other people have tried. That detective from years ago. The doctor at the hospital. The shrinks my parents sent me to. Even the counselor at St. Cecilia's, and if anyone would have been able to get me to remember, it would have been Sister Rosa."

"Erin . . ."

She shook her head. "It's been a long day," she said. "I buried my father today. Surely you can understand how exhausted I am."

Dark circles rimmed her pale eyes and her shoulders slumped. He was tempted to reach for her again, to comfort her, but clearly she didn't want that from him. Had anyone ever offered her comfort?

Instead of taking care of and treasuring her, her family had shipped off Erin to another country. To protect her or to protect themselves?

"I'm sorry," he said. And he wasn't just talking about her recent loss but all the losses she'd suffered.

"Please," she implored him. "Just leave me be . . ."

He would. For tonight . . .

She was exhausted, too exhausted for any more questions. But he had more. And he intended to ask them before she left again.

Wondering how much time he had, he asked one question. "How long are you staying?"

She shrugged. "I don't know . . . now that my father left me with . . ."

A big mess. Others might have appreciated his bequest, but Rafe could tell that it only created more problems for Erin with her family than she'd clearly already had.

She sighed. "I don't know."

That seemed to be her standard answer for everything. But he wondered if it was the truth, or if Erin knew far more than she was willing to admit. . . .

CHAPTER FOUR

Twenty-four years ago . . .

Erin wanted so badly to remember what had happened that night, so badly that she'd brought herself to Sister Rosa. Again . . .

The nun stared at her across her desk, her dark eyes soft with kindness and understanding. Her coppery skin was smooth and pretty. She didn't look much older than Anna Beth had been, but she was already some kind of doctor.

She talked to the other girls. Helped them with their problems.

She'd talked to Erin before, too, but she hadn't helped. No one had. "Why can't I remember?" she asked her, her voice cracking with her frustration.

Sister Rosa offered her one of her quick smiles, but this one had a tinge of sadness to it. Of pity. "Maybe you can't remember because there is nothing to remember."

"What do you mean?"

"You had a serious concussion, Erin. Someone hit you hard with something. It's possible you were unconscious the entire time you were missing. It's possible you don't remember anything because you weren't awake or aware enough to remember anything."

Was that true? Erin had wondered then. Would she never be able to remember anything because there was nothing to remember—at least nothing in *her* mind?

Now . . .

Erin wondered the same thing now, as she had all those years ago in Sister Rosa's office. That meeting had been before the sightings of Anna Beth. And Erin had been desperate to remember what had happened to her sister.

After those sightings, she really hadn't wanted to remember. She hadn't wanted it to be true that Anna Beth had staged the kidnapping, had taken the money and run away. Because that meant that Anna Beth was the one who'd hurt her . . .

And not just that night but every day—every moment— that she'd stayed away. Why?

Despite pleading for the detective to leave the night before because she was exhausted, Erin hadn't been able to sleep. Mrs. Markham had prepared the guest room for her with fresh bedding and some of the flowers from the funeral, but it hadn't been comfortable to Erin. Nothing was.

This wasn't home for her. She'd felt more at ease in some of the third-world countries she'd visited, where she'd slept on dirt floors with snakes and rats scurrying around her. Maybe that was the problem here, too, that everyone felt like a snake or rat that might attack her at any moment. But the detective . . .

Erin wasn't sure what he was, except distracting. She'd

thought of him entirely too much while she'd lain awake the night before. He seemed to honestly just want to solve an old mystery. And maybe his curiosity had piqued hers because she found herself standing in Anna Beth's room the next morning. Sunshine poured through the sheer curtains, casting a pink glow on the hardwood floor. The fuzzy pink rug was gone now, and beneath where it had been, the wood was darker than the rest of the floor. One area was particularly dark, as if it had been stained. But even in the darkness, there were tiny dots of glittery light, like sparkling diamonds. She leaned down and studied those spots closer and realized the dots were actually pieces of crystal.

Of the lamp . . .

That must have been what had hit her that night—what had brought about the flash of so much pain before darkness had claimed her, had pulled her under the surface of consciousness. Had she spent all those hours unconscious until she'd awakened so much later in the maze?

Where had Anna Beth been?

"Don't hurt—"

That had been her voice, the one who'd uttered those words. Anna Beth had been there. Where was she now?

Had that been her outside the cemetery, or just someone pretending to be her? Reporters always speculated that both scenarios were possible. That Anna Beth had staged the kidnapping and that someone had hired a girl who looked like her to make people believe she was alive.

Some reporters had speculated that her father had hired the girl. But he was dead now. He couldn't have hired her to show up at his funeral. And no, he wouldn't have hired her at all. He'd missed Anna Beth as much as

Erin had. She saw it now in the room he'd left as a shrine to his missing daughter. To his dead daughter?

Erin shivered and hurried out of the room. She'd already spent too much time in it, in the house. In Lake George. Daddy was buried, and no matter what his bequest was, he couldn't get Erin to stay. Neither could Detective Rafe Montego.

Though he tempted her . . . with those dark eyes of his and his deep voice and . . .

The intercom buzzed, and her pulse quickened. Was that him? Had he come back to continue with his questions, questions she couldn't answer?

She rushed over and pushed the button. "Hello?"

"Erin?" a deep voice asked. But it wasn't the detective.

"Who is this?" she asked, wondering if a reporter had showed up at the gate. There had been a couple the night before, but Ethan had handled them, had threatened them with trespassing charges and restraining orders and civil lawsuits. They'd left quickly then.

"It's Michael," the man replied. "Michael Andover."

"Oh . . ." She should have been excited, would have been excited if she'd still had her crush on him. While he'd aged well and was still as good-looking as she remembered, she had changed. Now she found herself drawn more to tall, dark, and brooding than to Michael's golden good looks. She doubted he was here for anything more than a neighborly visit.

"I'm sorry to bother you," he continued. "But I wanted to check on you, make sure you have everything you need."

"That's considerate," she said. Especially because she

hadn't seen him since she was a child. She quickly pressed the button to open the gate. "Please, come up to the house."

Mrs. Markham had yet to arrive, so she'd prefer company to being alone—as long as the company didn't hate her as her family did. She expected they would be back sometime today, trying to convince her or coerce her into giving up the estate. She met Michael at the door and found that he wasn't alone. Mrs. Markham had arrived with him.

"I'm sorry I'm late, miss," she said.

"You're retired," Erin reminded her. "You don't need to keep coming back."

"I'll be here as long as you are," the older woman told her. "Now, I'll get some coffee going for you both." She slipped down the hall then, toward the kitchen.

"How long are you staying?" Michael asked.

She sighed. "I don't know." She had no idea how much of a mess her father had made of her life. She'd have to talk to O'Neill—to see if he could easily undo what Daddy had done. "How about you?" she asked. "Do you still live in Lake George?"

He chuckled. "Oh no. Like you, I prefer to travel. But Father has been having some health issues, so I've had to come back to take care of him."

A twinge of guilt squeezed her heart. Would her father be alive yet if she'd done the same? If she'd come back to make sure he'd taken care of himself? If he'd stopped smoking and drinking so much and started eating healthier? Tears filled her eyes, but she blinked them away. "That is very sweet of you."

Why hadn't she been as good a daughter to her father

as Michael was a son to his? Had she let Mother and all those articles get to her? Made her suspect her father?

"Don't give me too much credit," Michael said with a self-deprecating smile. "I have help. There's a nurse who comes in regularly."

"So it's serious," she said. "I'm sorry."

He reached out and squeezed her hand. "You're the sweet one. I came here to offer you my condolences. I wasn't sure I got the chance yesterday in all the excitement. *Was* that Anna Beth who showed up outside the funeral home?"

She shook her head. "I don't know." The only thing she knew for certain was that she said that entirely too often. Maybe it was past time she got the answers the detective sought.

"You haven't seen her yourself over the years?" he asked. "She hasn't reached out to you?"

She shook her head again, and fought hard to ignore the ache in her heart. "I haven't seen her."

"But all those pictures over the years . . . surely she's alive?"

"The girl doesn't know," Mrs. Markham answered for her as she carried in a tray with a silver carafe and two cups on it. "You sound like that detective, Mr. Andover, with all the questions."

Michael's face flushed. "I'm sorry; that was rude of me." Something about his tone suggested he considered Mrs. Markham just as rude if not ruder for rebuking him.

Erin, on the other hand, appreciated her interference and smiled at her.

Despite being rebuked, Michael resumed his questions.

"What detective? Surely nobody's investigating a runaway after all these years?"

"It was a kidnapping," Mrs. Markham corrected him. "And I'm surprised Detective Montego hasn't talked to you. He's talked to everyone who was here that night."

Michael shook his head. "I haven't had the pleasure."

Surprisingly, Erin had found some pleasure in talking to the detective despite all his questions. For the first time in years she'd felt as if she'd connected with someone, someone other than the girls she'd met all those years ago at St. Cecilia's. Rayne had sent her a text that morning, letting her know she was in her thoughts.

Rafe Montego was the one who had filled most of Erin's thoughts last night.

"I should go out and get more provisions, Miss Mac-Donald," the housekeeper said. "Do you know how long you'll be staying?"

"Not much longer," Erin said. At least she didn't think so.

"Your father has just been buried. You'll have to stay at least a few days," Mrs. Markham said, and now her disapproval was all for Erin.

Erin nodded. "Yes, of course."

The older woman turned away then and headed back toward the kitchen.

"So you're not going to stay here permanently?" Michael asked. Then his blond head bobbed in a quick nod. "Of course there are probably too many bad memories for you here. You were hurt that night."

She sighed. "I don't really remember any of that, or

anything at all. Someone must have hit me with that lamp in Anna Beth's room."

"Do you think Anna Beth hit you?" he asked.

She shook her head. "No. I think she was telling somebody not to, but it was so dark. I couldn't see anything. And then it got much darker after I was hit."

"You're lucky you weren't killed," he said. "That was a heavy lamp."

She *was* lucky she had survived. Had Anna Beth?

"Miss MacDonald," the housekeeper said as she rushed back into the room. "Your mother just let herself into the gate."

Of course she had. She would know the code.

Erin grimaced. And Michael raised his blond brows. "Not someone you want to see?"

She sighed.

He raised his hand. "No need to explain. My mother and I have a difficult relationship as well, since she divorced my dad. Would you like me to stay?"

"Thank you," she said. "But I don't want to subject you to another scene like yesterday." As everyone had been subjected to at her father's funeral. She stood then and showed him out just as her mother was showing herself in.

The older woman stopped and stared at the blond man. "You look familiar . . ."

"Michael Andover," he said. "My father's home is next door."

But with the size of the estate, next door wasn't close. The property Daddy had left to Erin was bigger than the park at the entrance to the cul-de-sac, the one where the million dollars had been left so long ago.

"Of course," Sylvia Sloan said with a familiar and flirtatious smile. "Michael . . ."

"Michael was just leaving," Erin said, to rescue him from her mother's flirting and from her own embarrassment.

He took the opportunity to rush out the door and draw it closed behind himself.

Her mother sighed. "He left in a hurry. What did he want?" She flicked a glance over Erin, who wore yoga pants and a T-shirt, and with just that glance, she dismissed the thought from her mind that he might have been at all interested in Erin.

"He was being neighborly," Erin said.

Her mother shrugged. "He's not your neighbor. You're not going to stay here."

"I'm not?" Erin asked.

"You don't stay anywhere," Sylvia said.

And she wasn't wrong. The only place Erin had stayed was St. Cecilia's, and that had been just because, as a minor, she'd had no choice.

"So you might as well sign the house over to me," her mother said, as if it was that simple. "You don't want it."

"Why do you?" Erin asked, though she realized it was probably just to spite her ex-husband, to circumvent that prenup she'd fought so hard. "Why would you want the house where something so horrible happened?"

Her mother might have furrowed her brow—if it had been possible. As it was, her face barely moved, but she expressed her confusion with a, "What are you talking about?"

"Mother—"

"Your sister disappeared," she said. "You don't know that she's dead."

"You've thought she was," Erin reminded her. "You told reporters that she was. Especially when you were going through the divorce with Dad, you made it sound like you suspected him or his kids of killing *your* beautiful daughter." As if Anna Beth had belonged only to her.

As if Daddy hadn't been suffering just as much. No. Daddy had suffered more because he'd actually loved Anna Beth.

Sylvia hadn't. While she described Anna Beth as her beautiful daughter to differentiate her from Erin, Sylvia hadn't been able to handle Anna Beth being more beautiful than she was. Had she been like the wicked queen in *Snow White*? Had the mirror turned her into a killer?

Lake George was not a high crime area. While there were some break-ins and domestic disputes, there were very few murders. And usually those were the results of domestic disputes. Maybe that was why Rafe was so fixated on the old kidnapping—because it was the most interesting thing to ever happen in Lake George.

His fixation hadn't gone unnoticed, though. When he ducked under the crime scene tape and stepped through the motel doorway, the shift sergeant remarked, "Hate to pull you away from your old case to something you actually should be working on . . ."

"What should I actually be working on?" Rafe asked

as he glanced around the room. Some needles and a white substance were strewn across the coffee table. This motel was the most rundown one in town. Actually, it wasn't even in town, just barely on the boundaries of their jurisdiction. Its clientele had earned it a bad reputation. He stepped closer to where a woman lay, facedown on the unmade bed, her scraggly brown hair covering her face. "Looks like an overdose."

The sergeant snorted. "And you're the detective?"

Rafe had gotten the promotion over the sergeant, and the older man hadn't forgiven him for it. Just as Erin's family would probably never forgive her for inheriting her father's estate even though she'd had nothing to do with his bequest.

Or had she? Was her family right that she might have manipulated her father or blackmailed him into leaving her everything? They certainly would know her better than he did. Or would they . . .

She'd been so young when she'd been shipped off to boarding school. She couldn't be particularly close to any of them. Whereas Rafe had felt very close to her last night, so close that he'd shared details about his personal life with her.

Now he wasn't just fixating on that cold case but on Erin. He shook his head to clear it of thoughts of her and focused on the *crime* scene again. Was it really a crime?

"Have the techs processed the scene yet?" he asked. "Taken photos?" Just in case the sergeant was right . . .

The older man's bald head bobbed in a nod. "Of course. I know how to work a crime scene."

Rafe wasn't as convinced. The man had been known to look the other way for other crimes, like some of the rich residents driving while inebriated or their kids vandalizing school property.

Sergeant Meyer had done those favors, so he could advance in the department, as others had in the past. But with the recent reforms in law enforcement, there was more accountability now. Officers were expected to be fair and impartial and unbiased. Rafe sighed. He wasn't exactly being unbiased himself right now. He was making assumptions about the victim because of where she was.

So he pulled on some gloves and reached for her. When he moved the hair away from her face, he saw the bruises: not just on her cheek but on her neck as well. She hadn't overdosed. She'd been strangled.

"This is a real murder, Montego," the sergeant said. "It's a real case. Not like the one you're obsessed with. You're chasing some little rich girl that ran off with her boyfriend."

"That case isn't a simple runaway situation," Rafe insisted. "A seven-year-old was nearly killed." And he wasn't sure whether the fourteen-year-old hadn't been.

But, as Meyer had pointed out, that case was cold. This one was fresh, so Rafe focused on the scene now. The woman was probably his age, maybe a little older. And she was tall and almost painfully thin. From the tracks on her arms, she was obviously an addict.

Had her dealer killed her? Maybe she hadn't been able to pay him.

But Rafe knelt next to the bed and peered beneath it. "You said the techs processed the scene?" he asked.

The sergeant snorted. "Yeah, why?"

Rafe held up the money band he'd found beneath the bed. There had once been a lot of money in this room.

The killer must have taken it with him. So the woman hadn't been killed because she hadn't been able to pay.

Rafe lowered himself to the nearly threadbare carpet, looking for what else might have been missed. And he found a contact—one that was tinged a very pale blue with a dark rim around it.

It must have been specifically made. He eased back onto his knees and inspected the body again. And on the back of the woman's sweater he noticed the long, pale blond hair.

A gasp slipped through his lips.

"What?" Meyer asked. "What is all this stuff?"

"Stuff your techs missed," Rafe remarked. "A contact, blond hair, money band . . ."

The sergeant shrugged. "What does it mean?"

"That you're right," Rafe said. "This is a murder." But it hadn't drawn Rafe away from the cold case at all. In fact, it made the cold case very, very hot again.

Because if Rafe was right, this was the woman who'd impersonated Anna Beth at the funeral home. The one he'd caught just that glimpse of as she'd run across the cemetery.

Whoever had killed her must have been the person who'd hired her. So that person was cleaning up loose ends now. Did the killer think Erin remembered more than she said she did?

Would she be the next loose end he or she wanted to clean up?

CHAPTER FIVE

Twenty-five years ago . . .

Tears streamed down Erin's face, and a little moan of fear and pain slipped between her lips.

"Shh, it's all right," Anna Beth assured her. "You're going to be okay. . . ."

Her arms wrapped tightly around Erin's body, holding her close. Anna Beth was taller than her, so tall, but she was thin. And even though she tried, she wasn't that strong.

She wouldn't be able to save them.

Could anyone save them?

Now . . .

Erin jerked awake and found herself on the couch in her father's den. She'd intended to look over all the papers the lawyer had left for her, the will, the stock holdings, the business documents, as well as the papers she'd found in her father's desk, the reports from all the private investigators he'd hired to find Anna Beth. She'd read those quickly enough; there hadn't been much to read. Once she'd started on Ethan O'Neill's papers she must have dozed off. But even in her sleep, she'd dreamed of Anna Beth.

Or had that been a memory resurfacing?

Had Anna Beth comforted her in the dark on that night? Had Erin actually remembered something between being hit and awakening in the maze? Or was that memory from one of the many other nights Erin had sought out her older sister for comfort, for Anna Beth to soothe her fear of the monsters that lurked in the shadows?

There were shadows in Daddy's den now. Shadows the banker's lamp on his desk wasn't quite able to dispel. But Erin wasn't as afraid of the dark as she used to be. Once she had had no one to comfort her over her fears, she'd had to force herself to deal with them. To deal with the darkness and with being alone.

She drew in a deep breath now to push down the surge of anxiety that darkness always compelled to rise inside her. And she breathed in that sweet lingering scent of Daddy's cigars, of Daddy.

It was like he was still here. And in some ways it was like Anna Beth was as well. Like she whispered in the dark to Erin like she used to . . .

After Anna Beth hadn't returned with her that night, Erin hadn't wanted to be here anymore. Leaving for St. Cecilia's had been as much a relief for her as it had probably been for her parents. She'd suspected then that they'd wished Anna Beth had come back instead of her.

And so Erin hadn't come back . . . until now.

And now she wondered . . .

Had Anna Beth ever really left? Because it was almost

as if Erin could feel *her* presence here. She jumped up from the couch, the leather squeaking beneath her, and as she moved across the hardwood floor to the doors, the wood squeaked as well. The house was old, but like that night of the party, it felt alive to her. More than just a house . . .

It was a legacy. Her legacy now. Should she keep it? Should she stay here?

"Hello?" she called out.

Mrs. Markham hadn't managed to go shopping today, not with Michael's visit and then Erin's mother's, so she'd left early. Enough food from the caterer's remained in the fridge that Erin wasn't going to go hungry. And for some reason, even with the housekeeper gone, she didn't feel alone.

"Anna Beth?" she called out. "Anna Beth?"

Had she been at the funeral? Had that been her in person or . . .

She smiled at her fanciful thought. Some of the girls at St. Cecilia's had believed the old convent was haunted, but the only ghosts Erin had ever seen there had been her own. The ones she'd brought with her from her childhood. Those nightmares.

Like awaking alone in the garden.

She walked through the kitchen to the French doors that opened onto the stone patio that stretched along the entire length of the back of the mammoth house. The stones were cold beneath her bare feet. She must have kicked off her shoes in her father's den. But she didn't turn back. Instead, she kept walking toward that maze.

It was different now—so much taller and denser than it had been back then. But when she'd been seven, it had looked like this to her, so maybe nothing had changed. But her . . .

She wasn't as afraid as she'd once been. She stepped willingly into the maze now. Anna Beth had told her so many times how to navigate it, which turns to make, which ones to avoid.

Had they ever made it all the way to the other end, though? Or had they always turned back because Erin had been too scared to go on?

Because of the dark . . .

It was dark now, but for the glow of the moon over-head. It was a full one and bright in the sky, but even its light couldn't dispel all the shadows in the maze. And even though there was no wind, some of the branches of those thick shrubs rustled around her.

Animals?

Birds?

She had no idea what shared the space with her . . . beyond her memories. And in her mind she recalled all the turns Anna Beth had told her to take, all the ones she'd told her to avoid.

And she found herself deeper and deeper in the maze and farther and farther from the house.

When she tipped her head and looked up, she couldn't see the moon yet, only pieces of it through the trees that hung over the shrubs. She'd wandered so far out that she'd found where the forest had crept over the maze. And finally . . .

She found the other end of the maze . . . in those woods. Was this where she'd come from that night? Where she'd been that entire day she and Anna Beth had been missing?

"Anna Beth?" she called out. "Anna Beth?"

Was she out here yet? All these years . . .

She shivered. The cold had moved up from her bare feet until it gripped her everywhere—even deep inside. She needed to go back to the house. Needed to get out of here.

But for some reason she couldn't turn back.

She kept peering out of the maze into those woods. The trees were nearly as thick as the tall shrubs of the maze, the branches low to the ground. Vines wound around some of them. And from within the vines, something glinted—reflecting back what little moonlight penetrated the thickness of the woods.

Glass. There was something inside those vines . . . beneath those trees. She stepped out of the maze, off the soft grass and on to the sharp branches on the forest floor. She gasped as they poked and scratched the soles of her feet. She needed to turn back, she thought again.

She knew . . .

But she kept walking toward that glinting piece of glass.

There was more. A full window of it, the rotted panes barely holding in the pieces. And next to the window was a door, a padlock hung open from the handle.

It was old and rusted, like the metal roof of the shed that was nearly covered by the vines and branches. If not for the vines holding it together, the shed probably would have collapsed long before now. She reached for the door, and it creaked open . . . just a bit before the vines caught it, holding it closed . . . as if trying to keep her out.

She should stay out.

She knew that.

But she couldn't help but wonder . . .

Was this where they'd been that night?

Was that why she'd awakened in the maze . . . because her journey had begun at the end of it? At this shed?

Hoping to find a clue, she tugged harder at the door. It opened farther, the crack wide enough that she was able to squeeze inside it. But once she was inside, it snapped closed behind her. Had the vines done that?

Had they pulled it shut? Had they wrapped tightly around the shed to keep her inside?

She shivered again. She'd opened it once. She could open it again. But when she pressed her shoulder against it, it didn't budge. She pressed harder and harder against the wood. Then she hammered at it with her fists. But the door held, and against that handle the padlock rattled.

Had someone snapped it shut? Deliberately locking her inside? She moved toward the window then, checking to see . . . and through its dirty glass she glimpsed a shadow moving toward the maze. Someone had been in it with her, stalking her through it or leading her toward this place?

Her vision began to blur through that window . . . or so it seemed until she coughed and realized that it was smoke rising outside and in . . .

Whoever had locked her inside had also set the shed on fire.

The gates were open when Rafe drove up. He doubted Erin would have knowingly left them open; she wouldn't have wanted her family or the reporters to have easy access to her. She wouldn't have wanted Rafe to just drive through them either, like he was now, even though she had let him in the night before. She had answered what she'd been able of the questions he'd had for her. He wasn't here with more questions. He was here to make sure she was all right. His heart pounded fast and hard, with a sense of fear and dread.

He had a feeling she wasn't. That something had happened.

The rental vehicle was parked yet in the drive. She hadn't left. She was here.

He parked behind it, threw open his door, and ran up the stone steps to the front entry doors. His finger shook as he pressed the bell. The chimes echoed throughout the interior, but nobody came. Could she have been sleeping?

With the gates open? He doubted that.

He fisted his hand and pounded on the wood, and as he pounded, the door opened beneath his fist. It hadn't been locked either.

"Erin!" he yelled. And now he ran through the house, checking the rooms. Only one light burned in what must have been her father's den. It still smelled of cigars. A sheaf of papers lay on the floor next to a pair of shoes.

She'd been here, reading.

What had compelled her to leave? Had she gone upstairs? Was she in one of those many rooms off the wide hallway? No. She would have shut off the light. Maybe she'd just gone into the kitchen for something . . .

He headed back into that room, which was dark but for the moonlight streaming through the French doors. One of the doors creaked and opened, as if someone had pushed on it, or at least not shut it tightly.

He walked out then, onto the patio. "Erin!"

Was she out here? As she'd been that night so long ago? Was she in the maze?

He started across the lawn toward the high wall of shrubbery, and as he walked, a gust of wind kicked up, sweeping across the yard . . . carrying with it the smell of smoke. This wasn't the sweet smoke of cigars but something lighter, like fresh wood burning.

"Erin!"

Had she started a fire somewhere? Or had someone else?

"Erin!" he yelled again.

And finally he heard a reply: a scream of terror.

His instincts had been right. She was in danger. But was he going to be able to find her in time to save her?

CHAPTER SIX

Twenty-five years ago . . .

Erin's head pounded so hard that it felt as if it was going to shatter. As if she was going to fall into pieces. "Anna Beth . . ." she murmured. "Anna Beth . . ."

Where was she?

Why wasn't she holding her now?

Erin had to find her. So she forced herself to open one eye. But it was like it was still closed . . . because everything was so dark. Where was she?

This wasn't Anna Beth's room, wasn't her bed . . .

Erin was cold. And the floor beneath her was hard. She shifted a bit and a sliver of wood caught her nightgown, ripped into her skin. She tried to sit up, but her head hurt so much, was so heavy, that she fell back against the hardwood again.

And everything went black . . . just as it had in Anna Beth's bed . . .

Now . . .

Erin's lungs burned, struggling to draw in air through the smoke. All the smoke. Her eyes stung and teared up. She blinked to clear them and noticed a shadow looming over her before it pulled back. Then the moonlight bathed her, and she stared up at the night sky. Smoke drifted in front of the moon, hovered over the top of her, over the top of the walls of shrubs. She was in the maze again.

She coughed and sputtered, her lungs aching even as they drew in more oxygen.

"Are you all right?" a deep voice asked.

She turned her head and saw him kneeling beside her. The detective . . .

Rafe Montego . . .

"How . . . how did you find me?" she asked, her voice hoarse, her throat scratchy and raw.

"The smoke," he said. "Thank God the trees and vines were too green to burn and there was no gasoline, or you would have . . ." His voice cracked.

Burned up . . .

She would have burned up, just as someone had nearly burned up her friend a while ago. Rayne. Someone had tried killing her like that. Had someone just tried to kill Erin?

"Why?" she murmured. "Why would someone lock me in there? Set the fire . . ." She coughed and sputtered on the fear rushing over her and the smoke still burning inside her.

"You must know something, Erin, something more than you remember . . ."

She shook her head. "No . . ." She coughed. "I—"

"Shhh," he murmured. "An ambulance is on its way. You need more oxygen. Just rest."

The ambulance was close . . . because sirens rent the air. Despite the noise, her eyes drifted closed, and she slipped back into oblivion just as she had that night in the shed so many years ago.

She was gone.

The paramedics had taken Erin to the hospital over an hour ago. Rafe had wanted to go with her, to make sure she would be all right. That she'd be safe . . .

But he'd sent along another officer to protect her while he stayed behind and protected the scene. Too much had been missed all those years ago, too little in the case files to prove there had been any sort of investigation.

He was going to make sure that didn't happen again, that more things weren't missed as they'd been missed in that motel earlier today.

The hair.

The contact.

The money band.

All clues the killer had left behind, as he must have left clues behind all those years ago. If it was the same person . . .

If he or she had been a killer all those years ago . . .

Was Anna Beth dead? He suspected she was. Or nobody would have had to impersonate her. And the story—that she'd run off with a boyfriend—didn't add up with what he'd seen in her room. The posters of kitties and puppies and all the pink had indicated that even at fourteen, she'd still been a child. She hadn't had pictures up of boy bands or celebrity crushes, like he'd had that poster of her on his wall. Her only pictures had been of her little sister. That was who she'd loved, probably too much to willingly leave her alone—because even though she'd had other family, Erin had been alone after Anna Beth disappeared.

Rafe could understand not wanting to leave Erin. She was too vulnerable, in too much danger . . .

Yet somehow she had survived that night. Just as she would survive this one.

There had been no gasoline, and the vines and tree branches were too green to burn easily. Even the wood of the shed had been too full of moss and mold to do much more than smoke and smolder.

Which was fortunate for Erin. She hadn't burned up, and there had been enough smoke to lead Rafe through the maze to her. Then he'd had to break down the door, because the padlock, although rusted and old, or maybe because it had been rusted and old, had held the door shut. Rafe watched the crime scene techs take that padlock into evidence, as well as shoe imprints from the ground around the shed. Erin had had no shoes on when he'd broken into the shed and carried her out.

Someone else—someone besides her and him—had been out here. Had locked her inside, tried to kill her . . .

Why? What did she know that she didn't remember?

What had drawn her out here?

"Is there anything inside?" Rafe asked the head tech, Linda Wilson, as she stepped out of the shed. He'd personally requested the older woman at the scene; she hadn't been at the motel or that evidence wouldn't have been missed. He hadn't wanted anything missed again.

Her expression grim, she nodded. "Yes, you need to see this. . . ."

Rafe hadn't looked around the shed earlier—not with the smoke filling it. He'd just grabbed Erin and carried her out. Now he looked at it—at the age and neglect of the place. It had been here for years. "What . . ."

Then he saw it: the hole in the floor, the tattered edges of an old rug sticking out of it, the stringy hair spilling over the top of that rug and from the skull of the skeleton. And he knew why someone had had to impersonate Anna Beth, because she had been here this entire time. On the edges of her family's estate . . .

She'd never been in all those places she'd been photographed. She'd never left the grounds. She'd died the night she and Erin had been taken. That was why only Erin had returned—because only Erin had survived.

Just as she had survived again tonight. But would she survive the next attempt? Because Rafe had no doubt that there would be another attempt.

CHAPTER SEVEN

Twenty years ago . . .

"Could it be her?" Rayne asked, her misty, gray eyes narrowed as she stared down at the magazine Beatrix had tossed into Erin's room just a short while ago.

Erin had barely glanced at the photo herself. She just shrugged now.

"Don't you want to know?" Rayne asked.

Erin had given up on trying to remember what had happened that night. Maybe it *was* as Sister Rosa had said; maybe there was nothing to remember.

"But if it's her, why wouldn't she come back?" Beatrix asked from the doorway. Of course she would have waited around to see how Erin would react to the pictures, to the latest sighting of her missing sister.

Erin was always very careful not to react. She'd given up hope long ago that she would ever see Anna Beth again. She wasn't even sure why, though . . . because what if everyone was right? What if she'd had a boyfriend? What if they'd run off together?

But there had never been a boy. Whenever anyone had

paid her that kind of attention, Anna Beth had gotten creeped out. She hadn't been interested.

"She could get in trouble if she came back," Rayne suggested. "She could go to jail for kidnapping and . . ."

Assault . . . because Erin had been hurt. But Anna Beth would never have hurt her. She'd been the only one who'd ever really cared about her. Who'd protected her . . .

Erin looked at that photograph and shook her head. That girl wasn't Anna Beth. Sure, she looked like her, but she . . . she just wasn't . . .

Erin wasn't sure how she knew, but she did.

Now . . .

The last time Erin had nearly died at home she hadn't wanted to stay there, and after being at St. Cecilia's, she hadn't wanted to ever return to it. But this time . . .

This time she'd checked herself out of the hospital against doctors' orders. They'd wanted her to stay for observation. But after the X-rays and the oxygen treatments, Erin had felt well enough to return. It was late, though— so late that all the other police vehicles were gone when the officer drove her back to the estate.

Even he was surprised. "They processed the scene quickly," he remarked.

"With the fire, there probably wasn't much left to process," she replied. She didn't remember the flames or the heat, though—just the smoke. It clung still to her hair, to her skin, and her clothes.

She couldn't wait to get inside, couldn't wait to shower off that stench—to cleanse her body and her mind of the horrors of being trapped in that shed.

"The fire didn't do much damage," the young man said, as if reassuring her.

As if Erin cared about some old shed that had been so neglected that nobody had even known it was there. Or had they? Had someone known?

"They were able to recover the body," the officer continued. "Even the rug it was wrapped in . . ."

Erin gasped. That fuzzy pink rug . . . that had matched the blankets on Anna Beth's bed, the curtains at her windows . . .

That was why it was gone. It hadn't been taken for evidence. Yet . . .

But now it was part of the evidence that had been found in the shed . . . along with her sister's body.

"Oh my God," the officer said. "You don't know—of course, you don't know. I just thought that maybe you found it, maybe you found her while you were locked inside the shed."

Had she found her? Like the night of the abduction, she couldn't remember much about being in the shed. Just pounding and kicking at the door, and the smoke and the window and the shadow moving into the maze . . .

She shuddered. She could have died there. *Would have* died there if not for Rafe Montego rescuing her. He'd gotten her out of the shed, and then he'd given her CPR. The doctor had told her that, had told her that she wouldn't have survived if the detective hadn't acted so quickly.

There had been no one to rescue Anna Beth that night.

"Her . . ." That was what the officer had said. The body had been female. Maybe he knew; maybe he was just guessing.

It was a fair guess. Only one other person had disappeared all those years ago, and Erin had showed back up. Unlike her sister . . .

Anna Beth. It had to have been Anna Beth. All these years she'd been here. Unlike Erin, she'd never left.

"I'm sorry," the officer said again, his voice shaky with remorse and nerves. "The detective is going to kill me for upsetting you. He told me to make sure that nothing happened to you."

"I'm fine," Erin assured him. "I just want to go inside and rest."

But another car bore down on them, the headlights blinding them so that Erin had to squint.

"It's probably Montego now," the officer said as he squinted against the light. He stepped out of the vehicle and touched the switch on his door that unlocked her side, too.

Erin could open her door now, and she pushed hard at it, anxious to get out of the police car. She was even more anxious to see Rafe, to thank him for saving her life and for finding the body. Finally she knew for certain that Anna Beth hadn't left her.

She'd left Anna Beth.

She'd been the only one to make it out of that shed. That night so long ago, and again tonight.

But it wasn't Rafe Montego's long, lean body that stepped out of the vehicle parked behind the patrol car. It was her mother's.

Sylvia Sloan rushed toward her, but she stopped in front of her, stopped before she threw her arms around Erin. Not that that was probably what she'd intended to do . . .

Erin couldn't remember her mother ever hugging her, as Anna Beth had.

"You're alive," Sylvia exclaimed. "I heard in town that the police were out here. That a body was found . . ." She shuddered now, as Erin had moments ago.

"Were you really worried that it was me?" Erin asked. "Or did you know that it was Anna Beth?"

"They know it's Anna Beth?" Sylvia glanced at the officer.

"I—I don't know if the body's been identified yet," he admitted.

"But who else could it be?" she murmured before turning back and asking Erin, "Are you okay?"

"I'm fine," she said. Or she would be, once she showered off the smoke and processed what the officer had revealed to her, what apparently everyone but she had already heard.

A body had been found. Anna Beth had been found. As her mother had stated, who else could it be?

"I can help you into the house, Miss MacDonald," he offered. Apparently he'd noticed how exhausted she was. Or the doctor had shared with him that he'd wanted her to stay.

"I will help her," Sylvia insisted. "You can leave now. I'm here. I'll stay with my daughter."

"Detective Montego assigned me to protect Miss MacDonald."

She shook her head. "She doesn't need protection from me," she assured him. "And I'll make sure nothing will happen to her. Montego has no authority here. You need to leave."

I'll make sure nothing will happen to you . . .

That was what Anna Beth used to say to her, when Erin had slipped into her bed, crying over a nightmare, over the dark . . . over the monsters . . .

Her mother had never said that to Erin, had never comforted her. What had changed? Had she?

Erin doubted it. But she was too tired to fight. So she let her mother chase off the officer; she even let her follow her inside the house. But then she stopped in the foyer and turned toward her. "What are you really doing here?"

"I was worried about you," her mother replied.

"I'm fine. You can go."

Sylvia shook her long mane of brittle blond hair. "No. I'll stay. I know you don't like to be alone."

"Didn't," Erin said. "I got over that a long time ago. Twenty-five years ago—when Anna Beth disappeared." Then, because she couldn't be with Anna Beth, she'd preferred to be alone.

"Your sister has been gone a long time," Sylvia said.

Was that why Mother wasn't upset? Why she wasn't surprised that body had been found? Had she known she was dead all this time?

"Your father is gone now, too," Sylvia continued. "And you've never had a relationship with your older siblings. I'm all you've got."

Erin suspected more that that was the other way around now. Her mother had remarried a couple of times after the divorce, but those marriages hadn't lasted even as long as her marriage to Gregor MacDonald had. And there had been no reasons for her subsequent divorces like the reasons she and Daddy had had to divorce, no kidnapping, no great tragedy . . .

Just her mother's inability to feel deeply for anyone but herself. She was a shallow, selfish woman. Anna Beth had been more of a mother to Erin than Sylvia Sloan ever had.

"I'm not alone," Erin said. She should have thought first of her friends, but the person who popped into her mind was Detective Rafe Montego. He was the one who'd saved her life. The one who'd breathed life back into her. He was the one she wanted to see now—not her mother.

She wanted to thank him for saving her life. And she wanted to thank him for finding Anna Beth. Finally she knew for certain that her sister was gone—really gone.

Rafe should have gone home, should have showered off the stench of the smoke. But there was nothing waiting for him in his empty apartment. Not that there was anything waiting for him at the estate either. He had no idea if Erin wanted to see him, but he wanted to see her—to make sure she was really all right. That she was safe.

So he called the young officer he'd assigned to protect her. "I just dropped her at the estate," Darren said.

"Dropped her? You were supposed to stay." He'd wanted more officers stationed there, to protect the scene, to protect Erin, but the chief had denied the expenditure. He'd said that the MacDonalds had a high-tech security system and enough money to hire their own bodyguards. They didn't need to use up police resources.

But that high-tech security hadn't been on earlier, when Rafe had found the gates open and Erin trapped in the smoldering shed.

"She's not alone," Darren said. "Her mother's there, and she wanted me to leave."

"She doesn't own the estate. Erin does." She owned everything now. Was that why someone had tried to kill her? Had it had more to do with her inheritance than with the past?

Who would inherit everything if Erin died? Her mother? Her siblings?

Not Anna Beth . . .

That had to be Anna Beth's body. The coroner had only done a preliminary examination at the scene, confirming that the skeleton belonged to a young female who'd been dead a long time.

Twenty-five years?

"Miss MacDonald didn't want me to stay either," the officer admitted. "I—I screwed up. I told her about the body."

Rafe groaned. He'd wanted to be the one to tell her, to comfort her . . . to hold her like he'd held her when he'd carried her out of the shed. He wanted to protect her. So it was no surprise that he found himself driving, not toward his apartment and his shower, but toward the MacDonald estate. He passed the park where the money had been dropped so long ago and followed the winding drive to the gates. They were closed now.

He lowered the driver's window and leaned out, pressing hard on the intercom button. "Erin? Erin?" he called out as anxiously as he had earlier, when he'd walked through the house and into the garden—when he'd just known something had happened to her.

That she was in danger.

They had a connection he hadn't expected because he'd

never experienced it before. Maybe after losing his dad and then his mother, he hadn't let himself get close enough to anyone else to have a connection. He hadn't wanted to lose them, too.

But he had lost so many other people. Men and women with whom he'd served . . .

He didn't want to lose Erin. "Erin!"

The speaker rattled, but he couldn't hear what she said—if she said anything—over the noise of the motor that opened the gates. They shuddered and rattled, too, as they drew back into the estate. And Rafe pressed on the gas, speeding toward the house. Toward Erin.

He'd almost been too late earlier that night. He should have gone with her instead of sending Darren. Her mother wasn't going to dismiss him. It looked as though she'd been dismissed because when he drove up, he found her walking toward her vehicle. It was empty. No driver waited for her this time, but at least she walked steadily toward it. She wasn't staggering. And when he stepped out of his vehicle and approached her, he didn't smell alcohol.

He couldn't smell anything but smoke. It burned yet in his nostrils.

"So you're the reason she was desperate to get rid of me," the older woman said, her pale eyes cold.

How could her eyes look so much like Erin's in color but in expression be nothing alike? Where her mother was cold and brittle, Erin was warm and sensitive. Too sensitive to have been raised by a woman like this.

Rafe narrowed his eyes. "I don't think she needs a reason to get rid of you, not after how quickly you got rid of her twenty-five years ago. How easily you shipped her off to Austria."

The woman glared at him now, her thin lips twisting into a sneer. "You have no idea what you're talking about. Nobody does. We sent Erin away to keep her safe."

That might have been the reason her father had enrolled her in the boarding school. He must have cared about Erin; he'd left everything to her. But this woman . . .

Had she cared enough about Erin to want to protect her?

How could a mother just give up her seven-year-old to someone else to raise?

"There had to be other ways to keep her safe," Rafe insisted.

She sighed. "I just know that she wasn't safe here."

"Still isn't . . ." Rafe murmured.

"I knew that if she stayed here, she would wind up like her sister."

"Most of the world presumed that Anna Beth was still alive," Rafe reminded her. "Because of all those photographs . . ."

"Most of the world didn't know my daughter. She was photogenic. She was . . . magic. . . ." She shook her head. "Those photos weren't of her."

"So you knew she was dead. But how could you be so certain?" Because she was the one who killed her? "Her body was never found. While those pictures weren't of her, she could have been out there somewhere yet."

"I knew she was dead because I knew he killed her," she said.

He tensed. "Who?"

"Her father—who else? That's why he fought me so

hard to keep this place. He probably didn't want anyone to find her body—to find out the truth. That's why there were those sightings of her, to take suspicion off him."

That had been the speculation. Even Rafe had considered that theory. "But he's dead, so who locked Erin in that shed? Who tried to kill her tonight?" Not to mention the other woman, the one who'd showed up at his funeral wearing the wig and the contacts.

And then Rafe had found the money band in the woman's motel room. Had that been from the million-dollar ransom?

Linda Wilson had vowed to find out. To trace the paper and find out how old it was and from what bank it had been issued.

Sylvia Sloan shivered and wrapped her thin arms around her thin body. "I—I thought it was an accident."

"Erin getting locked in that shed, it being set on fire?" He shook his head. "None of that was an accident. Someone tried to kill her tonight."

They'd failed, but now he wondered about Gregor MacDonald. Had Erin's father's death been what everyone claimed it was? A heart attack brought on by all his years of drinking and smoking? Or had he been murdered just as someone had tried to murder his youngest daughter?

He would need to exhume the old man's body. It might be easier to convince Erin to authorize that than a judge right now. He hadn't even been able to get extra protection for her.

"Where is she?" he asked with a glance toward the house. Why hadn't she stepped onto the porch?

Her mother studied him through narrowed eyes. "She's inside. Waiting for you . . ."

Just as Rafe had been waiting for her all these years.

Since becoming detective, he'd been waiting for her to come home, so that he could question her about the case, about the kidnapping. But now he realized he might have been waiting for her for an entirely different reason . . .

One he hadn't even known himself.

Erin MacDonald was quickly coming to mean something to him. Too much for him to lose her, but he was afraid that he would. That either the killer would get her, or the attempts on her life might chase her away.

Was she inside waiting for him? Or was she packing to leave?

CHAPTER EIGHT

Twenty years ago . . .

Why had Sister Maria called her to her office? Erin hadn't done anything bad. She wasn't like Lucy, who popped the heads off her Barbie dolls and scared the other girls with them. Lucy didn't scare her, though. Rayne wasn't scared of her either.

Maybe it was because they'd watched too many of Lucy's mother's movies, and they understood her. They understood what it was like to have a mother like hers . . .

Like theirs . . .

One who cared more about herself or men than they cared about their kids. Was Mother even trying to find Anna Beth? Or was she happy that she was gone?

Erin wasn't happy. Maybe that was why Sister Maria had called her here. Maybe she wanted her to talk to Sister Rosa again. She knocked on the door of the headmistress's office.

"Come in," Sister Maria said.

And once Erin pushed open the door, she caught the scent of cigar smoke, and she knew: Daddy was here.

Daddy was looking for Anna Beth. He'd told her that—told her that he would never stop looking. Even though Erin had.

She'd stopped looking at all those pictures Beatrix brought to her. She'd stopped looking for Anna Beth. Maybe it was better if she didn't find her. If she didn't know . . .

"Hey, there, girlie!" Daddy called out around the cigar chomped in his mouth. He didn't pick her up like he had that night in the maze. He just reached out and patted the top of her head, her curls scrunching beneath his big hand. "Ready to go home?"

"Home?" she repeated, and she glanced at Sister Maria. What were they talking about? Had she been bad? Had she gotten kicked out without knowing it?

"Yeah, honey," Daddy said. "Your mama and I finally settled things. The house is mine for sure, despite her best efforts to smear me. It's ours. You can come home now. We can be together there."

Panic pressed on her. She didn't want to be there—not without Anna Beth. She shook her head. "No, no! I can't! I won't!" And she turned and ran, not back to class but to her room. And when she was there, she slammed the door and locked it. Sister Maria had a key. She could come and get her, but Erin didn't want to leave. She could never go back home.

Now . . .

Erin could have stepped out of the foyer onto the stone steps at the front of the house, but then she'd have to see her mother again. And she'd just managed to get rid of her.

No. Detective Montego's voice emanating from the intercom speaker in the kitchen had gotten rid of Sylvia Sloan. For some reason the former supermodel didn't want to talk to this man. Which was unusual for her . . .

She liked to have the admiration of every man. Like Michael . . .

She'd flirted with him the other day. Maybe she actually was out there now, flirting with Rafe. Maybe that was what was keeping him. He'd had to make it to the house by now. He had to be here. Remembering how he'd called her name through the intercom had Erin's pulse quickening. He'd sounded concerned, like he cared. . . .

And even though he was a stranger to her, she trusted his concern more than her mother's. She didn't trust her mother at all. And over the years of her ranting about him being responsible for Anna Beth's disappearance, she'd undermined Erin's trust in her father. She stood now in his den, breathing in the scent of him, missing him.

"Oh, Daddy . . ." She should have come home with him all those years ago, when he'd come to St. Cecilia's to get her. She should have spent more than the holidays with him.

While she'd had the friends she'd made at the boarding school and in college and on her travels, her father had had no one. Sure, Ethan was always around him, but that was because he was on retainer. Had they really been friends?

Had her father ever had anyone in his life who hadn't

just wanted his money? That was all that Sylvia Sloan had wanted from him. His money and this house.

And now she wanted those things from Erin. She'd once considered signing them over to her and leaving. But not now.

She knew her mother would obliterate every trace of Daddy and Anna Beth from the house, from the grounds, and Erin couldn't let that happen. She couldn't let either of them disappear. Anna Beth had already been gone too long.

"I knew I'd find you here," a deep voice murmured.

She whirled away from her father's desk toward the doorway. And she found herself rushing forward, throwing her arms around the detective. She clung to him, shaking in reaction to everything that had happened, everything that she'd learned. "Thank you," she murmured. "Thank you for saving me tonight."

Had she thanked him in the maze? She couldn't remember. She could only remember seeing him kneeling beside her, his handsome face taut with concern for her. He cared.

His hands clutched at her back for a moment, holding her against him. His heart pounded hard against hers, in the same frantic rhythm. "You're okay?" he asked. "You don't have any damage to your lungs?"

She stepped back, just enough to peer up at his face, and she shook her head. "No. I'm fine." But her voice was still hoarse, her throat still raw, and the smoke clung yet to her hair and clothes. She needed to shower, but at the moment she felt as if she needed him more. "Thanks to you, I'm fine."

"I just knew you were in danger . . ." he murmured as he stared down at her so intently.

"How?"

"A body turned up earlier—"

"In the shed," she said. "I know."

"I'm sorry you learned about it from Officer Darren," he said. "I wanted to tell you myself."

"Thank you for finding her," she said. "For finding Anna Beth . . ."

"I didn't find her," he said. "The crime scene tech did, and I'm not sure it's Anna Beth, but . . ."

"The officer said she was wrapped in a rug. It has to be the one missing from her room. And who else would it be?"

He nodded. "I know, but we can't confirm her identity yet."

It didn't matter. Erin knew. "I never really believed any of those photographs were of her. Everybody speculated, but I just didn't feel any recognition when I looked at them. It was like looking at a stranger."

"She was a stranger," he said. "That's whose body I saw earlier in the motel. From the colored contact and synthetic blond hairs found with her, I'm pretty sure she was the woman who was impersonating Anna Beth."

She pulled back entirely now. "You found the impersonator?"

"A maid did," he said. "But I was called out to the scene. I found the hairs and a contact. It had to be a special order . . ."

"To look like Anna Beth's eyes . . ." she murmured.

He nodded. "That's when I got worried about you. She

was murdered, and it occurred to me that whoever had killed her might come after you next, might have been concerned that you'd remembered something from back then."

She shivered. "I remembered the shed," she admitted. "I remembered waking up in it."

"Was anyone with you?" he asked.

"I was alone," she said. As she'd been so often over the past twenty-five years . . . "And then I passed out again, and I don't remember how I got out of it, how I wound up in the maze . . ."

"You don't have any idea who it could have been? Who took you and Anna Beth out there?"

She shook her head. "My mother probably told you it was my father. But I know it wasn't."

"He's dead. He couldn't have murdered that woman in the motel. He couldn't have locked you in the shed, but maybe he hired someone to—"

"No," she insisted with a twinge of guilt over the doubts she had had in the past. "He wouldn't have hurt me. And he wouldn't have hurt Anna Beth."

"Do you think someone could have hurt him?" he asked. "Do you think he could have been murdered?"

She gasped. "I—I thought it was a heart attack. That's what the doctor said. He had clogged arteries."

He sighed. "Maybe that's all it was, but there wasn't an autopsy to confirm the cause of death. A doctor had been treating him for his heart issues, so he'd signed off on the death certificate."

"I want an autopsy," she said. "I want to know."

"I'll have the paperwork drawn up," he said. "We can

have his body exhumed and confirm if his death was natural causes or . . ."

"Murder," she said. "Anna Beth was murdered and that woman, and tonight someone tried to kill me."

His arms closed around her, and he pulled her back against his chest. "I won't let anyone hurt you," he vowed. "I'll keep you safe."

Anna Beth had made that promise too. And then she'd died.

Her body stiffened in his embrace, and Erin pulled back, pulled away from him. "You can't make that kind of promise," she told him. "You can't keep it."

She was right. And usually Rafe didn't make promises. He knew there was too much beyond his control, too much that he couldn't stop, too much violence, too much loss . . .

But to her, for her, he wanted to make promises. "I can try," he told her. "I can keep officers at the estate to protect you." He might have to have her lawyer make that call, though. Maybe the chief would listen to him, just as he had in the past when he'd warned Rafe to stop harassing Gregor MacDonald, that the old man was not going to talk about his daughters' kidnapping case anymore.

"Why?" she asked.

"Because you're in danger," he said. "Because someone wants you dead."

"What do you want, Detective?" she asked, and she stared up at him with those fascinating eyes of hers, watching him, waiting for his reply.

Did she see it in his face? The attraction he felt for her,

that tingled inside him, that had him gasping for breath as he had in the shed? Like she had when he'd done mouth-to-mouth on her?

He wanted to feel her lips beneath his again, but moving, kissing him back.

And he found himself leaning forward, brushing his mouth across hers. She kissed him then, kissed him with all the passion that was burning inside him, like he'd worried she was going to burn. He wanted to pick her up and carry her away—from this house, from this town . . .

To any of those beautiful places she'd visited and photographed and written about . . .

He wanted to protect her from everything. But the only thing he could really protect her from right now was himself. So he pulled back and, panting for breath, he released her. He was shaking with the desire coursing through him. He couldn't remember ever wanting anyone as much. "I'm sorry," he murmured. "I'm sorry . . ."

"Why?" she asked. "Because I'm not Anna Beth? Isn't she the reason you were so fascinated with this case?"

His brow furrowed as he stared at her in confusion. "I—I don't know what you're talking about. . . ."

"Everybody preferred my sister to me," she said. "Even me. She was so beautiful. So sweet. So selfless."

"Erin . . ."

"She was the one who should have come back," she said. "She was the one everyone wanted. I saw it on their faces, you know. Saw the regret that it wasn't her who showed up that night. That it was me."

"Erin . . ." He reached for her again, but she held up

her hands, held him back. "Is that why you've stayed away? Why you never came back?"

"I didn't think there was anything for me here anymore," she said. "Anyone who really cared. But Anna Beth was here. She was here all this time." Tears rolled down her face, forging streaks through the soot on her freckled skin.

"Erin . . ." He wanted to tell her that he cared, that she mattered to him. But they barely knew each other. And why would she trust him when she couldn't really trust anyone else? Not even her family . . .

"You can go," she told him. "I'll be okay all alone. I've been okay all these years."

"I can't leave you alone," he said. "Not with someone out there wanting to hurt you. I'm going to make sure there are police here."

She nodded. "That's fine. But you can go. I can't help you solve this case, and that's what's most important to you."

It should have been. Solving cases was his job. And now he had two murders and an attempted murder to solve. He needed to get back to work. But he couldn't leave yet, not until she had the protection he'd promised her.

A promise he shouldn't have made.

"Are you going to stay?" he asked.

Or would she leave him like everyone else had? His dad. His mom. His comrades in arms . . .

"I'm going to go upstairs and shower now," she said.

He nearly groaned at the thought of that, at his overwhelming desire to join her. But he'd already gotten too personally involved in this case, too personally involved with her.

His losing perspective wasn't going to help him find the killer. It would only help the killer get away with his crimes all over again. Rafe couldn't let that happen. Not for her sake . . .

Or for his.

Because the only way he could keep his promise to her was if he caught the killer and stopped him from trying to kill her again.

CHAPTER NINE

Twenty-five years ago . . .

Erin's lashes fluttered—up and down—and through them, she studied the prisms of light dancing across the ceiling. She loved Anna Beth's lamp, loved how the bulb was inside the crystal obelisk so that the whole thing lit up, glowed, bounced that light around the room.

It was as if it was alive.

And just that light could make her feel less alone, as she was now, as she waited for Anna Beth. The party was still going full force as her mother's parties always did, lasting so late that sometimes when she and Anna Beth woke up in the morning, the guests were still there, eating breakfast in their party clothes, shoes dangling from their fingertips, black ties hanging loose around their shirt collars.

The sounds of the party lulled her to sleep until she awoke to the darkness. The light was off. The bed was warm.

Anna Beth was talking in whispers; maybe trying not to wake her. "What are you doing here? Get out . . ."

Who was she talking to?

"Who's there?" Erin asked.

"Don't hurt—"

Then that flash of pain—that agonizing flash of pain—before all the darkness. The never-ending darkness . . . of oblivion and ignorance . . .

Now . . .

In her sleep, restless with her memories, Erin jerked, and the creak of the leather as her body shifted against the couch awakened her fully. Despite the afternoon sunshine streaming through the windows, shadows lurked yet in the corners of the dark-paneled room. She'd fallen asleep in Daddy's den again. Just being here made her feel closer to him. But now she didn't think just of him in this room; she thought of Rafe, too. Of how they'd kissed.

Of how she hadn't wanted to stop kissing him.

But he'd pulled back; he'd pulled away from her.

And it had felt like getting dumped at St. Cecilia's School for Girls all over again. But even before that moment, before that kiss, Erin had pulled away from him. He wanted to protect her, and she was pretty certain that was how the last person she'd loved had died, protecting her.

"Don't hurt—"

She hadn't heard the rest of it, but she could imagine what Anna Beth had said. *"Don't hurt her!"* But whoever had swung that heavy crystal lamp at her head had hurt her.

Badly.

But then that person had gone on and hurt Anna Beth even more. He'd killed her. Had that been his intention all along? Or had it been just about the money, and Anna Beth had died because she'd tried to protect Erin, as she always had?

As Rafe Montego had promised that he would protect her . . .

He wasn't here, though. But as he'd promised, he had an officer stationed inside the house. So Erin wasn't alone. But she was still afraid.

She was afraid she was falling for the detective and afraid that he was going to get hurt. That she was going to lose him just as she'd lost Anna Beth all those years ago. And Daddy . . .

He was gone, too. Had he died of natural causes, as she'd thought? Or was Rafe right to suspect murder?

The only one Erin could think that would want her father dead was her mother. Sylvia Sloan had hated Gregor MacDonald—even when she'd been married to him. The former model had cringed whenever he'd touched her. All she'd wanted from him was his money.

But she hadn't gotten that when she'd divorced him. Did she think she would get it now that he was dead? Had she actually believed that he would leave her anything in his will?

Or had she known he would leave it all to Erin?

Erin had yet to write up a will for herself. So who would get everything if she died? Next of kin? Her mother? Her siblings?

She needed to talk to Ethan, needed to draw up something that would protect her, and maybe it would protect Rafe, too. If she took away anyone's motive for killing her, he wouldn't be hurt trying to protect her.

And the money had to be the only motive.

She had no memories of that night, no idea to whom Anna Beth had been speaking before that heavy lamp had struck her, had knocked her out for so many hours. And sometime, during all those lost hours, that person had killed Anna Beth. Erin hadn't been able to help her sister then.

But she would do what she could to help the person she cared about now.

To help Rafe.

Rafe hadn't gotten a good look at the corpse when it had been wrapped in the blanket in the shed. He'd seen only that blond hair protruding from the skeletal remains. But now, laid out on the slab, even he could determine the cause of death. He didn't need the coroner to tell him, though the man confirmed it anyway.

"Blunt force trauma." Dr. Thiel pointed toward the shattered skull. "A heavy blow to the side of the head. But this . . ." He pointed toward the face. "This was vicious." He shuddered at the sight of all those broken bones. "Someone wanted to destroy her face."

This was more than a kidnapping gone wrong. Had it ever been about the money? Or something else?

Obsession?

Jealousy?

And where had Erin figured into it all?

Had she just been in the wrong place at the wrong time? Maybe the killer hadn't known she was going to be in her sister's bed. Maybe this had been his—or her—

intention all along: to kill the budding supermodel. People from that industry had been at the party that night.

Photographers.

Other models.

Her mother . . .

Was that the person who'd been the most jealous of Anna Beth's success?

Sylvia Sloan had once been a model herself. But in the short amount of time Anna Beth had modeled, she'd already eclipsed her mother's career. She'd already eclipsed her mother's beauty.

"Could a woman have delivered blows like that?" Rafe asked the coroner.

The coroner studied the damage and nodded. "Sure, if the weapon was heavy enough . . ."

"And this . . ." Rafe gestured toward the other victim, the one lying on a slab next to Anna Beth. He pointed toward the bruises around the mystery woman's throat. "Could a woman have done that?"

The coroner stepped over to that table, pulled out a ruler, and measured the bruises. "If she had big hands . . ."

Sylvia Sloan was a tall woman with long arms and legs. And hands?

He remembered her pointing at him. Her fingers were long as well, her hands big. She could have done this.

"And this . . ." he murmured as he pointed toward the next gurney, the one that had just come in from the cemetery. The sheet still covered the body on it.

The coroner pulled down the sheet, exposing Gregor MacDonald's face. His eyes were closed, but his lips were curved into a slight grin. As if he'd found something funny just as he died . . .

If he'd died of a heart attack, wouldn't he have grimaced in pain? Or cried out for help? His housekeeper hadn't found him until hours later, hours after he'd been dead.

"What did he die from?" Rafe asked.

"I haven't had a chance to examine him," the coroner remarked. "You're keeping me too damn busy, Montego. What the hell's happening in Lake George?"

Rafe turned back to that first body: the skeletal remains that very likely belonged to Anna Beth MacDonald. "It's because of her . . ." he murmured.

"What do you mean?" Dr. Thiel asked.

"If her body had been found all those years ago, if her killer had been caught, I don't think these other bodies would be here." And he didn't think someone would have tried to kill Erin either. She would have been safe.

"We don't know that Gregor was murdered," the coroner said. Dr. Thiel was an older man; he'd lived and worked in Lake George for many years. "And even if he was, that old man made a lot of enemies in his lifetime."

Could that have been why someone had taken his daughters? MacDonald had paid the ransom, but he'd only gotten one of them back. Someone had gotten their revenge on him then. And probably for all the years she'd been missing . . .

Because Anna Beth's father would have wondered where she was, what had happened to her. Just as Rafe had wondered . . .

"You think his daughter did this?" Dr. Thiel asked as he lowered the sheet farther down MacDonald's body.

"What?" he asked with shock. Sure, Erin had inherited everything, but she'd seemed shocked when she'd learned that information at the funeral. She couldn't have known. She couldn't have hurt her father or anyone else.

He didn't think she was capable. But then, he really didn't know her.

"Sally's a strong woman," the coroner remarked. "I've seen her go after that last husband of hers. Beat the crap out of him. Didn't kill him, though."

Sally MacDonald. Rafe had forgotten all about her. She certainly resented her youngest sister. Had she resented Anna Beth even more? Enough to kill her?

Rafe would question her and Sylvia Sloan. But there was someone else he wanted to question first, someone he should have questioned years ago, though the chief and other officers had told him to back off.

That the detective who'd investigated the kidnapping twenty-five years ago had done the best he could to find the missing girl. To find out who'd kidnapped both girls.

But now Rafe had proof that the man hadn't done a thorough job at all. Because Anna Beth MacDonald had never left the estate.

How the hell hadn't Detective Voller found her body? How could he have missed the shed?

Unless he hadn't wanted to find it.

He hadn't wanted to find her.

Like the woman found dead in the motel, had the detective been paid off? Had he accepted some of that ransom money or something else . . .

Sylvia Sloan was still beautiful now, in a kind of cold, plastic way. But twenty-five years ago . . .

She might have been able to manipulate a man into looking the other way, into letting her get away with her crimes.

CHAPTER TEN

Fourteen years ago . . .

Erin peered out from the stage in the auditorium of St. Cecilia's School for Girls. The chairs were filled with the family and friends of the young women graduating today, cheering them on with applause and whistles.

Nobody sat out there for Erin. Mother had probably forgotten. Daddy had sent flowers with a note apologizing for missing her special day; he hadn't been able to get away from his business. He'd felt so badly about not coming that he'd called, too, with excuses about mergers and stocks and government sanctions.

As the last of the recipients received her diploma, the stage cleared, the graduates joining their families. Erin didn't want to intrude, but she also didn't know where to go.

Sister Maria must have noticed her hesitation because the headmistress approached her. She looked no older than she had when Erin had first arrived at St. Cecilia's eleven years earlier. Her hair had already been white then, and perfectly coifed. Maybe it was her apple cheeks that kept her face from aging. She studied Erin through the wire-rimmed glasses that kept sliding down and nearly off her small nose. "Miss MacDonald, what are your plans? Going home?"

Erin shook her head. "I don't have one anymore."

The older woman's brow furrowed. "Yes, you do." Then she reminded Erin, "Your father tried to take you home years ago."

And Erin had refused to go. Was it because of all the things Mother said about Daddy? All the things she'd accused him of? Was that why Erin had been afraid to go back?

"I'm going to be fine." Erin forced a smile to assure the headmistress. "I've already been accepted to that art college, the one that specializes in photography, and once I finish that course, I'm going to travel. There are so many places I want to see." And seeing all those places would keep her too busy to go home.

"What about the truth, Erin?" Sister Maria asked. "You used to see Sister Rosa, used to ask her to help you remember what happened."

Erin shook her head. "And maybe there's nothing to remember."

"Maybe not," Sister Maria agreed. "But there are other ways to learn the truth. You could talk to people—to your family—the ones who might remember more than you do about that night."

She shuddered at the thought, and then she finally admitted, "Maybe I don't want to know what the truth is."

Maybe it was better to believe that those infrequent sightings of Anna Beth meant that she was alive yet, that nobody had killed her—most of all, no one Anna

Beth had known and loved had killed her. Nobody Erin knew . . .

Now . . .

The laugh was high and forced and raised goose bumps on Erin's skin. Her mother was here, desperately flirting with the officer outside the door. That was how she was— how she'd always been, coldly dismissive one moment and frantically charming the next.

At least with men . . .

With her family, she'd always been coldly dismissive.

Erin drew in a breath and forced herself to open the door.

"See, Officer, I told you that my daughter would be happy to see me," Sylvia Sloan insisted. She turned from smiling at the officer toward Erin, and her eyes were so frigidly cold that Erin nearly shivered.

"That didn't take long," Erin murmured.

Ethan had left just a short time ago. But he'd been so gleeful that he must not have been able to wait to tell the others.

"Your father would be so proud of you," he'd praised her.

And Erin thought of that little half smile he'd worn in the casket. . . .

Maybe he'd known she would wind up doing this. He would have found it funny for certain.

Her mother pushed past her and walked through the foyer, the scent of her perfume nearly choking Erin.

"Do you want me to come inside, Miss MacDonald?" Officer Darren asked. Her mother hadn't fooled or beguiled him though she'd tried.

Erin shook her head. "No. I'll be fine." Her mother wasn't going to kill her now. Unless she could get her to change her will, she had nothing to gain.

Except revenge . . .

Was that why she'd killed Anna Beth?

But could even Mother be so cold as to murder her own daughter?

"What the hell are you thinking?" Sylvia asked when Erin joined her in the den. "Are you trying to be as spiteful as he was?"

"You've always said that I'm more like him than you," she reminded Sylvia. That she had that unruly red hair and pudgy body . . .

That was what she'd overheard at those parties, whenever anyone had mentioned her youngest daughter to Sylvia. She'd laughed and remarked, "The poor thing takes after her father, while Anna Beth is the spitting image of me."

"Oh, I think she's even lovelier," one hapless party guest had replied.

Only to be tossed out of the party.

But he'd been right. Anna Beth had been lovelier because her beauty had been much more than skin deep.

"Is that what this is about?" Sylvia asked. "You're lashing out at me because I wasn't some warm and fuzzy mommy to you? Because I abandoned you at boarding school like that detective accused me of doing?"

A smile tugged at Erin's lips. Rafe really was trying to protect her, or at least defend her.

"God, you even smile like he did," Sylvia murmured with disgust. "Like I told the detective, you were sent to St. Cecilia's to protect you."

Erin snorted at the thought of being safe there. Another girl had died there. Surely her mother would have heard about that; it had been all over the news at one point. "I was sent there because I wasn't the daughter you wanted back. Because I wasn't the one who got you any attention."

Her mother snorted now. "Like I need anyone else to get attention for me. I'm famous."

"Was that it, then?" Erin asked. "You didn't want to compete for the attention?"

Her mother laughed now. "You were never competition for me, darling. You never will be . . ."

Erin flinched, as hurt now as she'd been in the past by her mother's dismissive comments. But her feelings didn't matter here. The truth mattered. She realized that now; that she deserved to know the truth. It couldn't be any worse than Anna Beth being dead.

"Is that why you killed her?" Erin asked. "Because Anna Beth was competition for you? Because she was prettier? More photogenic?"

Her mother flinched now, as if Erin had struck her. "How dare you accuse me of killing her!"

"You were so jealous of her," Erin insisted.

A muscle twitched along Sylvia's tightly clenched jaw, but she didn't deny Erin's claim. Instead, she lifted her chin and stared down her nose at her younger daughter. "At least she was useful. She would have supported me—unlike you. She would have taken care of me."

"And it's all about you . . ." Erin murmured. "Don't you care what happened to her?"

"Do you?" Mother asked. "You've been gone for years.

Your father hired private investigators to search for her. You haven't done anything."

Heat rushed to Erin's face. Her mother was right. Anna Beth had given up her life for Erin and she'd done nothing to find her killer. Nothing to make sure there was justice for her sister, for Erin's savior. "That's changing now," she insisted. "Now that I know she's really dead. Now I'm going to figure out who killed her."

Her mother sighed. "It wasn't me. Why do you think I had Anna Beth start modeling? I wanted her to make enough money so I could get away from your father, from all men." She shuddered. "That's why I started modeling in the first place, to get away from my father."

"Oh . . ." Realization dawned on Erin. She suddenly understood so much. "He hurt you?"

Sylvia shrugged. "It was a long time ago, and I got away."

"Did you really believe Daddy was hurting Anna Beth like that? Is that why you told those reporters those horrible things?"

Sylvia shrugged again. "I don't know. I was upset. I was . . . scared . . ." Her voice cracked with the admission. She hadn't known how to get away from him then. So she'd gone on to another man, and another . . .

Tears stung Erin's eyes. "He didn't," Erin told her. "I was always in Anna Beth's bed. I would have known."

Sylvia nodded. "I know . . . you two were inseparable."

Until that night.

That night someone had separated them forever.

"I have never been as close to anyone as you two were to each other," Sylvia admitted.

And maybe that was another reason Mother had been jealous of Anna Beth.

"I'm sorry," Erin said. So very sorry for her mother.

"Sorry you're leaving your father's money to charity?" she asked.

Erin shook her head. "No. I will do that when I die. But in the meantime, I'll pay your hotel bill. I'll also provide you an allowance."

"Your father wouldn't like that," Sylvia said.

Erin wasn't so sure. "Did you ever tell him? Did he know about your past . . . ?"

She shook her head, and her brittle blond hair swished over her thin shoulders. "No. Nobody knows . . ."

"If he had, things would have been different," Erin assured her. "He would have cared." But instead of opening up with each other, they'd lashed out at each other. Hurt each other . . .

And Erin had been hurt in the process . . . without Anna Beth to comfort her, protect her.

"I'm sorry," Sylvia said now. "I'm sorry Anna Beth died so young. I'm sorry you lost your sister and you never really had a mother . . ."

Anna Beth had been her mother. The person who'd nurtured her most.

Nobody had nurtured or protected Sylvia Sloan but Sylvia Sloan. For the first time in her life, Erin understood her mother. She closed the distance between them and wrapped her arms around the older woman.

Sylvia stood stiffly in her embrace, as if she could hardly bear being touched. Then something happened, as if something snapped, and she hugged Erin back, clutching her close like Rafe had clutched her last night.

And for the first time in her life, Erin felt as if her mother cared about her. "I'm sorry, too," Erin said. "So sorry for what you've gone through . . ."

Sylvia stiffened and pulled back then. "That was a long time ago."

But she'd never recovered from it.

"I'm also sorry I accused you of hurting Anna Beth."

Her mother nodded. "I know I wasn't a good mother. That I wasn't a mother at all. But I didn't . . ." Her voice cracked.

Erin believed she hadn't hurt Anna Beth, but . . .

"I authorized Detective Montego to exhume Daddy's body," she said.

Her mother laughed. "Are you warning me? You think I killed him? I would have done that before we divorced if I was a killer, Erin. Then I actually would have gotten something out of it besides just a deep sense of satisfaction."

Erin couldn't be sure she hadn't done it now—for that deep sense of satisfaction.

"Your father died of a heart attack, which is ironic because I never really believed he had one," Sylvia said.

"There was no autopsy," Erin said. "There will be one now."

"If somebody did in that old bastard, there will be many more suspects than me," Sylvia said. "Magnus and Sally and even old Ethan."

"Ethan?"

"You don't think he had his hand in your father's pockets all those years? That he wasn't helping himself . . . ?" She laughed. "He was no true friend to your father because your father had no true friends, just people who wanted to benefit from him—myself included."

"But Ethan . . ."

"He was here the night of the party. He might have wanted a bigger paycheck than your father was giving him," Sylvia suggested. "Like a million dollars more . . ."

Erin shivered. Just a short while ago she'd been alone with Ethan in this room.

He hadn't hurt her then, but the officer had been outside the door. Had he tried to hurt her last night?

Was he the one . . . ?

Erin's head began to pound as it had that night with the pain and the confusion. She hadn't understood what was happening then. She needed to understand now. She needed the truth.

"I need the truth," Rafe said when the retired detective finally opened the door of his cabin.

"Who the hell are you?" Voller asked. "Another damn reporter?"

"Have reporters been here?" Rafe asked. He'd had a hell of a time finding out where the retired detective lived; he'd had to threaten Sergeant Meyer that he was going to report him to Internal Affairs if he didn't tell him. He didn't have anything specific on the sergeant to report, but Meyer had been worried enough that he'd given Rafe the address. The cabin was directly on Lake George—with a substantial amount of frontage.

On his salary, Rafe would never be able to afford such a place. How could Voller?

He pulled out his badge and showed it to the guy. "I'm

surprised Meyer didn't call to warn you that I was coming."

"Reception's lousy here," Voller admitted. "And I don't have a landline."

While the lake frontage was substantial, the cabin was not. Rafe could see through the log structure to the patio doors that opened onto a rickety deck hanging from the back.

"So you haven't talked to anyone?" Rafe asked. "You don't know?"

"Know what?" Voller asked. He pushed a hand that shook slightly through his thick, gray hair. Gray stubble lined his jaw, too. He'd retired before Rafe had joined the force, so Rafe had figured he was old. But now he wondered if Voller was as old as he looked, or if guilt and alcohol had aged him.

"The body was found."

Voller sighed, but he didn't ask what body. Obviously the reporters who sought him out only asked him about one case, the only crime of any notoriety that had happened in Lake George. He also didn't ask where the body had been found; he just stepped back from his door and walked through the open sliding one onto his deck.

Rafe followed him out. "You knew she was dead."

The wind rifled through the older man's overly long hair as he stared out over the deep blue water of the lake. "No."

"But you must have suspected?"

He shrugged. "Easier to hide a dead body than a live one."

"Did you even look for her?" Rafe asked.

"Of course I looked."

"Then how did you miss her? How didn't you find the shed on the estate?"

"That place is huge," Voller replied. "And that crazy maze where the little girl turned up, it was harder than hell to get through . . ."

"So you know that's where the shed was," Rafe surmised. "At the end of the maze . . ." His stomach churned with disgust. This man hadn't just known about the murder; he must have helped cover it up.

Or had he done more?

Had he been the killer?

Maybe he'd wanted more than the small payoffs some of his coworkers, like Sergeant Meyer, had taken for looking the other way. Maybe he'd wanted that million dollar payoff.

Rafe reached for the holster beneath his jacket. "We should have this conversation down at the station," he said. Where Rafe could record it.

Voller shook his head. "Nope. I'm not going anywhere. If you want to talk, we talk here."

Where there were no witnesses . . .

Where nothing he said would be admissible.

Rafe wanted the truth so badly, he didn't care. If Voller confessed, he would damn sure find a way to make it stick. And he would make certain this guy never got anywhere near Erin again.

"Let's talk then," Rafe agreed.

"You won't be able to prove anything," Voller said, as if he'd read Rafe's mind, as if he'd known he intended to make charges stick even without a confession.

"Why not?" Rafe asked. "Along with her body, other evidence was recovered. It's currently being processed. DNA is going to show up on it."

The old man snorted. "DNA. That's all you young guys talk about these days. You use it to make your cases, to find your suspects. It's sloppy. It's lazy."

"It gets convictions," Rafe reminded him.

"It was an accident. That's all any of that will prove."

"Anna Beth's death was an accident?" Rafe asked.

The older man nodded. "Of course. She fell. She hit her head."

Rafe snorted now. "Then after she'd smashed the back of her skull apart, she turned around and bashed in her own face until every bone was broken, until she would have been entirely unrecognizable? What the hell kind of monster are you?"

The older man's face paled and he gasped. "I—I'm not a monster. I had nothing to do with her death."

"But you know who did," Rafe said. "And you helped cover it up all these years."

The older man was shaking now, his body and his head. "No, no, no . . ." he murmured. "You have to be wrong. You have to be . . ."

"We can go down to the morgue right now," Rafe offered. "You can see for yourself that this was no accident. Anna Beth MacDonald was brutally beaten."

"But her sister, she just had that bump on her head."

"A concussion that had her unconscious for hours," Rafe reminded him. "But still, she's lucky to be alive. Anna Beth wasn't so lucky. Somebody made damn certain that she was dead."

Voller kept shaking his head. "No, no, no . . ."

"Who told you it was an accident? Sylvia Sloan? Sally MacDonald?" Either of those women might have swayed an old man like Voller. The first with her wiles, the second with tears.

While Rafe had never met him, he'd heard plenty of stories about Voller. He was a chauvinist. His disrespect of his female coworkers was one of the reasons he'd retired so early. He hadn't been given much of a choice.

Voller's brow furrowed. "Who? The mother? The sister? What are you talking about?"

"Who told you it was an accident?" Rafe asked. "Who lied to you and made you complicit in a murder?"

"Complicit?" Voller shook his head. "No. You can't prove that. You need to get out of here. You need to leave right now!"

"Whoever you helped get away with murder has started killing again," Rafe said. "They're tying up loose ends." He stared hard at the detective. "I don't think there are any looser than you are right now."

The old man's whiskered throat moved, as if he struggled to swallow. "What do you mean? Who died?"

"Gregor MacDonald—"

"That was a heart attack," Voller said.

Rafe shrugged. "We'll know for certain soon enough. But there's no doubt that the woman impersonating Anna Beth was murdered. She was strangled to death in a motel room. And then . . ." His voice lowered with anger, making it gruff. ". . . someone tried to kill Erin MacDonald last night."

"Erin? The little girl? She's back?"

He nodded. "And she's in danger. And you're going to damn well tell me who she's in danger from." He tightened his hands into fists now. He had never understood the detectives and police officers who'd resorted to the old school tactics of beating confessions from perps—until now.

Now that he was desperate to keep Erin safe.

CHAPTER ELEVEN

Twenty-five years ago . . .

Mother stood in the doorway, sneering at Anna Beth. "Don't you think you're a little old to be playing with dolls?"

Anna Beth knelt on the floor beside Erin, dressing a Barbie doll. She ignored what Mother said.

"She's playing with me," Erin said in her sister's defense. "I asked her to . . ." She'd asked Mother to play before, but Sylvia Sloan had turned her down with a sneer, just like the one she was giving Anna Beth now. She knew now to never ask her again. And Daddy . . .

He was always too busy. "Making money to buy those dollies for you, girlie!"

Anna Beth was busy, too. There was always some photo shoot or commercial she had to go to.

Like now.

"You're going to be late if you don't get going," Sylvia threatened. "And you're not going to embarrass me like that." She turned toward Erin then, sneering at her. "This one is enough embarrassment."

"She is not!" Anna Beth said. "She's just a little girl."

"You're not," Sylvia said. "Now hurry up and get ready. We need to leave!" She slammed the door on her way out.

And Anna Beth uttered a groan of frustration. "I'm sorry," she told Erin. "I have to go . . ." Tears filled her eyes.

"It's okay," Erin assured her. "I know you're too old to play dollies with me. You have to work."

Anna Beth sighed now, and one of the tears rolled down her beautiful face. "I wish I was like you."

Erin's mouth fell open in shock. "Me? You're the beautiful one. The smart one . . ."

Anna Beth shook her head. "You're beautiful. You're smart."

"You are, too," Erin insisted. "Why do you want to be me?"

"I want to be seven," Anna Beth said. "I want to play with dolls and go to bed early and get up for school, not work. . . ." Her voice cracked. "And I don't want everyone staring at me, especially the boys. . . ." She shuddered.

"You don't like boys?" Erin asked.

"Not the creepy ones," Anna Beth said. Then she blinked away her tears and forced a smile. "It's okay, though. This will be a short shoot today. Mother has the party planned for tonight."

Erin groaned now. She hated the parties. Hated all the strangers filling their home. She wanted to be alone. Well, not alone. She wanted to be with Anna Beth. "Can I come with you?" Erin asked.

Anna Beth smiled. "Mother will say no," she warned

her. "But I'll tell her it's the only way I'm going—with you. . . ."

Now . . .

That was how she'd died—with Erin. Erin couldn't re-member the details of that night—not after getting struck so hard with that lamp—but she knew she must have been there when her sister died. She walked around Anna Beth's room now, trying to summon what memories she had of that night, of that moment . . . before everything had gone black.

Why couldn't she remember more?

Was it like Sister Rosa had said all those years ago? That there was nothing for Erin to remember?

But she'd remembered the shed . . . once she'd been in it. She'd remembered awakening on the floor of it. She'd been alone then, though.

Anna Beth had already been dead.

Who had killed her? And why . . .

Anna Beth had been so sweet, so beautiful, so loving. She had always tried so hard to make everyone happy—Erin, Mother, Daddy, the photographers who'd worked with her, the other models . . .

But the creepy boys . . .

Who had she been talking about?

Had she had a stalker? Someone obsessed with her beauty who hadn't realized that Anna Beth would have rather played with dolls with her little sister than had a romantic relationship?

It could have been any of those photographers. But would Anna Beth have called them boys? They'd been older than that—much older. Maybe the male models with whom she'd done some shoots . . .

But how would one of them have known where Anna Beth's room was? None of them had ever stayed in the house. If they were as young as Anna Beth, they'd had chaperones at the shoots and at the parties.

It had to have been someone who'd had more access to the house. Ethan? Was Mother right? Had he been involved?

Anna Beth would never have called him a boy, though. No . . .

Erin's eyes were getting gritty with exhaustion, the way they'd been the night of the party. Except for her nap in Daddy's den earlier, she hadn't had much rest since being locked in the shed. Even after showering off the smoke the night before, she'd been too unsettled to sleep—too upset over what had happened, over learning that Anna Beth had been here this entire time.

And that maybe Erin had known where she was . . .

She was tempted to crawl into Anna Beth's bed like she used to when she was a child. But she knew she'd find no rest there, only more nightmares—more flashes of memory of that heavy lamp coming down so hard on her head.

Heavy . . .

She'd known it was heavy because she had barely been able to move it along the bedside table when she'd tried pulling it closer to her. But someone else had recently remarked on how heavy it was.

Someone that wouldn't have known unless . . .

Her blood chilled as realization finally dawned on her.

He'd slipped up when he'd said that, when he'd admitted to it being heavy.

Why hadn't she noticed his mistake?

He must have—that must have been why he'd locked her in the shed last night. Because he'd been trying to kill her before she'd shared his admission with anyone.

Her hand shaking, she reached for her cell phone. She had an officer outside the door, so she didn't need to call 9-1-1. She wanted to call Rafe, wanted to share with him what she'd learned.

But she didn't have his number.

Had he given her his card?

It didn't matter. Officer Darren would know how to reach him. She rushed out of Anna Beth's room and ran down the wide hallway to the front stairwell. It would bring her down to the foyer, closer to where Officer Darren had been stationed. Was he still here, or had his shift ended? If it had, there would be a replacement on duty—someone else who would undoubtedly know how to reach the detective.

The Lake George Police Department couldn't be that big; everybody had to know everybody else. Just as everybody knew everybody else in this neighborhood . . .

Just as they went in and out of one another's houses and yards . . .

That was how he'd known about the shed, about Anna Beth's bedroom.

About how heavy the lamp was—because he'd picked it up, he'd swung it at Erin.

Her heart pounding with her excitement to talk to Rafe, she pulled open the door and gasped. Michael Andover stood on the front steps. Alone.

He flashed her a wide grin. "I was just about to ring the bell."

She glanced around him. The patrol car was parked in the driveway behind Erin's rental. Where was the officer?

What had he done to him?

She couldn't get past Michael to get to her car. He was too broad, too big. So she stepped back.

"Erin? What's wrong?" he asked, that wide grin slipping just a little.

She saw the creepiness then. What Anna Beth must have seen when they'd all just been kids yet, when, at seventeen, Michael would have still been a boy to her. But he hadn't been a boy; he'd been a monster.

Erin turned then to run. But he reached out, his hand grasping the ends of her hair. Ignoring the pain, she tugged free and ran—through the house—out the patio doors in the kitchen and through the backyard.

Night was beginning to fall, shadows looming all around the yard and that massive wall of shrubs that was the beginning of the maze. It was the only place for her to hide, so she ducked into it.

She'd probably made a mistake—as she had the night she'd walked willingly through that maze, trying to remember. Michael undoubtedly knew this maze and the grounds better than she did. She wouldn't be able to escape him.

He didn't have her number. Rafe couldn't call and warn her. So he dialed Darren instead. But the man's cell went right to voice mail. As it should.

He was on duty.

So Rafe had the dispatcher put him through to the officer's radio. It should have been clipped to his shirt collar. He should have answered it, but there was no response. Panic clutched at Rafe's heart, squeezing it. He could think of only one reason why Darren hadn't answered. And it wasn't good.

"Get a unit out to the MacDonald estate as fast as you can," Rafe told the dispatcher. If only the damn chief had authorized more of a police presence . . .

But maybe the chief had looked the other way for the same reasons that retired Detective Voller had. Maybe they'd known who the killer was all this time.

"He was just a boy . . ." Voller had said. "He didn't know what he was doing."

Rafe had snorted then. Michael Andover had been old enough to know exactly what he was doing, and so had his father when Peter Andover had probably paid off this detective and maybe the chief, with the money they'd collected as ransom from Gregor MacDonald. Ransom for the man's two daughters when they'd known they were only going to be able to return one of them.

"Little Michael had been sneaking drinks and probably other things at that wild party," Voller had continued to defend him. "He was out-of-his-head drunk and high . . ."

"So how the hell did he manage to clean up a crime scene as much as he had?" Rafe had asked. "How did he get two bodies out of the house without being seen? Because he had help, didn't he? Was it you?" It had to have been him—though Voller had claimed that Peter—Michael's father—had only admitted to him later what had happened.

Voller had shaken his head vigorously. "Of course

not . . . if I'd seen what you said . . ." His voice had cracked. "What he did to the girl . . ."

"Smashed her face to bits," Rafe had ruthlessly added, hoping to appeal finally to this man's sense of decency. If he had any . . .

"That wasn't an accident," Rafe had persisted. "And killing that woman in the motel and trying to kill Erin . . ." His voice had cracked then, when he'd realized exactly how much danger she was in.

Her neighbor had killed her sister. Someone Erin knew and probably still trusted.

"God!" Rafe had exclaimed. "He was at the funeral, talking to her . . ." He'd shuddered then, before whirling and heading toward the door. He'd already been pulling out his cell phone to call Darren and then the dispatcher.

So Rafe was in his car now, heading toward the estate. But would he get there in time? Would he be able to keep the promise he never should have made to Erin?

Would he be able to protect her?

CHAPTER TWELVE

Twenty-five years ago

"You always find me," Erin complained when Anna Beth peered over the back of the bench in one of the many dead ends in the maze.

"That's because you always hide in the same spot," Anna Beth told her. "Mix it up. Hide someplace I would never think to look for you."

"But then you might never find me . . ." Erin murmured, fear rushing up to clog her throat. She couldn't bear the thought of being out here somewhere on the property—alone. Tears welled in her eyes.

Anna Beth jumped over the bench and pulled Erin into her thin arms, holding her close, comforting her. "I'll always find you," she promised. "I'll never stop looking until I do."

Now . . .

Erin shouldn't have stopped looking for Anna Beth. She should have kept searching until she'd found her. But she'd been so young . . .

She'd had no control—no way to stop her parents from shipping her off to St. Cecilia's. But when she could have come back, when Daddy had come to get her, she'd refused.

She'd been scared to return, scared of all the memories that were rushing over her now. But she was even more scared now, with a killer stalking her around the property. A killer who knew the estate better than she ever had . . .

Hide someplace I would never think to look for you . . .

Anna Beth's advice from so long ago echoed in Erin's mind. Erin had known where Anna Beth wouldn't think to look for her—anywhere dark and far from other people. Because Anna Beth had known how Erin hated to be alone in the dark.

But Michael didn't know Erin. And she certainly hadn't known him. She'd thought he was cute. That he was nice. She hadn't seen the creepiness that Anna Beth had.

Poor Anna Beth . . .

"It's no use, you know," Michael called out, his tone as charming as ever. "I used to watch the two of you play out here. I know where you're going."

To the bench. Not damn well likely.

She wasn't going to be trapped in that dead end. She had to remember what Anna Beth had told her: count the turns, follow them to where the maze came out in the woods. By the shed.

Surely he wouldn't think she'd go back there, to where he'd nearly killed her once, to where he'd hidden her sister's body all those years ago.

But once she'd entered the maze, there was nowhere else she could go to escape him.

"Come on, Erin," Michael called out. "I just want to talk to you, to explain what happened that night."

So he wasn't even going to bother denying that he had murdered her sister. But then, how could he deny it now that her body had been found?

"It was your fault, you know . . ." The charm had slipped away from his voice, as he grew more breathless, running through the maze to catch her.

She could hear the branches rustling, hear his feet pounding on the lawn. She was moving fast, too, but quietly. If only she could squeeze through the branches the way she used to . . .

But the only way out now that she'd entered was by the shed. As she got closer to the woods, the sky got darker, the shadows deeper. Was she heading in the right direction?

"It was your fault!" he yelled, as if expecting her to deny it—to react. "If you hadn't been there that night, if you hadn't been in her bed . . ."

He still would have killed Anna Beth. Erin had no doubt of that, because she knew that Anna Beth hadn't been expecting him, wouldn't have welcomed him showing up in her room. She'd just wanted to stay a little girl, like Erin was. And, in a way, she had. She'd never gotten older, had never had to deal with any more ugliness after that night.

"I would have never hurt Anna Beth!" he yelled.

But clearly he had no compunction about hurting Erin.

And maybe it was time she hurt him back. Instead of hiding, instead of running, as she'd been doing all these years, maybe it was time that she fought him.

She nearly missed the opening to the woods, probably

would have if not for the strand of yellow tape stretched across it. The yellow glowed in the dark. She caught it in her hand and tugged it off the branches. Maybe he would miss the opening. Maybe he would keep running—right past it to the dead end beyond it.

She ran now toward the thick shadows where the shed stood, just a little charred in places from the fire that hadn't taken off. Or she would have already been dead . . .

If it was a garden shed, surely there had to be tools in it. Something she could use as a weapon.

That night she'd been locked inside; she'd been too scared, too panicked to look around, or maybe she'd remembered it more than she'd thought. Because another memory flitted through her mind . . .

Blood.

So much blood.

Her hands had been covered in it, sticky with it.

"Anna Beth . . ."

Had that blood been hers or her sister's?

She shook her head, trying to clear the memories from it. She needed to focus on the present now, so she wouldn't wind up like Anna Beth. She rushed toward the shed. More tape had been strung across the open doorway. The jamb was broken, the door tossed on its side next to the shed. Rafe must have done that when he'd rescued her.

She couldn't count on him doing that again. He thought she was safe; he'd left the young officer as her protection. But Officer Darren had needed protecting, too. How had Michael snuck up on him?

Because he knew the property so well . . .

She wasn't going to get trapped in the shed again, as he'd trapped her the night before. She just ducked her head inside and scanned the shadows for anything she could use as a weapon. But before her eyes adjusted to the shadows, hands pressed against her back, shoving her into the dark space.

She reached out, grasping for anything to stop her fall. And her hands slipped over a wooden pole or handle propped against the wall. She caught it, grasped and swung it toward the door. Brandishing it like a bat, she kept swinging and swinging.

The blade of the shovel at the end of the pole connected with a body. Michael cursed and stumbled back, falling to the ground outside the shed. She stepped out with him, and she could have swung again, would have, but then he pulled a gun, the barrel glinting in the faint light of the sun setting above the many trees.

Still holding the shovel, she ran back toward the maze. Shots rang out, the bullets rustling through the shrubs. They were small enough to make it through the walls of the maze, small enough to penetrate the branches and her body. She might have been able to outrun Michael on her way back to the house, but she wouldn't be able to outrun the bullets.

Rafe reached through his open window and pressed his finger on the intercom button. His hand was shaking. His whole damn body was shaking. Nobody answered. Was he too late?

Because he had no doubt that Michael Andover would try to kill Erin again. He must have believed she'd remembered something from that night, the night he'd killed her sister. The night he could have killed her.

"Erin!" Rafe shouted. But it was no use. No one was answering that intercom. Because they couldn't?

Shots reverberated from somewhere on the property, ringing out so clearly and loudly that birds rose up like a cloud from the trees. Panicked.

Afraid.

Rafe was, too. So much so that he pressed hard on the accelerator and rammed the gates with the front bumper of his car. Metal screeched and crumpled. He backed up and then pressed the accelerator again, hitting the gates harder, with such force that they opened even as the front of his car crumpled more.

He stopped it and jumped out, and squeezed his body through the opening the vehicle had made. He drew his weapon, holding it against his side as he ran down the long drive toward the house. Next to the fountain, he found the body.

Rafe had worried that he'd find Darren like this. Dead.

The officer lay facedown on the driveway, blood pooling beneath his head. Someone had struck him hard, just as Erin had been struck that night.

And Anna Beth . . .

Rafe knelt beside him and felt the officer's neck, but there was no pulse. No sign of life. The blow had killed Darren, just as it had Anna Beth. Not only had the young officer lost his life, but his weapon was also missing. Rafe wasn't sure if he'd even had a chance to draw it, or if Andover had snuck up on him from behind and taken it after hitting him.

Rafe kept swiveling his neck as he listened for more shots. Where had they come from? The front door stood wide open, as if Andover had forced his way inside or someone had run out of it.

"Erin!" Rafe called out as he stepped into the dim light of the foyer. He glanced into the den, but it was empty except for the furniture and that faint scent of cigar smoke. So he hurried down the hall toward the kitchen. Like the front doors, the patio doors stood open to the backyard.

As he crossed the kitchen toward them, shots rang out again, echoing off the stone patio. They were close.

The shooter was close.

Rafe rushed toward the maze, but before he could step inside, something swung at him, nearly striking him. He ducked back and cursed.

"Rafe!" Erin exclaimed. "Oh my God! It's Michael. He has a gun!"

More shots rang out. Close. Loud. The bullets whizzing through the branches. Rafe jerked her out of the maze. "Get out of here! Run straight out to the street—backup is on the way."

He didn't look to make sure she ran; he couldn't pull his attention away from the entrance to the maze. Andover had to come out this way. And he would have to get through Rafe to get to Erin.

She would be safe.

Backup should have been there already, though. Where the hell was it?

Why couldn't he hear sirens yet? Why couldn't he hear anything but the ringing in his ears from those shots being fired?

Andover was close. So close that Rafe heard the click of the empty chamber. He'd run out of bullets.

"It's over," he told the other man. "You're under arrest. Come out of there."

And he waited, his attention on that opening. Branches rustled; the shrubs closest to Rafe were shaking. Was Andover trying to come through the wall? He peered through the gathering darkness at the shrubs. The wall seemed to loom taller than it had just moments before.

Then he realized: Andover had climbed it. And now he jumped down—onto Rafe—knocking him to the ground. Rafe clutched his weapon tightly, so he didn't lose it, as Darren might have lost his. But a hand covered his as Andover grappled with him for the Glock, trying to turn the barrel toward Rafe.

Onto Rafe . . .

Michael Andover was trying to take Rafe's life, just as he'd taken so many others, starting with Anna Beth.

CHAPTER THIRTEEN

Twenty-five years ago . . .

Erin was helpless.

"No, I don't wanna go . . ." she murmured, tears choking her as she watched Daddy pack up her clothes and toys.

"Girlie, you'll be safer at St. Cecilia's than you were—than you are—here," he told her.

"Yes, safer," her mother said from where she leaned against the open door of Erin's room, but she was staring at Daddy.

She barely looked at Erin ever, but especially not now, not since Erin had come back and Anna Beth hadn't.

Erin knew why they were really sending her away—because they wished she'd stayed away. Because they wished Anna Beth had come back and not her.

Erin wished the same. She wished Anna Beth was here, making everything brighter, happier, safer.

But Erin couldn't bring her back.

And she couldn't keep herself here. She was being sent away, and she was too little—too weak—to stop them. To stop anyone . . .

Now . . .

Erin wasn't weak anymore. She wasn't helpless. She'd been running too long from her past, from the truth, from this killer. . . .

So she hadn't listened to Rafe; she hadn't run out to the street for help. She wasn't going to leave him to fend for himself. She'd hovered nearby, watching, waiting to make certain she didn't lose him as she'd lost Anna Beth that night so long ago.

And it was a good thing she had waited . . .

Because just as Michael had taken her by surprise that night so long ago, he'd taken Rafe by surprise, leaping down from the wall of the maze to tackle him to the ground. The two men rolled around, both grappling for the weapon.

And Erin couldn't just stand by helplessly and watch. In the thickening darkness of night, it was hard to see them, hard to discern who was whom . . . but for the lightness of Michael's hair. So, swinging into action, Erin rushed forward and swung the shovel. The blade came down on the back of that blond head, and a cry of pain slipped from Michael's lips, just as a shot rang out. A shot from Rafe's gun.

As close as they were, the bullet couldn't have missed. At the thought of it striking Rafe, of hurting him, or worse, Erin screamed.

"Erin, are you all right? Did you get hit?" he asked, his voice full of concern—for her.

She shook her head. "No. I'm fine. Are you all right? Did you get hit?"

Rafe grunted as he pushed Michael's unconscious

body from his. "No," he said. "But I probably would have been . . . if not for you," he said. "You saved me."

She wasn't so sure. because even in the faint light, she could see spatter on his shirt. Blood.

"Are you sure?" she asked. "You're bleeding."

He pointed down at Michael. "He got hit—twice." He leaned down and felt for a pulse. "He's alive, though."

A surge of relief surprised her. After what he'd done, she shouldn't have cared. But while Erin wasn't helpless, she was no killer either. She didn't want revenge; she just wanted justice.

The wail of sirens grew louder as that backup Rafe had promised approached them. Too late to help.

Too late to do more than clean up.

"Are you okay?" Rafe asked. "He didn't hurt you?"

"Not this time."

But he had so many years ago. She knew now that it had been him. It had all been him.

Rafe drove through the crumpled gates of the estate and steered down the drive. He wasn't speeding this time. The threat to Erin was gone now. Once Michael Andover recovered from his gunshot wound, he would be locked behind bars for the rest of his life.

Erin was probably gone, too. There was nothing keeping her in Lake George. Her father was dead. He had been murdered, just as Rafe had suspected. But Erin's mother hadn't been responsible.

Michael had confessed to murdering Gregor MacDonald; he'd confessed to everything. To murdering Anna Beth so long ago and to nearly killing Erin . . .

Then. And now . . .

She was safe. That was all that should have mattered to Rafe. That she was safe and that a cold case had been closed, justice finally served. But more mattered to Rafe than that.

Erin mattered.

He didn't want her to go.

But how could he ask her to stay? They'd only just met a few days ago. They were strangers, yet he felt he knew her and she knew him, that there was a connection between them that Rafe had rarely—if ever—had with anyone else. He drew in a shaky breath as he pulled up behind Erin's rental car, which was parked beside the fountain. Rafe felt both a rush of relief and one of deep regret.

Poor Darren . . .

He'd given his life for his job, as so many of Rafe's comrades in arms had over the years. Andover would serve another life sentence for that murder, as he would for each of the others—at least that was the deal to which he and his lawyer had agreed.

Rafe and the prosecutor had spent the night hashing out the plea arrangement at Andover's hospital bedside, with the recovering murderer handcuffed to his bed railing. Rafe's eyes were gritty with exhaustion, his body aching with it, and from the fight with Andover. A fight that Rafe probably would have lost if Erin hadn't stepped in, if she hadn't saved him.

She was so incredible. Too incredible for him to let go without a fight.

Despite his sleepless night, Rafe rallied and rushed toward the door. The rental car was here; she hadn't left yet. He jabbed at the doorbell, hitting it twice before even giving her a chance to answer it. He wasn't sure what he was going to say to her; just that he had to say something. He had to shoot his shot.

Then the door opened.

From the dark circles beneath her beautiful eyes, she hadn't gotten any more sleep than he had. She looked exhausted and vulnerable, but he knew how strong she was. And she deserved to know the whole truth—about her family's tragedies and about his feelings.

She reached out toward him, as if she intended to touch him, but jerked her hand back to her side. "You didn't need to come here," she said. "The prosecutor called me. She told me about the deal."

"She was supposed to ask if it was okay with you," Rafe said. "Maybe you would rather have had the cases go to trial to make sure everyone learned the truth about your dad and your sister—that he never had anything to do with her disappearance. That his persistence in finding out the truth was why he died."

Tears pooled in her eyes, but she managed a slight smile. "He kept looking for her everywhere but here," she murmured.

"He wouldn't have thought she could have been so close, that her killer was so close . . ."

"From the reports I found in his den, he kept having Mother's people investigated: the photographers, the fashion designers, the other models," she said. "Michael wouldn't have had to kill him."

"Michael poisoned your father's scotch for the same reason he tried to kill you," Rafe explained. "He thought you'd both figured out he was responsible from a slipup.

While he was the one who'd slipped up with you, he thought his father had with yours. Or that he'd flat-out confessed. After Mr. Andover had gotten sick, his conscience had started bothering him. He wanted your father to know the truth, that his daughter was dead, but he wanted to use Michael's excuse, that it was an accident." Anger coursed through Rafe as he remembered how Michael had originally tried using that excuse during the plea meeting, until Rafe had shared the coroner's preliminary findings with the man's lawyer. Then he'd dropped it.

Erin shuddered.

"You're cold," Rafe said. "We should go inside."

She stepped back then, and he followed her into the mansion and closed the door. Then he glanced around the foyer, expecting to find her bags or some boxes packed up, any sign that she was leaving. Everything looked the same as it had before, yet it all felt so different now somehow.

"I'm not cold," she said. "I'm furious he would say that. He came into her bedroom that night. He was going to do *something* to her. . . ."

"He never got the chance," Rafe assured her. "Once he hit you, she started fighting him, trying to protect you. That was when he hit her, so nobody would hear her. If the party hadn't been going on, someone might have . . ."

"That was always the argument with my parents— blaming each other for that, for her disappearance."

"That was why you should have made the choice," Rafe said. "Not the prosecutor. Terrible accusations were made about your father being involved in your sister's disappearance, speculation that he'd even hired the impersonator."

"There was more than one over the years," she said. It was no question; she must have recognized, as Rafe had, that the women had changed more than just that they'd aged.

"Yes," Rafe said. "He claims this is the only one he killed. The only one who knew who had hired her, and he was worried that even though he'd paid her, that she might tell someone."

She nodded. "That she might tell *you*. You reopened the investigation. You started talking to people. You're the reason I know the truth now. For certain." Her voice cracked as it trailed off. "I know that Anna Beth didn't choose to leave me. She fought for me."

"None of that was your fault," he said. Because Andover had tried to use that excuse to the prosecutor as well, he might have said something earlier to Erin, when they'd been alone together, when he'd been chasing her through the maze.

"I know," she said.

But he wasn't sure that she did. "You were *not* responsible. He was going to hurt her sometime. He probably would have earlier—but you were always around, always with her. You kept her safe, too, until that night."

She nodded again. "He said that. That he watched us play . . ." She shuddered. "That's why Anna Beth mentioned the creepy boys."

Heat rushed to his face for a moment, and he was embarrassed even as he was compelled to admit, "I had one of her posters up in my room all those years ago."

She smiled again—but just slightly. "I think a lot of boys did. That didn't make you creepy."

"That's not why I pursued this case," Rafe said. And not why he wanted to pursue her now. He needed to make that clear. "I outgrew whatever crush I thought I had years ago. I just wanted to solve the mystery, close the case."

"And you did," she told him. "You did. You should get credit for that. Is that why you're questioning the plea deal?"

"Not at all," he said. "I got what I wanted. Justice. That's all that matters. I don't need any credit, especially because I don't really deserve it. That woman died, your father . . . I should have solved the case five years ago and they would still be alive." Erin wouldn't have lost her father. Would she forgive him for that?

"Just as Anna Beth's death is not my fault, their deaths aren't yours," she said. "It was all Michael's fault—all of it."

He released a shaky breath of relief that she believed that, that she didn't blame herself or him. "And you're fine if the rest of the world doesn't find out that Michael—not your father—was to blame for everything?"

She sighed. "I don't think that'll be a problem. I think there will be plenty of stories about the case being closed. I've been turning reporters away all night . . . until Ethan threatened them with harassment and trespassing charges again."

"Did you get any sleep?" he asked.

She shook her head again. "Doesn't look like you did either."

He glanced down at his rumpled and torn suit. "I guess I look like hell . . ." He should have gone home and showered and changed. But he hadn't wanted to risk her leaving before he could talk to her.

"You look . . ." Her voice cracked.

"What?"

She shook her head, and tears welled in her eyes.

"Erin?"

He reached for her again, but this time she didn't jerk back. Her arms slid around his shoulders, and he clasped his behind her back, pulling her against his chest. His heart pounded madly.

"Thank you," she murmured. "Thank you . . ."

"I'm the one who needs to thank *you*," he said. "You saved my life." And not just when she'd knocked out his assailant. She'd saved his life by making him care again, by making him risk getting close to someone.

"You saved mine," she said. "You literally breathed life back into me. I feel like I've been lost, just wandering around alone like I did that night in the maze so many years ago. . . ." She shuddered.

He clasped her closer. "You're not alone anymore, Erin. You'll never be alone . . . if you would consider staying, giving me a chance . . ." Emotion rushed up, choking him.

She pulled back and peered up at him, her pale-blue eyes wide with shock. "What?"

"I know it's crazy," he said. "I know we barely know each other. But I feel this connection to you, and I know this is a terrible time, that you're going through so much and you're vulnerable and I'm a fool . . ." He trailed off, ashamed of himself for taking advantage of her. "Your dad just died and you've been through so much . . ."

"So have you," she said. And it was as if she knew . . . *everything.* "You've experienced loss and close calls with death. So you understand, better than most, how important life is and how precious and rare any connection is."

He released a shaky breath as his anxiety began, finally, to ease. "You are the one who understands," he said. And because she did, perhaps she would stay.

She nodded. "I do understand completely. I feel the same way, that there could be something special for me here . . . with you. I'm not leaving."

"But your career . . ."

"I've traveled enough for now, enough that I have all the research I need for a book I've been contracted to write. And this is the perfect place to do that."

"In your father's den," he said, where he kept finding her.

She nodded. "Yes, I feel close to him here. Close to Anna Beth. Maybe that's why he left me the house, and not just to spite my siblings and my mother. He'd been trying for years to get me to come home again."

"That's all I wanted to do—during my deployments—was to come home again," he admitted. "But it never really felt like home, not with my parents both gone, and so many of my fellow marines not coming back. I felt so alone."

"I've felt that way for years," she shared.

"But now," he continued, "with you here, everything feels different, feels right again."

She smiled widely now, and her blue eyes sparkled. "That's exactly how I feel, like everything's right again." She rose up on her tiptoes and brushed her mouth across his.

Despite how tired he was, his pulse pounded and his breath caught in his lungs. "So very right . . ." he agreed.

"And neither of us will be alone again."

EPILOGUE

Ten years later . . .

They were inseparable—just as Erin and Anna Beth had been so many years ago. Erin sat on the lounge chair on the patio, watching the two little girls who played together near the opening to the maze.

Rafe had suggested years ago that they should cut it down, but Erin had resisted. She'd had good memories in that maze as well as bad ones. And she clung now to every memory of Anna Beth.

It was no longer all she had of her sister, though.

One of those little girls, with her light-blond hair and pale-blue eyes, looked exactly like her namesake. Exactly like Anna Beth.

Her twin sister was named for Rafe's mother, Tessa. Her hair was darker, a strange mix of blond and brown and red, and she had dark eyes like her father. Eyes that expressed her every emotion, just as his did. Love, that was in them every time he looked at Erin, as he looked at her now as he leaned down and pressed a kiss to her forehead and his hand to her swollen belly. "You're sure there's just one in there?" he teased.

She smiled and nodded as her heart swelled with love for her husband and for their family. "There's just one. Our son."

He would be named for his father and both his grandfathers: Rafael Emilio Gregor.

The girls had already started calling him Regi.

"Your friends—Lucy and Rayne and their families—will be here soon," he said. "Are you sure you're up for a party?"

Parties didn't scare her as they once had. She actually enjoyed entertaining now. "I'll be fine. It's not as if Mother is letting me do anything anyway."

Sylvia Sloan's voice, giving orders to the staff, drifted out of the open patio doors, and then she drifted out. She only spared Erin and Rafe a brief glance and a smile before heading directly to her four-year-old granddaughters. "Look what Grammy brought you . . ." She held out a plate of cookies to them.

Instead of reaching for the cookies, both girls reached for her, wrapping their small arms around her. Instead of flinching or pulling away, Sylvia Sloan clutched them both close to her. She knew now how important family was; that in opening herself up to Erin and Rafe and the kids, she was no longer alone.

That with love and family, none of them would ever be alone again.

Connect with

Us

Visit us online at
KensingtonBooks.com
to read more from your favorite authors, see books
by series, view reading group guides, and more.

 Join us on social media

for sneak peeks, chances to win books and prize packs,
and to share your thoughts with other readers.

facebook.com/kensingtonpublishing
twitter.com/kensingtonbooks

Tell us what you think!

To share your thoughts, submit a review,
or sign up for our eNewsletters, please visit:
KensingtonBooks.com/TellUs.